A PRIVATE WALTZ

"Smile and close your eyes," David said.

"Close my eyes?" Samantha's eyes opened even wider at his instruction. "But why should I do that?"

"So that you shall be able to hear the music more clearly. And do not worry about trodding on my toes, for I shall simply move them out of the way if you miss a step. All you must do is listen to the music and allow me to guide you in the pattern of the waltz. It is so simple, even I can do it. And so shall you."

"But you do not know how very clumsy I am."

"You may have been clumsy with Mr. Pauley as a partner, but you shall not be so with me. Be assured that if you trip, I shall steady you. And if you fall, I shall catch you. Now let us move to the music."

Samantha moved as David's hand exerted pressure, and after a few faltering steps, she was soon moving about the room with a modicum of assurance. A smile replaced the frown on her face as she glided over the carpet in David's arms. She felt light as a feather, tethered to the earth only by his warm fingers on her waist.

Gradually, inevitably, the music box wound down, its tinkling notes playing slower and slower until they stopped altogether. Samantha opened her eyes, the magic of her first successful waltz still upon her, and gazed up into David's dark blue eyes. She wanted to tell him how marvelous their dance had been, how enthralled she had felt in his arms. But Samantha was speechless, her lips slightly parted, the color high on her face. And then David's lips lowered to hers and she sighed as he softly kissed her. . . .

Books by Kathryn Kirkwood

A MATCH FOR MELISSA

A SEASON FOR SAMANTHA

Published by Zebra Books

A SEASON FOR SAMANTHA

Kathryn Kirkwood

Zebra Books
Kensington Publishing Corp.

http://www.zebrabooks.com

This book is for Jami.

ZEBRA BOOKS are published by

Kensington Publishing Corp.
850 Third Avenue
New York, NY 10022

First Printing: February, 1999
10 9 8 7 6 5 4 3 2 1

Printed in the United States of America

One

Samantha Bennings uttered a most unladylike curse as she rounded the bend and spotted the carriage that sat near the entrance to Hawthorne Cottage. It was a somber black and its finish gleamed richly in the sunlight that filtered through the branches of the trees, rubbed to a high gloss by a stable boy who dared not shirk his duties. The horses that drew it were also black, a perfectly matched pair that stood obediently by the whitewashed gate, their heads lowered somberly. Their master was also somber; Samantha had never observed him clothed in any color save black. The stately equipage belonged to the church, one of the many perquisites that the Vicar Turnbull enjoyed by virtue of his ecclesiastical position.

Reining in her horse, Samantha came to an abrupt halt. She was not in a proper frame of mind to deal with the vicar today. Opting for the path through the woods in lieu of the broad gravel lane that led directly to the front of the cottage, Samantha wound her way round to the stable and quickly dismounted.

"He shall be gone, God willing, before I am finished with my duties here." Samantha spoke to her horse, Red Thunder, which had been her uncle's favorite mount. The beast seemed to understand her words for he whinnied softly and nuzzled her arm as she led him to his stall.

Red Thunder's saddle was heavy, but Samantha slung it off expertly and carried it to the block. Once she had rubbed Red Thunder down and stabled him, she moved to the saddle and rubbed it down as well. Then she smiled in amusement as she considered the dressing-down that Vicar Turnbull would surely have given her, had he observed her using this particular saddle. It had belonged to her uncle and the design did not allow her to ride in the manner that was required of proper young ladies. Samantha had been mounted astride Red Thunder's broad back and even more shocking, she had clothed herself in a pair of her uncle's breeches which she had altered to fit her slender waist. Samantha was well aware of the fact that ladies did not wear breeches, but clothing herself in a manner befitting a decorous young miss should only hamper her in her work.

"Perhaps I should have permitted him to see me." Samantha grinned at Red Thunder. "My improprieties should have been fodder for his next sermon."

Red Thunder nickered softly in response and Samantha laughed. Then she opened her saddlebags and began to unpack her equipment. She took particular care with the instruments, cleansing them thoroughly and then placing them in a pot of water that she put on the stove to boil, precisely as her uncle had always done. Aunt Phoebe had not allowed her husband's equipment in her kitchen and for this reason, Uncle Charles had installed a small stove in the barn.

Samantha was quite alone in the stable, for the groom had long since been dismissed. Her aunt had decided to dispense with his services as Red Thunder was their sole horse. When her uncle had died, he had bequeathed his satchel of instruments and his favorite mount to Samantha so that she might continue his work, and Aunt Phoebe had sold the remainder of his cattle to augment her widow's portion.

Samantha knew that her aunt had little worry financially. Though she was not affluent, by any means, Aunt Phoebe had received the necessary funds to maintain Hawthorne Cottage and pay for all of her necessities. There was even enough to keep Rosy, their maid-of-all-work, and provide Aunt Phoebe with the means to enjoy an occasional visit to her sisters in Dorset.

Uncle Charles had been the second son of a wealthy country squire. He had developed an early affinity for animals and his father had arranged for him to study veterinary medicine. Once those studies had been completed, Uncle Charles had returned home to treat his father's cattle and to build a practice in the area. Over the years, his diagnostic skills had become legendary; he had once been summoned to treat several ailing wild beasts that His Majesty had housed in the royal zoo.

When his father had died, Uncle Charles had inherited Hawthorne Cottage. He had continued to treat his father's cattle, which his older brother now owned, and he had trained Samantha to follow in his footsteps. Samantha had studied from her uncle's books and notes, and had accompanied him on his rounds. Though Aunt Phoebe had felt that such training was not seemly for a young girl, Uncle Charles had effectively quelled his wife's protests and Samantha was now as skilled as her uncle had been.

As she waited for the water to bubble, Samantha sighed wearily. She had been awakened at daybreak by a summons from Mrs. Harper. The children's missing dog had returned home at last, but he had been sadly the worse for wear. Samantha had cleansed the dog's cuts and stitched them neatly while the eldest of the Harper boys had held the squirming pet. She had applied a salve and then bandaged the pup, cautioning Mrs. Harper to send for her immediately if the young canine chewed them off. After assuring the two boys that "Jersey" would recover nicely if he were kept in the house for a few days, Samantha had ridden to Squire Wadsworth's country manor to inquire after his prize thoroughbred mare.

She had found her uncle's elder brother in quite a taking. The mare had been preparing to foal, but it had promised to be a difficult birth as the foal had presented itself in the breech position. It had taken all of Samantha's con-

siderable skill to turn the foal and achieve a happy conclusion.

Squire Wadsworth had been full of praise for Samantha's resourcefulness. Once the foal had gained its legs
and the mare had recovered from the difficult birth, he
had pressed a heavy purse on Samantha in payment for
her services. Though she had tried to refuse, the squire
had insisted she accept it and Samantha had ridden off to
her next appointment with a pleased smile.

The Widow Browne had been waiting for Samantha with
a full tray of lemon spice cakes. Samantha had lanced the
boil her milk cow had developed, left a salve for her to
apply, and availed herself of a still-warm cake before the
neighbors should arrive.

Neither the widow, who had baked for this express purpose, nor Samantha had been disappointed. Samantha
had barely swallowed her last bite before the Widow
Browne had shown in Samantha's first visitors.

Though her training was primarily in the treatment of
animals, people often sought Samantha's services as well.
Like her uncle before her, Samantha had learned that
many of the tinctures, salves, and creams that she prepared
for her four-legged patients were also effective for human
ailments. She had given Farmer Hicks the salve that she
had mixed for his rash, removed a deeply embedded splin-
ter from his wife's palm, and dispensed a cream to a neighboring girl who wished to reduce the size and coloring of
her freckles. After treating several more neighbors for various ailments, Samantha had ridden back to Hawthorne
Cottage only to find that Vicar Turnbull was paying yet
another call on her Aunt Phoebe.

The vicar had been a recurrent visitor of late and
Samantha suspected that the purpose for his frequent presence at Hawthorne Cottage had little to do with the care
of Aunt Phoebe's soul. It was rumored that Vicar Turnbull
was seeking a second wife and Aunt Phoebe had dropped
many not-so-gentle hints that once dear Samantha was

married and had a home of her own, she should then be free to live with her sisters in Dorset.

Samantha had just finished repacking her instruments when Rosy appeared in the doorway of the stable. "She's waiting for you in the parlor, miss. She told me to say it was a matter of extreme importance."

"I shall be in directly, Rosy." Samantha knew it was anatomically impossible, but her heart seemed to drop to her toes. She suspected she knew the reason for her aunt's summons. Samantha's eighteenth birthday had come and gone, and she was of marriageable age. Indeed, young ladies were permitted to wed much younger, but thus far, no one had offered for Samantha. Just last month, Aunt Phoebe had remarked that she feared her dear niece was destined for the life of a spinster if she did not change her unladylike ways.

Hoping to subvert the alliance that Aunt Phoebe was attempting to make for her with Vicar Turnbull, Samantha had embarked upon a campaign to make certain that news of her unladylike behavior reached his ears. She had thought to force him to choose someone more suitable, but perhaps the man was too dim-witted to realize that she was such a stunningly imperfect match. Samantha turned to Rosy with a frown. "Is the Vicar Turnbull still with my aunt?"

"No, miss. The vicar took his leave some time ago. But there's something in the wind, Miss. She was smiling like the cat who got into the cream pot when she sent me out here to fetch you."

The moment Rosy left, Samantha changed her clothing. It would never do for her to be inappropriately dressed when she answered the summons from her aunt. She hung her uncle's breeches on a nail in the corner of the stable and shook out her skirt to free it from wrinkles. Then she smoothed her short, curly, red hair and studied her reflection in the polished piece of tin that served as her mirror.

All things considered, she was well put together, Samantha decided with a smile. Her blue eyes were bright, nicely set off by the blue scarf she wore at the neck of her creamy white blouse. Her color was high, lending a healthy glow to her smooth complexion, and her generous lips were an acceptable shade of rose. She washed a smudge of dust off her nicely-shaped nose, slipped into her shoes, leaving her boots in the stable, and took a deep breath as she exited the place that she had come to think of as her refuge.

Samantha sighed as she headed down the path that led to Hawthorne Cottage. She had never held a high opinion of Vicar Turnbull. His sermonizing about sin and God's retribution was depressing at best, and he seemed to find no good in mankind. He was a dry, humorless widower in his early fifties and Samantha found him about as appealing as the pool of stagnant water that gathered in Squire Wadsworth's north field every spring.

Though Vicar Turnbull was far from the perfect match that an innocent young miss might envision, it was not his physical appearance or even the disparity in their ages that concerned Samantha. She was not at all repulsed at the prospect of wedding an unhandsome older man who shared her interests. But Vicar Turnbull had made it clear that he did not approve of Samantha's "doctoring," even going so far as to proclaim that such work interfered with God's will.

When the vicar had suggested that she give up her ungodly work, Samantha had asked him if he regarded animals as God's creatures. As she had expected, he had answered in the affirmative. She had then asked if he regarded her as God's creature. Again the answer had been in the affirmative. Samantha had then argued that since she was God's creature and capable of providing aid to another of His creatures, would not God surely wish her to do so? This reasoning had earned her a lecture from Aunt Phoebe about respecting those learned individuals who held offices in the church, and an even sterner one from Vicar Turnbull's pulpit on the following Sunday. His subject had been the sin of conceit, and the vicar's eyes had singled out Samantha when he'd cautioned those amongst them who were so full of conceit that they should presume to interpret the Almighty's will.

Samantha hesitated at the cottage door, loath to enter into the altercation that should be certain to occur with her aunt. Given the choice, Samantha would prefer to sit on the shelf for the rest of her life than to marry a man like Vicar Turnbull. Unfortunately, she would not be afforded the luxury of refusal. If Aunt Phoebe had approved the match, there was little Samantha could do to avoid it. Any objection on her part would be regarded as willful and improper, and she would be censured by all of their acquaintances.

Taking a deep breath for courage, Samantha opened the door and went directly to the parlor. She found her aunt waiting, a tea tray on the small piecrust table beside her and a satisfied smile on her countenance.

"I have delightful news, Samantha." Aunt Phoebe's hand was trembling with excitement as she gestured for her niece to take a chair. "The Vicar Turnbull has offered for you!"

Samantha nodded and took the chair that her aunt indicated. There was no need to make queries, as her Aunt Phoebe was naturally loquacious and would tell her all that had been discussed in due time.

"It is a far better match than I had dared hope you should make." Aunt Phoebe wore an expression of supreme contentment. "Such a worthy man! So kind! And you need have no concern that I have deceived him. The good vicar knows all."

Samantha nodded. "Then the vicar does not find it distressing that I have no dowry?"

"Not in the slightest, child." Aunt Phoebe laughed merrily. "Vicar Turnbull has addressed that failing with exceeding good grace, pronouncing that the gift of your hand in marriage is all the dowry that he could wish. He has even been so kind as to promise never to mention your mother's scandalous conduct."

Samantha's interest was immediately piqued. "Scandalous conduct? You have not spoken of this before, Aunt Phoebe."

"Oh, dear!" The color rose on Aunt Phoebe's countenance. "I had not meant to make mention of that!"

"But you did make mention of it and now you must tell me." Samantha refused to let her aunt off that easily.

Aunt Phoebe nodded reluctantly. "I daresay you are correct, Samantha. Charles and I agreed to keep it from you when first you came to us, but now that you are soon to be wed, you must come to terms with your mother's indiscretion."

Samantha reached out to pour her aunt a cup of tea, as that unfortunate lady was undeniably distressed. When her aunt had taken several sips of the bracing brew, she proceeded to relate the tale.

"You were but a babe when you came to us, Samantha, far too young to remember either of your parents. Your uncle insisted that when you asked, we should tell you that both of your parents had expired in a carriage accident."

"Then this is not true?" Samantha's eyes widened. She had always believed the story that her aunt and uncle had told her.

"I fear it was only half the truth. Your father, my youngest brother, was killed in the mishap, but your mother was not with him at the time."

Samantha frowned. "Where was she?"

"She had left my brother to run off with another man." Aunt Phoebe's lips tightened in anger. "To make matters even more intolerable, she was already in an interesting condition. When you were born, your mother brought you here and ran off that night, never to return."

"But I am my father's child, am I not?" Samantha clenched her hands together tightly to keep them from trembling.

Aunt Phoebe's lips tightened. "I suspect you are not, for you bear no resemblance, either in appearance or in temperament, to any other in my family."

"What of my mother?" Samantha swallowed with difficulty. "Has there been any word of her?"

"None. Your uncle insisted that we make inquiries regarding her whereabouts though the cost was exceedingly dear. He was told that she fled to France with a nobleman of dubious distinction and died there of the fever."

Samantha sat in silence for a moment, doing her utmost to compose herself. The only family she had ever known, her Uncle Charles and her Aunt Phoebe, had been reduced to the status of strangers. "When you discovered all this, why did you keep me?"

"Charles convinced me that it was our Christian duty to do so. And he had developed no little affection for you by the time that we learned of your mother's death."

Samantha nodded. Uncle Charles had been the kindest of men and would never have allowed her to be placed in an orphanage, whether she had been relative or foundling. Should her aunt have been the one to decide, Samantha suspected that her fate should have been much different.

"Let us not speak of these distressing matters any further." Aunt Phoebe smiled resolutely. "We shall consider instead your upcoming nuptials and rejoice in the fact that such a fine man has chosen you for his wife."

Samantha frowned. Contemplating marriage to Vicar Turnbull was every bit as distressing as the unfortunate circumstances surrounding her birth. Only one cheering thought entered Samantha's mind. Her engagement to Vicar Turnbull might well be lengthy, considering the encompassing duties of his office. This would give her ample time to engage in even more outrageous behavior so that he should be forced to cry off.

"I should prefer that you have a large wedding, but my purse is not adequate for any but the simplest affair." Aunt Phoebe sighed and Samantha hid a smile. Though her aunt had ample resources, she was impossibly penurious. "Vicar Turnbull and I have discussed the problem at length and we have decided to hold the ceremony here in the garden. It shall be delightful, Samantha. The dogwood shall be in full bloom for your nuptials."

Samantha drew a deep breath of relief. The dogwood bushes were just beginning to bud. They would be in full bloom in a week or so and then they would not bloom again until the following year. This meant that she would have ample time to force the vicar to break their engagement.

"Does this meet with your approval, Samantha?"

Aunt Phoebe was waiting for an answer and Samantha nodded quickly. "Yes, Aunt Phoebe. Next spring will be a perfect time for the wedding."

"Next spring?" Aunt Phoebe frowned. "No, Samantha. That is not what I meant at all. Vicar Turnbull is eager to take you to wife and your wedding will be held in one week's time."

Samantha sat numbly as Aunt Phoebe continued to rhapsodize over the plans she had made with the vicar. There would be a fine cake that the vicar himself had promised to procure, and his colleague would be performing the ceremony. Samantha would have a new gown for the affair. The vicar had agreed to stand the cost out of his own pocket. His only stipulation was that it be serviceable for the other church functions that Samantha would attend as his wife.

Samantha managed to utter the appropriate words when her aunt paused for a response, but her mind was not on the arrangements that had been made for her nuptials. She was desperately searching for a way to extricate herself from this most distressing predicament and effect an escape from Vicar Turnbull's unwelcome affections.

Two

Aunt Phoebe had retired to her bedchamber at last, seeking her afternoon's rest. The moment her aunt had quit the parlor, Samantha had escaped to her own chamber to attempt to plan a way out of her difficulties. This was not an easy task. If Uncle Charles had been alive, he would not have forced Samantha to marry against her will. But Uncle Charles had been buried for almost two years and Samantha was alone with her aunt.

During their converse in the parlor, Samantha had tendered several objections to the marriage that had been so handily arranged for her, but they had held no weight with her aunt. Aunt Phoebe was determined that Samantha should wed the vicar at once and she would brook no nonsense. According to Aunt Phoebe, every young woman experienced doubts when confronted with her impending nuptials. Indeed, it was quite natural for a proper young miss like Samantha to be reticent. Samantha's aunt had been of the opinion that if wiser heads did not prevail during this period immediately preceding the ceremony, very few brides would come to actually speak their vows. Samantha had been assured that she would come round once Vicar Turnbull had taken her to wife, and she should then be certain to appreciate the honor that he had bestowed upon her.

Samantha sighed and sat down on the edge of her bed. She was trapped and there was naught she could do to save herself. There was no acceptable way of refusing the vicar's suit, and from her aunt's comments, Samantha was certain that Vicar Turnbull would not cry off. There was nothing for it but to wed the vicar and resign herself to an unhappy marriage and an even unhappier life.

But was that her only option? Samantha got up to pace the floor. Squire Wadsworth, her uncle's older brother, would provide her no aid. He was most deferential to Aunt Phoebe and would surely throw his chips in with her. There was no one else in her small circle of acquaintances that Samantha could approach with her problem. Vicar Turnbull was greatly respected and they should all chide her for her reluctance to become his wife.

It was at this exact moment that a solution occurred to Samantha, a radical plan but one that would surely succeed. If Aunt Phoebe was truly no relation to her, she had no familial obligation to defer to her wishes. Samantha Bennings was an orphan and must needs please only herself.

Samantha stopped pacing and stood perfectly still, a smile spreading across her countenance. Aunt Phoebe claimed that her only reason for remaining at Hawthorne Cottage was to discharge her Christian duty toward Samantha. It should make little difference whether Samantha moved to the vicarage as a bride or took leave to seek her own fate. The end result should be exactly the same. Once Samantha was no longer in residence, Aunt Phoebe could seek a new owner for the cottage and move to Dorset with her sisters.

The only creature Samantha would be sad to leave was Red Thunder. She had come to love her uncle's favorite horse, but Squire Wadsworth had offered to buy his brother's mount, and Aunt Phoebe should be certain to accommodate him. Red Thunder would have a new home in the squire's well-kept stables and the noble beast would enjoy the company of the squire's other cattle.

Her problem solved, Samantha began to plan her escape. Aunt Phoebe would surely attempt to stop her if she made her intentions known so all must be done in secret.

Since her aunt always rested for at least two hours of an afternoon, Samantha decided that there was no time like the present to take her leave. Thanks to the contents of Squire Wadsworth's purse, she had gained the blunt that was necessary to begin her journey.

Samantha's first task was the packing of her belongings and she accomplished that in short order. There was not much that she could call her own: a few items of clothing, her uncle's books and his satchel of veterinary instruments, and one or two keepsakes. She penned a message, explaining the reason for her actions, and left it in her room where it would be found in due time. Then she hurried down the stairs to take leave of Rosy and to assure that she had ample time to make good her escape before Aunt Phoebe came to realize that she was missing.

She found Rosy in the small kitchen, paring vegetables for their evening meal. The maid-of-all-work merely nodded as Samantha explained that she had been summoned to care for several ailing animals.

"You will be riding then, miss?" Rosy looked up from her work.

Samantha shook her head, hoping that the whisker she was telling did not show on her face. "No, Rosy. A cart has been sent for me and it will also carry me home. The problem is serious and I fear it may occupy a considerable length of time. Neither you nor my aunt need wait up for me. I shall undoubtedly be exhausted and retire immediately upon my return."

"You'd best take some nourishment with you then, miss." Rosy began to pack a small hamper, filling it with bread, cheese, and several sweet cakes.

"Thank you, Rosy." Samantha smiled as she took the hamper. "This will be just the thing if they do not offer sustenance."

"Do be careful, miss." Rosy reached out to touch Samantha's hand.

"I will, Rosy. Never fear."

"I shall tell your aunt exactly what you have told me."

Rosy's voice was shaking slightly. "And I can't say I blame you, miss. It's been a hard life for you since your dear uncle stuck his spoon in the wall and the vicar is not for the likes of such a friendly young miss as you."

Samantha reached out to hug Rosy. Though her aunt's maid-of-all-work had tumbled to the scheme, Samantha was certain that Rosy would not betray her. With tears in her eyes, Samantha exited the kitchen, retrieved her carpetbag from its hiding place near the door, and left Hawthorne Cottage for the last time.

Samantha's last stop was the stable. It took only moments to retrieve her uncle's satchel of instruments and the clothing she'd worn earlier, and make certain that Red Thunder was content for the night. Then she walked quickly down the lane and out onto the road that led to her freedom.

As she walked down the dusty road, Samantha reviewed her plan. Her destination was the Two Feathers, a roadside inn only a few miles away. The place had a rather unsavory reputation and no one would think to look for her there. The moment she arrived, she would engage a room for the night and perhaps she would be fortunate enough to find a conveyance to continue her journey. It mattered not that her flight might be filled with hardship and, perhaps, an element of danger. Samantha was firmly convinced that any fate that befell her would be preferable to wedding a man that she so despised.

The shadows were deepening when Samantha reached the courtyard of the Two Feathers Inn. A coach had recently arrived, and she watched as the coachman handed down his female passenger and escorted her into the inn. The woman was dressed in a lovely traveling gown and a veil; by the style of her clothing, Samantha could tell that she was a lady of quality. It was highly unusual and most improper for such a lady to travel alone, without the company of a relative or female companion. Though she knew full well that it was of no concern to her, Samantha found the situation intriguing.

No sooner had the coachman and his charge disappeared from sight than another coach arrived. Four young gentlemen disembarked and after a brief glance in their direction, Samantha attempted to make herself as inconspicuous as possible. The four gentlemen appeared to be in raucous humor, shouting out for drink, food, and feminine companionship. Samantha easily surmised that they had indulged in a goodly amount of strong spirits before they had arrived at the Two Feathers Inn as, to a man, they were regrettably foxed.

Instead of going into the inn as Samantha expected they should do, the four gentlemen lounged on benches in the courtyard, sending their coachman inside to procure a bottle. They were quite near the door and Samantha knew she risked much by attempting to pass them and gain entrance to the establishment, but the sun was sinking lower in the sky and she could not stand in the courtyard all night.

With a deep breath for courage, Samantha slipped through the gathering shadows in a circuitous route to the door. She had almost gained her destination when she heard a shout behind her. One of the group, a veritable bear of a man with a barrel chest and massive arms, hurtled forward to grab her. He reeked of strong liquor and his laughter boomed loudly in her ear.

"And what have we here? A comely wench, if I do not mistake myself."

Though his words were slurred, no doubt the result of frequent libations throughout the day, his grasp on her arm was firm. Samantha struggled to free herself from his iron clasp, but all she gained for her efforts was a tear in her sleeve.

"She is a wildcat and I shall tame her!" the giant of a man bellowed to his friends.

Samantha ceased her struggles immediately. She had learned the art of self-defense by watching the local farm boys wrestle, and she bided her time patiently. She was much stronger, physically, than she appeared. The years of helping her uncle treat large animals had strengthened her muscles and prepared her well for this confrontation.

The large man seemed surprised at her sudden capitulation and his grip lessened slightly. Samantha was about to deliver a well-placed jab where it would be certain to cause the most discomfort when a fifth gentleman arrived upon the scene.

Samantha cast a quick glance at the newcomer. He was not one of the four who had arrived in the coach and he did not appear to be foxed. He appraised the situation at a glance and then he strode to her side. With seemingly little effort, he broke the big man's hold on Samantha's arm and pushed him back, where he could not reach her.

"Get your own! This one's mine!" the big man roared, stumbling slightly as he attempted to recover his balance.

"I fear you are mistaken, sir." The newcomer smiled, a dangerous glint in his eye. "There's time enough for carousing later, but not with this particular miss. She belongs to me."

"The hell you say!" The big man frowned and lunged forward, but he was far too slow. The newcomer neatly stepped aside and the force of the big man's lunge carried him into a nearby bush.

Samantha was about to make a dash for the door when the newcomer did something she did not expect. He reached out and swept her up into his arms, as if she had no more weight than a feather, and carried her into the inn.

It was useless to struggle. His arms were like steel bands around her. Samantha looked to the innkeeper to see if he would come to her aid, but he appeared quite accustomed to this type of behavior. He merely winked at the newcomer, tossed him a key, and gestured toward the stairs.

As she was carried up the staircase, Samantha glanced up into the newcomer's face. What she saw did not reassure her and her eyes went wide with fright. He was a tall man with skin tanned bronze by the sun. His gold-colored hair was much longer than fashion dictated and his eyes were of such a dark shade of blue, they were nearly black. He was the most handsome man Samantha had ever seen, but his behavior made it clear that he was not a gentleman. She kept a tight hold on her carpetbag, remembering the satchel of sharp instruments inside. When he let down his guard, she would find a means to escape from this new peril.

The newcomer unlocked a door at the top of the stairs and carried Samantha across the threshold. Kicking the door shut behind him, he deposited her, quite unceremoniously, on the bed. Then he did something that Samantha found even more shocking than the actions of the crude lout who had initially accosted her. He laughed.

"I should like to know what humor you find in this situation!" Samantha spoke up without thinking. "You are no better than the other beast who accosted me in the courtyard!"

"Oh, but I am . . . much better, in fact. And you shall soon come to realize that."

Samantha's mind spun in frantic circles as he bent down and kissed her quite thoroughly on the lips. She could not seem to hold a thought. His lips were warm and insistent, and her will to resist came very close to vanishing in the heat that threatened to consume her. But she had not left the only home she had ever known and set out on a journey that was a testament to her independence only to be ravished by the first handsome stranger that she encountered. How dare he take liberties with her person! He did not even know her name!

Lips clamped firmly together, Samantha reached out for her satchel. He was regrettably mistaken if he assumed that she would not defend her honor! But just as she was about to lay hands on one of the sharp instruments, he abruptly released her and stepped back with a chuckle.

"You are woefully ignorant in the ways of pleasing a man." The newcomer's lips twitched in amusement. "I daresay you belong at home in the schoolroom."

Samantha glared at him, the color high in her cheeks. "And your manners belong in the stable, sir!"

"That is precisely where I should prefer to be." He laughed a trifle ruefully and raised his eyebrows. "It is obvious to me that you are ill-suited for the type of life that you have chosen. You have neither the qualifications nor the inclinations. Leave this place now, or you will surely regret it."

Samantha stared up at him in utter confusion. Though he spoke with the accents of a gentleman and his words were quite precise, she found that she did not catch his meaning. For what particular life was she ill-suited? She had not mentioned her occupation and he had no knowledge of her qualifications. Then quite suddenly, Samantha remembered the circumstances of their meeting and the wink that he had exchanged with the innkeeper. It was clear that he had mistaken her for a doxie!

"I am not what you believe I am, sirrah!" Samantha straightened her clothing and sat up primly. "And it was presumptuous, on your part, to have assumed that I was a . . . a . . ."

"A bit of muslin?" He laughed as he finished the sentence for her. "Perhaps you are not, but from your appearance I had no reason to believe otherwise."

"What is wrong with the manner in which I am dressed?" Samantha glanced down at her modest gown.

"It was not your gown that led me to my assumption. Will you deny that you were standing alone, outside the entrance of the Two Feathers Inn?"

Samantha shook her head. "I cannot deny it, for that is precisely where I was standing. I was about to enter when I was rudely accosted. Can *you* deny that the large gentleman in the courtyard acted improperly toward me?"

"He did nothing improper. Nor did I, for that matter. The Two Feathers Inn is well known for its willing female companionship and you were unescorted. Mistaking you for a lightskirt was entirely understandable on both of our parts."

Tears began to form in Samantha's eyes and she blinked them back. "But I did not know that this place was . . . was . . ."

"Yes. I see." He sighed and tossed her a bag of coins. "This will be more than ample to pay for your torn clothing and secure this room for the night. You will be safe if you stay inside and do not venture out until morning. And then, my innocent young miss, I advise you to go straight home to your parents and beg their forgiveness for running off as you did."

Samantha watched with utter amazement as he strode to the door and opened it. She was about to tell him that she could not, in all conscience, take his purse, when he turned for a final word.

"Unless you intend to solicit the fleeting attentions of traveling men, I would advise you to stay far away from the Two Feathers Inn in future."

The door banged closed with finality and Samantha jumped to her feet. She rushed across the wooden floor, heart beating rapidly in fear, and locked it securely behind him. Then she stood silently, listening to the sounds of his receding footsteps. Her legs were trembling and she did not draw an easy breath until all was quiet in the corridor beyond.

Never one to dwell on a problem for long, Samantha walked resolutely to the bed and took another dress from her carpetbag. What a dreadful tangle she had nearly made of her first few hours of freedom! When she had washed off the dust of her journey and dressed in a clean gown, she sat down on the bed and thought about the handsome stranger. She was certain that he wasn't from these parts. His speech had been far too genteel for that of a farmer or a simple tradesman.

Finding herself exhausted by her ordeal, Samantha ate some of the food that Rosy had packed and then prepared for bed. As she lay there, listening to the rowdy crowd below the stairs, she wondered if the handsome stranger was amongst the merrymakers. He had not mentioned whether he was to stay or to travel on, but she found it quite easy to imagine him sitting at a table in the common room, flirting with the prettiest maid at the inn.

Samantha could picture the scene in her mind. The maid would be dressed in a gown that was crafted to display her buxom figure, and as she bent over to serve him, he would raise his brows in appreciation of her obvious charms. It would not matter to him whether she was unmarried or someone's wife, so long as she encouraged him with a smile. They would continue to enjoy their flirtation until she had finished her duties. And then, in the wee small hours of the morning, he would take her up to his chamber for the purpose of indulging the very same passions that he had so recently intended to enjoy with her!

The thought filled Samantha with an extremely uncomfortable emotion. This sentiment had all the attributes of jealousy, but Samantha told herself that it could not possibly be so. If his uncouth behavior toward her was an accurate indication, it would be very foolish of Samantha indeed to harbor any envy for his current companion.

With firm resolve, Samantha forced all thoughts of the handsome stranger from her mind and concentrated instead on falling asleep. It would be extremely foolish, perhaps even dangerous, to greet the morning with a muddled head. She should need all her wits about her so that she could safely continue her journey.

Samantha was about to slip into the waiting arms of Morpheus when a puzzling question popped into her mind. The handsome stranger had assumed that she was in the muslin trade when he had carried her up to this room. His first action had borne witness to that fact when he had tossed her onto the bed and kissed her most thoroughly. He had then pronounced her woefully inexperienced, well before Samantha had informed him of his mistake.

He had known, from a single kiss, that she was not a lightskirt. Samantha frowned up into the shadows. What action on her part had caused him to tumble to that conclusion?

Samantha reviewed the kiss in her mind and a pleasing warmth swept over her. Despite her initial fear, she had begun to respond to the heat of his lips and the delicious pressure of his mouth upon hers. Was her response so different from that of a doxie? It was most improper, perhaps even scandalous, but Samantha was desirous of encountering the handsome stranger again so that she could ask him.

Three

The sun had just risen over the horizon when someone tapped upon her chamber door. Samantha was already dressed, having given up her bed an hour ago and settled into a chair near the window. She had watched the sky lighten from ebony black to a gray that had, as the time passed, become increasingly tinged with rose. The rose had subsequently taken on a brighter glow, a color so lovely that Samantha had gasped in delight. Finally, the crest of the sun had peeped over the landscape and the miracle of morning had occurred once again, transforming the gray-black shapes of the trees and bushes into lush emerald green and prompting the birds to sing in a joyful cacophony of melodies to greet the new day.

Her eyes felt scratchy and Samantha rubbed them. She had spent a restless night. Her sleep had been disturbed by visions of the handsome stranger, and every sound from below had caused her to start and sit up on the lumpy mattress, peering into the shadows alertly. She had attempted to convince herself that her unease was caused by the unfamiliar surroundings and the ordeal that she had endured. But this was not the entire truth, for each and every time her eyes had flown open, she had found herself wondering what should have ensued if the handsome stranger had believed that she was a lightskirt.

Samantha crossed to the door on legs that trembled with exhaustion. Was her visitor the handsome stranger, come to offer an apology for his rude behavior? She hesitated, uncertain whether it was wise to release the lock. He had advised her to wait until morning to open her door, but it was most certainly morning. Should she throw open the portal, now that it was daylight, and risk encountering him again? She quickly decided that caution should be wise and she called out softly, inquiring as to the identity of her caller.

"My name is Olivia." A tentative female voice answered her query. "I know this is an imposition as you do not know me, but . . . but I most desperately seek your assistance."

Samantha took the precaution of arming herself with a heavy pitcher before she unlocked the door. She would not put it past the big man who had attacked her to use trickery to gain access to her chamber. But when she pulled open the door, she saw only the young woman who had arrived at the inn shortly before her.

"Oh, thank you for seeing me! I do not wish to take up too much of your time, but I find myself in a horrible tangle!"

Samantha put down the pitcher and gave a reassuring smile to the slight, golden-haired girl who stood in the doorway. She was tall, Samantha's equal in height, but her build was so slender she looked as if the very breeze should blow her away. There was more than a hint of trouble in the depths of her deep brown eyes and Samantha immediately felt a stirring of sympathy.

"Please come in, Olivia, and do sit down." Samantha gestured toward the chair. "I shall be happy to help you if I am able."

Olivia entered the room and settled herself on the very edge of the chair. "It is very kind of you to invite me into your room. I would never presume to put myself forward, but I simply do not know how I shall go on."

"You must tell me your concerns and perhaps we may devise a solution together." Samantha smiled again, hoping to give her new acquaintance more courage. By the strong light entering through the dusty window, she revised her assessment of Olivia's age. Samantha had, initially, thought her to be a mere child, but now she could see that Olivia was older, perhaps even of an age approximating her own.

Olivia nodded, taking a deep, bracing breath. "I am being carried to London against my will!"

"You have been kidnapped?" A frown furrowed Samantha's brow. If Olivia had been abducted, she had successfully managed to escape her captors.

"No, not kidnapped." A small giggle escaped Olivia's throat. "I did not intend to give that impression, though I can easily understand how you may have reached that conclusion. I am traveling to my grandmother's home. She has sent her coachman to carry me there."

"And you do not wish to go?"

"No! I cannot! It is my work, you see. I have promised to finish it and Grandmama will never allow me to do so."

Samantha nodded. She did not understand, but she was certain the young lady should tell her of her circumstances in due time. Her immediate concern was to allay Olivia's fears and to relax her sufficiently so that she should feel free to confide her troubles.

"I am making such a muddle of this." Tears gathered in Olivia's brown eyes.

"No, you are not." Samantha perched on the ledge of the window and smiled again. "Perhaps it would be best to start over, at the beginning. I am Samantha Bennings. And your name is Olivia?"

"Yes, Olivia Tarrington. My parents died three years ago and my mother's older sister had charge of me until two weeks past. That was when she died."

"How dreadful!" Samantha sighed compassionately.

"Not as dreadful as you might imagine." Olivia's lips turned upward in a small smile. "Quite naturally, I am sorry at her passing, but she only took me in because it was her Christian duty and she truly did not approve of me at all!"

Samantha stared at Olivia for a moment and then burst

into laughter. "Your aunt sounds much the same as mine. And now you are being sent to your grandmother?"

"Yes." Olivia smiled back and Samantha could see that she was becoming more comfortable. "My grandmother on my father's side has decided that I must have a Season."

Samantha noticed the anxious expression that swept across Olivia's countenance. "You do not wish for a Season, Olivia?"

"Heaven forfend!" Olivia winced. "I should never have the bottom to endure a Season in London, even if I desired one. I am painfully shy around strangers and it should be an agony for me!"

Samantha nodded. She had heard tales of the Season in London and it had sounded quite exciting to her, but perhaps it should not be so if one were shy and retiring. "Perhaps you should enjoy it, if your grandmother were to escort you."

"Oh, no! I am certain I should not! Even if I managed to endure all those routs and parties and balls, I cannot spare the time from my work."

"You mentioned your work before." Samantha nodded quickly. "Please tell me about it."

Olivia smiled and her enthusiasm was clear to see. "I am an artist and my painting master has assigned a series of paintings for me to complete. It is to be a nature folio and it is nearly finished."

"An artist!" Samantha breathed the words. "How marvelous!"

Olivia's brown eyes sparkled. "It is marvelous, indeed! Mr. Dawson assures me that I have the necessary talent, and I do not wish to spend time in London when I could be pursuing the elusive creatures that await my canvas. Painting is my passion and I . . . I wish to devote my life to my work!"

Samantha nodded. "I am sensible of your feelings, Olivia. Which particular species do you paint?"

"Birds." Olivia breathed the word almost reverently. "They are such magical creatures, Samantha. One has only to imagine the sights their eyes have seen to appreciate their wondrous qualities. To soar with the wind and fly above the treetops, with nary a care in the world! How I wish, just once, that I should have the opportunity to float above this lovely land and experience their sense of pure freedom!"

Samantha smiled as she attempted to imagine that feat. "It should, indeed, be a wonder. Have you painted many birds, Olivia?"

"Oh, yes! I have only a few more renderings to complete before I will have painted one of every kind. This is why I do not wish to be interrupted now. The timing is most critical."

"Why is that?"

"Mr. Dawson is to present my folio to a publisher at the end of the year and he has located a naturalist who is willing to write a brief description of each specimen, listing its characteristics and habitat. He envisions a type of reference manual for those who enjoy watching birds. Oh, I do so hope that my work will be published!"

"I am certain that it will be!" Samantha's eyes were sparkling, too. Olivia's enthusiasm for her art was contagious and she did not seem at all shy when she spoke of it. "I have no doubt that such a reference work should be most useful, indeed."

Olivia nodded. "There appears to be a need for such books. Mr. Dawson has set up a correspondence with another artist who has embarked on a similar work. His name is John James Audubon and he currently resides in America in a place called Kentucky. He hopes to publish also, when his life-size portraits of birds are complete."

"Then there will be two such books in print?"

"Yes. But Mr. Audubon paints the American birds while I portray ours." Olivia began to frown slightly. "And our methods are quite dissimilar."

"Please tell me how." Samantha was curious.

"It is a small difference, but I find it disturbs me excessively." Olivia sighed. "Mr. Audubon occasionally paints birds that have been killed and I have vowed never to do so. My specimens are captured and kept in a large cage for no more than a day before they are released back into their natural habitat."

"That is indeed a feat! How do you paint them so quickly as that?"

"I sketch them in detail and in a variety of poses by observing them as they move about the cage. Then I color the sketches with crayons so that I possess an accurate record of their appearance. After that step has been accomplished, they are released to resume their lives."

Samantha nodded. "Your methods seem quite humane. And you say that your folio is nearly complete?"

"Yes. I need only three more paintings. These particular birds inhabit the area around Bath and I intend to travel there as soon as I am able."

"Do you have the necessary funds to complete your folio?" Samantha thought of the purse the handsome stranger had tossed her and wondered whether she should offer it to Olivia.

Olivia smiled as she nodded. "I have saved a goodly portion of my quarterly allowance and Mr. Dawson has arranged for me to stay with his aunt while I am in Bath. She is also an artist and she has sent word that she shall be glad of my company."

"You must go then." Samantha declared. "Indeed, I should not hesitate if I were in your place. It is the opportunity of a lifetime!"

Olivia looked quite delighted. "You *do* understand!"

"Indeed, I do! Have you given thought to what you might do after your folio is published?"

"Oh, yes!" Olivia's eyes began to sparkle again. "I shall attempt another folio."

"You shall paint other creatures?"

"Oh, no!" Olivia shivered slightly. "Perhaps I should not admit to being so cowardly, but several of the larger specimens that I painted served to frighten me enormously. The eagles were quite fierce, and also the hawks and the owls. Though I admire the birds of prey enormously, I should not care to paint them again."

"But they were caged, were they not?"

Olivia nodded. "Most definitely. And I was never in any actual danger. But I could not help to think of the terror a small creature must experience at being caught up in their talons. Perhaps my aunt was right and I am too timid."

"If this is true, it is not a grievous fault." Samantha hastened to reassure her as Olivia appeared anxious once again. "Timidity may be less of a fault than being too bold. That is my fault, according to my aunt."

"How lovely to be bold!" Olivia sighed. "I admire you greatly, Samantha. How wonderful it should be if a small bit of your boldness might magically make its way to me."

Samantha smiled. "Perhaps it shall. And perhaps I may borrow just a bit of your restraint. But that is neither here nor there. You mentioned that you wished to begin another folio. What subject have you chosen?"

"Flowers. I should like to buy a small cottage in the countryside and cultivate my own subjects. I have decided that the paintings shall be of actual size and of great use to the naturalist. Perhaps I shall even include all of the indigenous flora."

Samantha was amazed at the scope of such a work. "But shouldn't such a project take years to complete?"

"Most assuredly." Olivia did not seem at all daunted by the prospect. "But I cannot think of a finer way to spend my remaining days upon this earth!"

"How shall you finance your endeavors? It should take a great deal of money to buy a cottage."

"That is, indeed, a problem." Olivia sighed deeply. "I am aware that the proceeds from my folio of birds should not be enough to pay for it all. My parents set aside funds for me and I shall come into this inheritance in two months' time. I had planned to use the monies for that purpose, but now I find that Grandmother has made that quite impossible."

Samantha frowned. "I do not understand."

"It is simple. Grandmother must sign a paper to release the funds and she will not do so unless I agree to take part in the Season."

"Then you have no choice." Samantha reached out to take Olivia's hand. "It will not be so bad, Olivia. The Season is short and surely you can spare the time from your work. And when it is over, your grandmother will sign the release and you shall be free to pursue your artistic endeavors."

"That is precisely the problem." A worried frown crossed Olivia's countenance. "I shall *not* be free. If it were solely the Season and nothing more, I should force myself to endure it. I should clothe myself in finery and sit with the Antidotes and the chaperones until it was over. But my grandmother's intentions extend much farther than requiring my attendance at assemblies and Venetian Breakfasts."

"What does she require of you?" Samantha was intrigued.

"Before she died, my aunt wrote to my grandmother to elicit her aid in securing a suitable match for me."

Samantha's eyes widened in sudden comprehension. "Oh, dear! And your grandmother has been successful?"

"Beyond my aunt's wildest dreams. Grandmother managed to arrange for my marriage at the conclusion of this current Season!"

Samantha began to frown. "But surely you can refuse to wed if it does not please you."

"No, I cannot." Olivia shook her head. "Now that my aunt has died, my grandmother is my legal guardian. Acting as guardian, she has already accepted the gentleman's suit on my behalf!"

"There is no way for you to object?"

"None whatsoever. My grandmother has written to inform me that my marriage will take place *before* I come of legal age."

"But she can't force you to marry." Samantha was horrified at this disastrous turn of events. "Such a thing is not possible . . . is it?"

"Not legally, no. I could refuse the gentleman's suit, but if I do, she will refuse to sign the waiver to release my inheritance."

"That's blackmail!" Samantha was shocked.

"Yes, but it is perfectly legal blackmail. And my grandmother is quite sincere in the belief that she is guiding my life in the proper fashion."

"What will happen to your inheritance if your grandmother refuses to sign the waiver?"

"I shall still receive the funds, but not until my twenty-fifth birthday. It is a very long time to wait to continue my work."

"Yes, indeed." Samantha sighed in sympathy. "It is unfair to force you to marry to receive the funds that are already yours."

"That is not the half of it! You see, Samantha, even if I do endure the Season and marry the gentleman that my grandmother has chosen for me, I *still* shall not receive the funds."

"Why ever not?" Samantha felt her mind begin to spin.

"Because once I am wed, my inheritance will become my husband's property, to do with as he wishes. It would be a rare husband indeed who would allow the funds to be used for the purchase of a country cottage for his wife, especially if she intends to retire there to pursue her solitary artistic career."

They sat in silence for a moment, pondering the dreadful tangle, and then Samantha sighed deeply. "There does not seem to be a solution to your difficulty, Olivia. If you marry, your husband will not allow you to use the funds as you choose. And if you refuse to marry, your grandmother will not allow you to receive the funds. I do wish your problem were as simple as mine for then I should know the solution."

"How thoughtless of me!" Olivia flushed in embarrassment. "We have discussed my situation at length, but I have not seen fit to even inquire about you. I apologize, Samantha."

Samantha smiled. "It does not signify as my problem is solved. My aunt decided that I was to marry the vicar, a man I could not abide. But there was no inheritance, nor even any family to consider. My aunt told me that she was not truly my aunt and thus the solution was simple. I packed my belongings and left yesterday, never to return."

"You ran away?" Olivia gazed at Samantha with admiration. "That is capital, Samantha! Indeed, it is exactly as I should have done, had I not been so timid and frightened. Where do you go and what shall you do?"

"I did not consider that when I fled Hawthorne Cottage. My thoughts were entirely of making good my escape. I shall seek employment, of course, but not until I am well away from this area."

"Then you truly do not know in which direction you will go?"

Samantha shook her head again. "Indeed, I do not. Any place is as good as another, I should think."

"Are you not in the least bit frightened?" Olivia wore an expression of complete amazement.

"No. Any fate that befalls me shall be preferable to wedding the vicar."

"But there will be no one to help you, Samantha." Olivia's expression grew anxious. "You will be forced to endure the company of strangers and make your own way in the world."

"I enjoy encountering strangers. Some of them are not to my liking. I should be a goose to believe that all strangers are good. But many others are but friends that I have not yet met." Samantha favored her new friend with an ironic smile. "Fate is strange, Olivia. In all probability, I shall be the one to lead the solitary life of a rustic while you shall experience the bustle and excitement of London. We should both be much happier if our destinies were reversed."

Olivia nodded, deep in thought. And then her eyes be-

gan to sparkle with excitement. "But they *can* be reversed.
You are truly wonderful, Samantha! You have just tumbled
to a way out of my difficulties, and it shall also serve you
well in the bargain."

"I have?" Samantha frowned slightly. Had the stress of
Olivia's predicament unhinged her senses?

"You shall take my place and I shall take yours! Please
say that you will do it, Samantha. From what you have told
me of your character, you should take great delight in my
London Season."

Samantha felt a rush of excitement as she contemplated
the wonders of London. Uncle Charles had told her of
the Royal Society for the Promotion of Natural Knowledge
and the learned professors that lectured there. How wonderful it would be to observe of these august gatherings!
There was also the Royal College of Physicians. Though
Uncle Charles had not been a fellow, he had corresponded
with several and had been highly respected in his field.
One fellow, Matthew Baillie, the notable Scottish patholo-
gist, had sent her uncle a copy of his book, *Morbid Anatomy
of Some of the Most Important Parts of the Human Body,* and
they had corresponded frequently concerning the relation
of animal pathology to human. Though Matthew Baillie
was now an elderly gentleman, his practice in London still
thrived. Samantha was certain that if she were to contact
this notable gentleman, he would extend every courtesy
to his country colleague's niece.

"I see this thought pleases you, Samantha." Olivia was
aware of the excitement that glittered in Samantha's eyes.
"You should like to travel to London, then?"

"Oh, yes! It should please me above all things! But such
a ruse could not possibly succeed, Olivia. Your grandmother will surely know that I am not you."

"But she will not!" Olivia sat up a bit straighter, a bit
of her confidence returning. "My grandmother has not
set eyes on me since I was in leading strings. She will have
no reason to believe that you are not her granddaughter

when you arrive in the very same coach that she dispatched for me."

"But your grandmother's coachman will know that we have traded places."

"No, he will not." Olivia began to smile. "I wore a veil in his presence. My eyes were swollen from crying at my predicament, and I did not wish for anyone to look upon my face."

Samantha thought about it for a long moment and then she nodded. "Then it *is* possible. But will your grandmother agree to release your inheritance if I take your place?"

"Of course! You shall pretend to be delighted with the choice she has made for your husband. You have but to tell her that you would use the funds for your dowry, and she will waste no time in contacting the solicitor to sign the necessary papers. The funds will be released to me on the date of my eighteenth birthday and I shall be there to collect them!"

"Yes, such a plan could succeed." Samantha nodded quickly. "But about the wedding? You told me that it was to be held *before* your eighteenth birthday."

Olivia nodded. "Grandmother will have grown to trust you by that time, and you shall think of a way to delay it. On the day that I collect the funds, I shall leave an envelope for you at the solicitor's office, containing half of my inheritance. We shall work out all the details so that you will know exactly what to do, and you shall have the funds to start a new life in a place of your choosing."

"There is no reason for you to be so generous." Samantha frowned slightly. "If I agree to do this, you need pay me only enough to leave London."

Olivia laughed. "Nonsense! My inheritance is exceedingly large and I could not possibly spend it all. There is more than enough for the both of us to enjoy a comfortable life. You must not forget that without your assistance, I should not be allowed to claim any of it. Please say that you shall do it, Samantha. I should be very grateful to you."

"It would be a wondrous adventure!" Samantha's eyes glittered in excitement. "But I fear I should soon give myself away. I know nothing of how to conduct myself in polite society."

"Nor do I! Do not forget that I was raised in the country by a maiden aunt who had only been to London but once in her life. Grandmother will not expect me to know anything of the *ton* and its ways. She will hire tutors and all you must do is to learn your lessons. And you shall not even have to remember a new name, for my second name is Samantha! All you need say is that you despise the name 'Olivia' and should much prefer to be called by your second name!"

"But what of your family?" Samantha was still concerned. "I know nothing of them or the relatives that your grandmother is certain to mention."

"That shall not present a problem, either, for I have met very few of them. Come to my room, Samantha, and we shall ring for a sumptuous meal to break our fast. And while we are eating, I shall tell you the story of my life so that you shall be prepared for any questions that my grandmother should ask."

Samantha hesitated for a moment and then she nodded, rushing to gather her meager belongings. If she went to London in Olivia's place, Aunt Phoebe and Vicar Turnbull should never be able to find her.

"Hurry, Samantha." Olivia stood at the door, her hand upon the latch. "You must take nourishment, listen to the story of my life, and dress in my traveling gown. And then you shall be off to London!"

Samantha nodded and hurried out of the room at Olivia's heels. So long as she did her part and their ruse was not discovered, this could be the grandest adventure of her life!

Four

Samantha's heart beat an anxious tattoo as the extremely proper butler led her to a room that he called the Blue Salon. Her baggage was being unloaded by several footmen, and Samantha had been assured that it should be promptly carried up to the chambers that she should occupy for the next two months.

"I shall inform Her Ladyship of your arrival." The butler, who had informed Samantha that he was called Spencer, intoned, "Her Ladyship has left orders that she wishes to see you immediately, before you are taken to your chambers."

With a slight bow, Spencer left the Blue Salon, and Samantha was left alone in the beautifully appointed room. When the door had closed behind him, she settled her skirts around her and pressed her hands together to keep them from trembling. In the brief time before she had boarded the carriage that was to carry her to London, Samantha had committed the salient details of Olivia's life to memory. They had even devised a means of one-sided communication, should an emergency arise. Since Samantha should play the part of Miss Olivia Samantha Tarrington, Olivia had decided to adopt Samantha's identity for her stay in Bath.

A hastily written message had been dispatched to Olivia's painting master, who had an affinity for intrigue and was certain to help them in their scheme. Mr. Dawson would inform his aunt that Miss Tarrington should not be coming to stay with her, as she had decided to join her grandmother in London for the Season. Another of Mr. Dawson's students should arrive in Miss Tarrington's stead, a Miss Samantha Jane Bennings, who preferred to be addressed by her second name, Jane. In the event that Samantha had reason to contact Olivia, she should address her correspondence to Miss Jane Bennings in Bath.

Samantha took a deep breath for courage. This first meeting between Samantha and Olivia's grandmother should set the tone for weeks to come, and Samantha knew how important it was that she play her part faultlessly. She was dressed in one of Olivia's best gowns, a traveling dress of midnight blue muslin with a cape of the same material. The color served to set off her auburn hair; Samantha's greatest fear was that the Dowager Countess of Foxworth should give one glance to her hair and know immediately that she was not Olivia.

As she waited for the dowager countess to greet her, Samantha carefully observed her surroundings. The Blue Salon was indeed lovely, the most beautiful she had ever seen. It provided access to a charming pleasure garden, immediately outside the arched double doors that were set into the far wall. Tall, arched windows, running the entire length of the wall, looked out over this pleasant aspect and Samantha found herself hoping that she would be here long enough to stroll through the garden, admiring the splendid and colorful blooms.

Turning her attentions to the interior of the room, Samantha's gaze traveled eagerly from one piece of lovely furniture to another. The style was elegant, highly polished with carved wooden frames that curved to hold cushions covered in a heavy silken fabric. Samantha was seated on a chair whose cushions were of a delightful shade of robin's egg blue. Other cushions were slightly lighter in hue and still others, darker. As an artisan, Olivia would have loved the Blue Salon as it enjoyed the entire range of the blue pallet.

The decorations of the salon were also of blue; a large

Wedgwood urn atop a lovely wooden cabinet, a tapestry woven in blue, green, and gold that depicted a mythical scene of epic proportions, and a painting of a Grecian goddess that had surely been done by an artist of some renown. As if that were not enough, Samantha also noticed an ornate oval mirror with a design of glittering blue sapphires set round the edge.

The draperies were of ice blue velvet, pulled back from the windows and held there with silken cords that were attached to the wainscoting. The parquet floor was covered in part by a beautiful Aubusson rug that was woven in shades of blue; the walls above the wainscoting were covered with a shade of blue silk that was so light, it approached pure white.

Samantha's inventory ceased abruptly as she heard the sound of approaching footsteps in the hallway. A moment later, the door was opened and an attractive older woman with silver hair strode into the room. Samantha rose to her feet immediately. She did not have to be told that the woman before her was Lady Edna Tarrington, the Dowager Countess of Foxworth, Olivia's grandmother.

Lady Edna was dressed in a gown of deep red silk. She held herself stiffly, as if she suffered from some inflammation of the joints but was unwilling to succumb to this weakness. The moment she spied Samantha, her color went pale and she stopped quite suddenly, her hand pressed to her heart.

Samantha hurried across the room, taking Lady Edna's arm quite firmly and helping her to a chair. "Be seated, Madame, and breathe deeply. This faintness will pass in but a moment."

With a second glance to ascertain that Olivia's grandmother would not topple from her chair, Samantha hurried to the sideboard and poured a small snifter of brandy. Then she wasted no time in returning to the chair to hold it to Lady Edna's lips. Olivia's grandmother took a sip and coughed slightly, a bit of color returning to her cheeks.

"Brandy? And it is not yet noon?" Lady Edna glanced

up at Samantha in some amusement. "Surely that is not what you were taught in your gentle aunt's home!"

Samantha shook her head. "No, Madame, it is not. My aunt did not drink strong spirits, nor did she allow their presence in her home. I should have given you water or tea, if it had been available. Unfortunately, I had no option and you were in dire need of an instant remedy."

"I was, was I not?" Lady Edna laughed softly. "The shock at seeing you quite overcame me, my dear. With that glorious red hair, you are the picture of my dear sister India."

Samantha bit back the smile that threatened to turn up the corners of her lips. It was quite impossible for her to resemble Lady Edna's sister as she was of no relation whatsoever. But people tended to see what they wished to see and Lady Edna was no exception. Olivia had been correct. Her grandmother had not thought to question Samantha's identity.

Lady Edna appeared to be waiting for an answer and Samantha searched her mind. Try as she would, she could not remember Olivia mentioning any relative of that name. "I am sorry, Madame, but I do not remember your sister."

"Of course you do not!" Lady Edna sat up a little straighter and smiled at Samantha. "India died young, long before you were born. Was your hair always that particular shade of red?"

"No, Madame. When I was born, it was much lighter—the color of gold, I was told. It remained that way until my fifth year and then it took on this color."

"And I saw you only once, when you were no more than three years of age." The woman nodded and then frowned slightly. "Why do you not call me Grandmama?"

"I did not wish to take that liberty, Madame, until you had invited me to do so." Samantha did her best to explain. "I shall call you whatever you wish, of course."

"Grandmama will do nicely. And I shall call you Olivia?"

The last was spoken as a query and Samantha answered quickly. "I do wish that you would not, Grandmama. I have been called Samantha for as long as I can remember. It is my second name and I much prefer it."

"Good!" The dowager countess nodded. "Olivia does not suit you at all. Samantha it is, then. Where is your abigail? I was told that you would bring her."

Samantha felt much relieved that Olivia had prepared her for this question. "She succumbed to carriage sickness, Grandmama, on the first day of our journey. It was extremely severe and, as we were passing quite close to her home, I sent her there to recover."

"Then you traveled alone? With no female companion to accompany you?"

"Yes, Grandmama." Samantha nodded. "But you need not fear that my behavior was in the least improper. Your coachman escorted me to the room that he had secured for me, and engaged the innkeeper's eldest daughter to stay there with me."

Lady Edna nodded. "Yes, Hawkins is quite resourceful. This is the reason I chose him to fetch you. Perhaps it is just as well that your abigail did not accompany you. I doubt that a country servant should have been able to perform the duties that shall be required as your dresser."

It was on the tip of Samantha's tongue to mention that she was entirely capable of dressing herself, but she quickly remembered that Olivia had been used to the services of an abigail. Lady Edna did not seem to notice her lack of response and Samantha breathed a bit easier as the older woman smiled at her.

"I shall ask my own dresser, Michele, to find someone suitable to attend you."

"Thank you, Grandmama." Samantha smiled politely. "It is most kind of you."

Lady Edna seemed pleased at Samantha's response. "You have brought your entire wardrobe as I requested?"

Samantha nodded. "Yes, Grandmama. Mr. Spencer informed me that my baggage was being taken to my chamber."

"Chambers." Lady Edna corrected her gently. "Come with me and I shall show you where you are to stay."

They climbed up the grand staircase to the third floor
and Lady Edna opened a door at the end of the hallway.
"This is the suite I have set aside for your use while you
are my guest."

Samantha's eyes widened as Lady Edna led her into a
lovely bedchamber, much larger than any she had seen
before. The dowager countess opened another door and
they stepped into the dressing room that Samantha would
use. Still another door led to a private sitting room that
was the size of Aunt Phoebe's whole cottage!

"La, Grandmama! Whatever shall I do with all this
space?"

"You shall fill it, of course." Lady Edna laughed. "You
are to have a new wardrobe as I have my doubts that any
of the things you brought with you will be acceptable here
in London. And you are certain to make friends during
your Season. You shall entertain them in your private sitting room. I refer to the young ladies only and not the
gentlemen. Gentlemen callers are not to set foot past the
formal Drawing Room on the first floor."

"Yes, Grandmama." Samantha nodded. Olivia had
warned her that her grandmother was a stickler for propriety, but Samantha was of the opinion that Lady Edna's
rules, thus far, were perfectly reasonable.

"And now you must rest after your journey." Lady Edna
crossed the room and turned at the doorway. "I shall send
up a maid with water for your bath. After you have bathed
and rested, we shall peruse your wardrobe together to see
what additions are required."

"Thank you, Grandmama." Samantha breathed a deep
sigh of relief as Lady Edna made to exit the chamber. But
the dowager countess turned once again, a frown upon
on countenance.

"I do hope there is something suitable that you might
wear this evening. I have arranged a small dinner party
and I should like you to look your best."

"I am certain there will be, Grandmama." Samantha

nodded quickly. "Though my clothing is not of the latest fashion, it is of good quality."

Lady Edna smiled. "We shall see. In any event, the duke will not be in attendance so it is of little consequence. Tonight's gathering will be quite informal, but it shall afford you the opportunity to practice your manners at table."

Samantha blanched at the thought. She knew little of proper table etiquette as Aunt Phoebe had never formally entertained.

"Whatever is the matter, child? You have gone as white as a ghost!"

Samantha swallowed with difficulty. There was nothing for it but to admit to the truth. "I fear that I shall be certain to disappoint you, Grandmama. I have never attended a dinner party."

"You have *never* attended a dinner party?" Lady Edna looked astounded. "What was your aunt thinking, to keep you so isolated?"

"She was unwell, Grandmama, and preferred a quiet, rustic life. I am certain she did not mean to neglect this aspect of my training, but such entertainments were beyond her limited capabilities."

"You are loyal to your aunt's memory and that is to your credit." Lady Edna gave her an approving nod. "I doubt, however, that your aunt was ever fond of entertaining. My son made mention of her cheeseparing ways in several letters that he sent to me."

Samantha dropped her eyes. Perhaps Olivia had not been exaggerating when she had claimed that her aunt was thrifty to a fault.

"That is neither here nor there." Lady Edna frowned slightly. "Though I did enjoy a correspondence with your aunt, she did not see fit to inform me that she was unwell. If she had, you may rest assured that I should have sent for you long before this!"

"Perhaps she did not wish to burden you with her problem, Grandmama," Samantha offered as an excuse.

"You may have the right of it, child." Lady Edna nodded. "Lady Honoria was a proud woman and not inclined to ask for assistance from any quarter. From what particular disability did she suffer?"

Samantha thought quickly. Olivia had told her that her aunt was far too stingy to entertain, but Lady Edna's question had provided her with a golden opportunity to use her skills for that good lady's benefit. Samantha took a deep breath and embarked on a Banbury tale of her own making. "My mother's sister was afflicted with a crippling inflammation of the joints that caused her intense pain. The doctor prescribed laudanum, but she did not wish to avail herself of such a strong drug in the dosage that was required to ease her pain. She complained that it adversely affected her senses."

"Yes. Such an effect should be an anathema to such a woman." Lady Edna nodded. "Laudanum does tend to leave one's senses reeling."

"Precisely. This is the very reason that I sought another remedy, one that should ease her symptoms but not affect her senses."

"And did you find such a remedy?"

Samantha nodded, gratified to see the eager expression on Lady Edna's face. "I did. It was twofold. I mixed a salve that loosened the afflicted joints. This enabled her to move more freely. And I prepared a tea of herbs and barks that reduced the inflammation and eased her pain."

"But she succumbed to this crippling disease in the end?"

"Oh no, Grandmama." Samantha shook her head. "She died in a carriage accident, on her way to visit an old friend."

"Then she had recovered sufficiently to travel?"

Samantha nodded. "Yes, Grandmama."

"How did you come to learn of this treatment?" Lady Edna frowned slightly. "From your aunt's letters, I had become convinced that painting watercolours of birds was your sole accomplishment."

Samantha nodded. "It is through my painting that I learned of this remedy. I chanced to meet a most unusual veterinarian who was engaged in the process of healing an eagle of a broken wing. While I sketched the bird, he told me of a salve he used on horses who had come up lame."

"This is quite fascinating." Lady Edna gave her an approving smile. "And the tea?"

"I learned of the tea through a Gypsy healer whose tribe camped near my aunt's home. The two remedies, correctly combined, proved of value to my aunt."

An expression of hope crossed Lady Edna's countenance, but she hid her enthusiasm quickly. When she met Samantha's eyes again, she looked only mildly interested. "I am glad you have told me of this, Samantha. My dresser suffers from the very same malady though she does not care to admit it. Could such a remedy benefit her?"

"I should think it would be just the thing, Grandmama." Samantha nodded quickly. She was well aware that Lady Edna was speaking of herself and not her dresser, but such a ruse did not bother Samantha. People had often come to her to seek remedies, claiming that they were for another. Her uncle had explained this strange phenomenon. Unlike animals, who had no pretenses, some people found it difficult to admit their own physical weaknesses.

"You are certain that it cannot harm her?"

Samantha smiled. "I am certain, Grandmama. The worst that can happen is that it will not help her. In any event, I strongly suggest that she try it. Would she agree to let me tell her of this remedy, or would she prefer that such news came from you?"

"From me, most definitely. She will admit her weakness to no other. If you will instruct me in the use of this remedy, I shall impart it to her."

Samantha quickly located her carpetbag and handed Lady Edna a jar of salve and a packet of crushed herbs and bark. "The salve is to be applied on the skin round the affected joints twice each day, once in the morning and once again when your dresser retires for the night. The herbal mixture is to be steeped like tea. One spoonful should be added to a cup of boiling water and allowed to rest for five minutes before drinking. You must warn her that the brew is bitter and a spoonful of honey may be added to make it more palatable."

"And how often must the tea be used?" Lady Edna took the packet and the salve.

"The tea should be consumed in the morning and again at night upon retiring. If the pain is severe, a third cup may be taken at midday, but I have found that it is usually not necessary."

"And this tea will not affect the senses?" Lady Edna still wore a look of concern.

"Not in the slightest. I would urge your dresser to begin the treatment immediately. It is not too late in the day for her to avail herself of the morning treatment."

"Thank you, Samantha." Lady Edna gave her a smile. "I shall see that she follows your instructions precisely. How do you come to have this remedy in your possession?"

Samantha thought quickly. It would not do to tell Lady Edna that she had brought all of her uncle's books and equipment, but there was a true reason why she carried the herbs and bark and there would be no harm in telling it. "I promised the Gypsy healer that I should never travel without it, Grandmama. Since I began to carry it with me, I have found that there is often an occasion when it can be of benefit to another. It is small repayment for the kindnesses that others have shown to me."

"Spoken like a true lady." Lady Edna smiled. "I shall leave you now, Samantha, and seek out my dresser to tell her of this remedy. I shall return in an hour or so, when you are refreshed and rested."

When Lady Edna took her leave, Samantha sighed deeply. She did not like to deceive Olivia's grandmother, but much good had come of her visit to this house. She had provided Lady Edna with the means to relieve her ailment and in the process, she had also passed her first test. Lady Edna had accepted her as her granddaughter and Olivia would be well pleased with Samantha's performance.

Five

Samantha stood on a pedestal with her arms raised slightly as the modiste's assistant helped her into one of her new gowns. This was the final day of fittings before her wardrobe was complete.

"Yes. This shall do very nicely." Lady Edna nodded and rose to her feet to smooth the teal blue sarcenet skirt of Samantha's gown. "You look lovely, my dear."

"Thank you, Grandmama." Samantha smiled at the older woman. She had noted the ease with which Lady Edna had risen from her chair. The remedy she had suggested had proved quite effective over the past two weeks. Lady Edna's movements were less constricted and it was now possible for her to walk in a natural fashion. The lines around her lips, caused by constant pain, had diminished considerably and Samantha had observed that she now descended the staircase without the need to grip the banister for support.

"Ah, Michele." Lady Edna nodded to her dresser who had just entered the room. "What think you of this gown?"

Michele moved forward and assessed Samantha's gown with a critical eye, walking round her in a circle and bending to observe the lines of the skirt. "Quite lovely, my lady, but perhaps the bodice could be a bit lower, no?"

"No." Lady Edna laughed. "This is Samantha's first Season and you know as well as I do, Michele, that a young lady's hidden charms are much more appealing than those which are fully displayed."

"This is true, my lady." Michele crossed the room to her mistress and quickly took the seat that Lady Edna indicated.

Samantha did her best to hide her amusement as another gown was brought out for their approval. Michele was approximately Lady Edna's age, and she also appeared to have grown more agile. It was quite apparent that the dresser had also suffered from inflammation of the joints, and Lady Edna had not been untruthful about her condition. Olivia's grandmother had merely been reticent to mention that she herself had suffered from a similar affliction.

"Oh, dear!" Lady Edna frowned as the gown was slipped over Samantha's head. "This color will not do at all!"

Michele nodded. "You are quite correct, my lady. It clashes most dreadfully with the color of her hair."

"You are both right." Samantha cast one look at the mirror and turned to smile at Lady Edna and her dresser. "I have never been able to wear this particular shade of pink."

Michele sighed. "There is no help for it, Madame. This gown must be dyed immediately."

"But to what color? It is a vivid hue and it cannot be dyed to a lighter color." Lady Edna frowned slightly as she turned to Samantha. "You are an artist, Samantha. Which color will serve us the best?"

Samantha was thrown into a dilemma by the question. She knew nothing of colors, but if she failed to answer correctly, Lady Edna could begin to doubt her, as Olivia was certain to have such knowledge.

"Let me consider it for a moment, Grandmama." Samantha glanced down at the bright pink hue of her skirt. Rosy, their maid-of-all-work, had owned a dress of this color and she had attempted to dye it black when Uncle Charles had died. Her first attempt had succeeded in part, but there was one area of the dress that had failed to take the dye. When Samantha had examined it, she had noticed that Rosy had spilled candle wax on that area.

Once the wax had been removed from the fibers, Rosy had re-dyed it successfully.

Lady Edna and Michele were waiting for her answer, as was the modiste who had come to deliver the gowns. Samantha took a deep breath and made her suggestion.

"I should think a dark brown with large pink flowers on the skirt would be lovely. All we shall need is a bit of candle wax and a brush."

The modiste turned to Samantha with a frown. "Candle wax? I have never heard of such a thing! For what would I use this candle wax?"

"It is quite simple, really." Samantha smiled at the disapproving modiste. "One melts the wax and paints it on the skirt of the gown, in the shape of flowers. Once the wax has hardened, the gown is immersed in the dye and then it is allowed to dry. When the wax is removed, the pattern is finished."

The modiste thought about Samantha's suggestion for a moment and then she began to smile. "How clever you are! The wax will keep the dye from the fabric and it shall not be colored in the areas where it is applied. I shall attempt this very ingenious plan this very evening! If it succeeds, such a process will be in enormous demand!"

"It will succeed." Samantha nodded quickly. "And it has an added benefit, Madame. It will enable your clients to choose their own designs."

The modiste's eyes began to gleam as she turned to Lady Edna. "Your granddaughter is indeed an artist, my lady! If this procedure is successful, I shall make you a gift of her entire wardrobe and I shall create several dresses for you, as well. But she must agree not to divulge the secret of this process to any other save me."

"I should think that such an arrangement could be made." Lady Edna's eyes were twinkling as she turned to Samantha. "What say you, Samantha?"

Samantha nodded. "It is agreeable to me, Grandmama."

"I must take my leave then." The modiste was smiling

as she motioned for her assistant to remove the vivid pink gown and dress Samantha in one of the gowns that had not needed alteration. "I shall return when this most ingenious gown is completed."

The modiste and her assistant hastily gathered up the gowns and hurried from the chamber. When the door had closed behind them, Lady Edna turned to Samantha with a smile. "How marvelous, my dear! Your clever suggestion has saved us the cost of two wardrobes. I shall reward you by taking you to any sight in London that you wish to see."

"Thank you, Grandmama." Samantha stepped off the pedestal and walked to Lady Edna's side. "There is only one sight in London that I truly wish to see."

"Astley's?" Lady Edna's eyes were still twinkling.

Samantha shook her head. "No, Grandmama. Though I have heard that Astley's is enjoyable, it is not the sight that I wish to see the most."

"Vauxhall Gardens!" Michele smiled. "Surely that is the one."

Again, Samantha shook her head. "There is no need to speculate for you shall never guess it correctly. My one desire is to attend a lecture at the Royal College of Physicians."

"The Royal College?" Lady Edna frowned. "I fear I do not understand you at all, Granddaughter! Attending a lecture at the Royal College should be the very pinnacle of boredom."

Samantha favored Lady Edna with a good-natured smile. "Perhaps you are right, Grandmama, but I should still like to do so. It has always been my fondest desire."

"It is an odd choice, Granddaughter. But if it is truly what you fancy, I shall send round a message to my old friend Matthew Baillie, and request that you be allowed to attend the lectures of your choosing."

"Your *friend*, Grandmama?" Samantha had all she could do to keep her jaw from dropping open in shock. The very person she had so wished to meet in London was Lady Edna's friend!

"He attended Oxford with your grandfather and we

have kept up our acquaintance over the years. When I conversed with him last, he was quite impressed with the remedy you devised for me."

Samantha bit back a smile. Lady Edna seemed oblivious to the fact that she had admitted the remedy was for her as well as her dresser, and it would be terribly unkind to call this lapse of the tongue to her attention.

"He had wished to meet you so that you might advise him of the ingredients. I had invited him to a small dinner party, four days from now, but I shall ask whether he is also available for tea this very afternoon."

"Oh, thank you, Grandmama!" Without another thought, Samantha put her arms around Lady Edna and hugged her unabashedly. Then she stepped back, aware that she might well have overstepped the bounds of propriety. "Please forgive me, Grandmama. I did not mean to be quite so . . . so overly enthusiastic."

Lady Edna smiled. "That is quite all right, my dear. You do realize, however, that such displays of open affection should be regarded as quite unseemly when we are in polite company?"

"Yes, indeed, Grandmama." Samantha felt the color rise to her cheeks. During her lessons in the past two weeks, she had been taught what was, and what was not, acceptable in polite society. "I shall promise never to so indulge my fond emotions for you in future."

Lady Edna looked bemused. "In polite company only, Samantha. In private, I should quite appreciate your charming lack of restraint."

"Damme!" Harry Fielding, the Duke of Westbury, swore as he raced down the road that led to his stables. His lips formed a tight line on his handsome face and his dark brows, which exactly matched the color of his hair, were knit together in a fierce scowl. He had promised to meet

David Brackney, his business partner and friend, at the entrance to the Westbury stables nearly an hour ago.

"No need to rush, Harry." David met him at the doorway. "When you said you were meeting with the Dragoness and Lady Fraidy, I took the liberty of assuming that you would be late."

Harry laughed, his good humor partially restored. David had known how to lift his mood, even when they had been boys together. Harry had been a lonely child, the third boy born to the Duke and Duchess of Westbury. The duchess had wanted a girl and she had let it be known that Harry's birth was a bitter disappointment to her. This baby was to be her last. The London doctor who had been called in to attend her had cautioned her so at the time. Since Harry's older brothers, Stephen and Robert, had fulfilled her husband's requirement of an heir and a spare, the birth of a third boy had distressed the duchess greatly. Instead of the companionship that a daughter should have provided her, she had been saddled instead with another rambunctious boy.

Harry was separated from Stephen by fifteen years. There was only a gap of ten years between Harry and Robert, but it might as well have been a lifetime. On the occasion of Harry's birth, both of his brothers had been off at boarding school and young Harry had grown up with no companionship to speak of. The duchess had left his care to a nanny, avoiding him almost completely, and the duke had been far too busy with his duties to take much interest in a third son.

Harry's only playmate had been the son of the stable master, and David and Harry had become fast friends. The servants had claimed they were closer than most brothers would be—the two boys had become inseparable. When the time had come for Harry to go off to Eton, he had approached his father with great trepidation and requested that David be allowed to attend the boarding school with him.

The duke had agreed quite readily, knowing that such a concession should place David's father firmly in his debt.

Freddy Brackney was the finest judge of horseflesh that the duke had ever employed. The stable master's skill at training racehorses, an activity of which the duke had been inordinately fond, was so well known in all of England that several other noblemen had attempted to hire him away to their own stables.

It was thus that Harry and David had gone away to Eton together, and then on to Oxford where they had both been polished and educated at the duke's expense. On the day of their joint graduation from that fine institution of learning, an event had occurred that had changed both of their lives forever.

Harry's family, with the exception of the duchess, who had taken to her bed with an ailment, had been traveling to Oxford for his graduation. Moments before the ceremony, both Harry and David had been called to the headmaster's office and told of the calamitous accident that had killed Harry's father and his two brothers. The duke's coach had tumbled over a cliff during a sudden storm and the headmaster had informed young Harry that he was now the new Duke of Westbury, a title that Harry had never thought, or possessed the slightest desire, to assume.

Harry had been shocked beyond belief by this disastrous turn of events. He would surely have faltered if not for the aid of David and Freddy Brackney. David's father had become Harry's agent, overseeing the lands and the tenants, and David had taken his father's place in the stables. During this time, the duchess had remained in seclusion, unwilling to face the loss of her husband and her two oldest sons. It was apparent that she expected Harry to carry on and did not wish to be bothered by the particulars. Though Harry had tried, his mother had refused his attempts to comfort her; the duchess had not emerged from her quarters for two long months. At the end of that time, she had summoned Harry, but only to inform him that she had sent for her widowed sister, who would make her home with them until such time that he married. When that event took place, Harry's aunt and his mother would take up residence at her sister's home in Brighton, where the society and the entertainments were more to their liking.

David had begun to call the duchess "Dragoness" when they were boys. It had been a childhood prank, of course, but the moniker that David had chosen had proven to be quite accurate. The duchess was indeed a dragon of the first water. Her sister, however, was not at all fierce. She was quite the opposite and appeared to be fearful of even her own shadow. David had named her "Lady Fraidy" and by referring to the two women thusly, he had caused his friend to view them in a humorous light. This banter had served Harry well as it made his mother and aunt's constant criticism much easier to bear.

"You are a lucky fellow, David." Harry sighed as he walked to the paddock with his friend. "Your father is a fine man and has always given you leave to live your own life. My burden would be much lighter if I had no family to attempt to please."

David nodded. "I do not doubt that in the slightest, and I have often said that it is folly for you to try to please the Dragoness and Lady Fraidy. It is an exercise in futility as you are certain to be unsuccessful."

"Just so. I am sure I do not know why I bother. They are continually bickering with me. If I say the weather is lovely, they tell me that a storm is surely in the making. And if it is raining and I mention that fact, they claim that the rain has almost ceased and it will turn out to be a lovely day. I have never known two women to argue so!"

David began to grin. "But you do enjoy jousting with the Dragoness and Lady Fraidy. Come now, Harry . . . admit as much!"

"It is true that I usually enjoy these matches, but this time I fear they have bested me. They caught me off guard and sank their claws into my back."

David frowned slightly. His friend seemed quite dejected, not at all the normal state of affairs for the fun–loving young Duke of Westbury. "What have they done, Harry?"

"I fear they have duped me and the results are disastrous. And all because I permitted them to ply me with a bottle of excellent brandy!"

"You have been outfoxed?" David laughed merrily at his pun and his dark blue eyes twinkled with good humor. "I mean, of course, that the Dragoness and Lady Fraidy arranged to get you foxed to extract some sort of promise from you?"

"You have the way of it exactly. And I am sorry to say that it was not merely a verbal promise. The Dragoness had written a letter, you see, and she requested that I sign it. I assumed that I was approving a chit for a new gown or some such thing. She is continually after me for things like that. Since I was far too muddle-headed to read the blasted thing, I simply signed where she indicated."

"Heaven forfend!" David began to frown. "Whyever did you do something so rash?"

"I tired of their voices and simply wished for them to leave me in peace. They did, of course, but only after I had signed the letter."

David groaned as his friend's words sank in. "And now your rash action has come back to haunt you?"

"It shall haunt me for the rest of my days! They have just informed me that I signed a letter of intent . . . a blasted marriage proposal! Without my knowledge or my approval, it seems that I have become betrothed!"

"To whom?" David's brows shot up with the question. It appeared that his friend was in a dreadful tangle.

"To the granddaughter of an acquaintance. I assume that she has the proper pedigree, or they should not have considered the match."

"Lineage, Harry." David made an attempt to lighten his friend's mood. "Cattle have pedigrees, young ladies possess lineage."

"Lineage then. I have no doubt that the young lady is exceptionally suitable. The Dragoness and Lady Fraidy would never permit me to marry beneath my station."

David took in his friend's tone of sarcasm and chose

not to comment on it. Instead, he nodded and searched his mind for a way out of the difficulty. "Perhaps you could talk to the young lady and explain that you were not in control of your faculties when you signed this letter?"

"That was my first thought. But they have just informed me that wedding plans are already in the making and I am expected in town in one week's time to meet my intended bride. Our engagement is official, you see, having been accomplished by proxy. To make matters even muddier, the document I signed insisted that we wed without delay at the end of the current Season!"

"What a horrible bumble-broth!" David was practically speechless. "You are to wed a young lady you have never met?"

"You have the right of it. I shall be caught in the parson's trap in less than two months' time!"

The two men stood in silence for a moment and then Harry sighed. "My fiancée has never set eyes on me. And should prefer to keep it that way! I do not wish to marry at all, but if I must, I most certainly do not choose to wed a stranger!"

David was thoughtful for a moment. He was aware that his friend had always been uncomfortable around young ladies—the required social banter was difficult for him. It was not that Harry disliked the ladies. It was rather a certain shyness that overcame him in the company of females. This David could readily appreciate. He was certain that if he had been cursed with the Dragoness as a mother, he should also be dreadfully uncomfortable among members of the opposite sex. "Tell me, Harry, did this young lady enter into this engagement willingly?"

"I assume that she did." Harry shrugged. "In any event, she would have no choice in the matter. According to the Dragoness and Lady Fraidy, all was arranged with her maternal grandmother, who hadn't set eyes on the girl since she was in leading strings."

"Then it is not impossible that she also feels trapped by these circumstances. You must meet her, Harry, and explain all. Once she understands this engagement was brought about through trickery, she may prove willing to cry off."

"Do you think so?" An expression of hope crossed Harry's face, but it was erased after a moment's consideration. "It will not fadge, David. Even if the young lady wished to cry off, her grandmother would never permit her to do so. She is quite penniless, you see, and will not come into her inheritance unless her grandmother approves. She would not dare to displease the lady who holds the purse strings."

David nodded. "I see. And the grandmother approves this match?"

"Most assuredly. I am considered the catch of the Season. Do not forget that I am a duke, and to make matters even more enticing, my solicitor tells me that I am as rich as Golden Ball."

"Quite true." David nodded. "Still, there must be a way of making you appear less suitable. I should think that you might develop some horrid flaw in your character, a flaw that should displease the grandmother so greatly that she will encourage her granddaughter to cry off."

Harry's brows shot up and a grin replaced his anxious frown. "This flaw should have to be horrendous."

"Indeed." David nodded quickly. "Let us think of the reasons a young lady might have for breaking her engagement."

"There is gambling. Margaret Whitmore cried off when her fiancé ran up too many vouchers in the hellholes he frequented."

"No." David shook his head. "Gambling will not serve you well, Harry. All you need do is remember our games of chance in college. You were forever losing your quarterly allowance."

Harry nodded. "What you say is true. I was forced to write my father for advances more times than I care to remember. But the fact that I am a foolish gambler might work in my favor in this instance."

"Perhaps, but you should have to lose a fortune and I do not think that you should like to see your name published as a bankrupt in the *London Gazette*."

Harry shuddered slightly. "No, I should not. I am proud of my family name and should not like to see it dragged through the dust. What of dalliance? If I am seen with an expensive bit of muslin, her grandmother may permit the girl to cry off."

"That will not serve, my friend. Many young ladies of impeccable breeding do not wish to be bothered with the physical side of life. She may be relieved that she shall not have to share your bed so often, and desire the marriage even more. You should have to embroil yourself in a scandal of some magnitude involving dozens of lightskirts, opera girls, and Cyprians if dalliance is to succeed as an excuse. And then you should be defeating your purpose of protecting your family name."

Harry nodded and looked a bit relieved. "Right you are. I suppose I could become a hopeless tosspot. That should sufficiently discourage her."

"Imbibing to excess is not for you, Harry." David gave a rueful chuckle. "You must needs remember that an over-indulgence in brandy is the very thing that placed you in this bramble! But consider what should happen if it came to light that you were promised to another. Then this young lady should be required to step aside."

"But I am not, and I know of no young lady who would agree to pretend to be engaged to me. Even if I happened to meet such an understanding young miss, *she* might then want to marry me and I should be in a similar tangle."

David considered the problem for a moment and then he sighed. "It is a pity you could not hire an actor to play the part of this young lady's intended. After all, she has never seen you and should not know the difference. The actor could then reveal himself the instant before the vows were to be spoken, and she should surely cry off."

"But I could not trust any actor who would agree to do such a thing. He should have to be someone I knew very well, someone I trusted implicitly. And there is no one who . . . David! You have come up with the perfect solution!"

"I have?" David reached up to run his fingers through his tousled honey-colored hair. "What did I say? You must repeat it, for you have left me at the starting gate."

"You can pretend to be me! I know it will work, David, and I would trust you with my life. All you have to do is introduce yourself as Harry Fielding, the Duke of Westbury, and no one will be the wiser."

David frowned. "But you must be acquainted with some of the notables of the *ton*. They will know that I am not you."

"I have no acquaintances in London, of the *ton* or otherwise. I have never even *been* to London. The Dragoness and Lady Fraidy have urged me to go to take part in the Season, but I have repeatedly refused them."

"But what of them, Harry? Surely the Dragoness and the Lady Fraidy shall travel to London for the Season if you are to be there."

"Not this particular Season." Harry smiled grimly. "I shall tell them that I will agree to finance their journey to the continent. They have been desirous of traveling, you see, and I have deliberately dragged my feet on the issue."

"I should think that you would be glad to be rid of them!"

"You are correct." Harry began to smile. "But you forget that they are contrary to the extreme. If they suspect that I should be happy to be shut of them, they should no longer wish to go. I must pretend to give my permission reluctantly, as if their arguments have convinced me."

"I did not know that you had it in you to be so devious." David regarded his friend with surprise.

"Yes, indeed. And it is to their credit as they have taught me to be so. I shall arrange for them to depart by the end of the week and furnish them with the blunt they will need to buy complete wardrobes while they are there. I shall give them the choice of attending my wedding or enjoying a six-month tour of the continent."

David laughed. "They will choose the tour. That is a foregone conclusion."

"Precisely! To further sweeten the pot I shall tell them that my new bride and I shall visit them there on our wedding trip."

"That should suffice to send them off and keep them away." David nodded. "But I *have* been to London, Harry. What if I am recognized?"

"Where, exactly, have you been in London?"

"I have attended the auctions at Tattersall's to purchase prime cattle for your stables."

Harry looked thoughtful. "While you were there, did you make the acquaintance of any titled gentlemen?"

"No."

"Then it should not signify. Even if someone should recognize your features and remember that you were present at Tatt's, it should not be unusual. Many gentlemen prefer to choose their own cattle. Which other locations did you frequent while you were in London?"

"Only one." David grinned. "But you need not be concerned, Harry. It is not a place where one gives one's name, and a true gentleman should never speak of it in polite conversation if he had spotted me there."

Harry was clearly puzzled for a moment, and when he caught the meaning behind David's words, his cheeks reddened in embarrassment. "You are correct, David. If you were seen in this particular . . . er . . . . establishment, it should not present a problem."

David tried not to smile at Harry's discomfort. His friend had never been easy when discussing matters of this nature. "If I do agree to go to London and masquerade as the Duke of Westbury, you cannot remain here. Someone should be certain to see you and uncover our ruse."

"That is easily solved." Harry smiled. "I shall tell all that I am departing for London, but I shall travel instead to Bath. I have long desired to visit a dear friend's aunt who resides there."

David shook his head. "No, Harry. Bath is not the place for you. You shall be certain to be spotted at one of the social gatherings."

"I shall not attend any such functions. My friend's aunt lives in a rustic cottage, some distance from the city. She does not take part in the social whirl of Bath."

"Who is this friend?" David was curious. "I have not heard you make mention of him."

"It is Charles Dawson. I have kept up a correspondence with him."

"Your old painting master?" David began to smile. "A nice chap, as I recall, and he seemed quite impressed with your landscapes. You must remember to give him my regards when next you send a letter to him."

"I shall be certain to do so. Charles wrote to me recently to tell me of his aunt's residence in Bath. He remarked that the area surrounding her cottage has a plethora of lovely vistas and he urged me to visit her there. It seems she has a fondness for artists and is herself a painter. He described her cottage as an artist's paradise and retreat."

David's smile grew wider. "You would travel there to paint?"

"Most definitely. Her invitation arrived in this morning's post, urging me to avail myself of her hospitality. I shall reply immediately and accept."

"It is a capital idea, Harry!" David's dark blue eyes warmed with affection. "You have neglected your painting of late and I am aware that it gives you great pleasure. I am also aware that the Dragoness has discouraged you in your passion."

Harry nodded. "It is difficult for me to paint in the face of her criticism. She regards the pursuit of art as unmanly, more suited to a woman's temperament than that of a gentleman."

"Her attitude is idiotish and I am most relieved that Rembrandt and Michelangelo did not have such a mother!"

David sighed deeply. "I truly believe you have the skill to become a formidable talent, Harry. The landscape you completed for me is one of my prized possessions."

Harry's smile was like a ray of sunshine as he reached out to clasp his friend's hand. "Thank you for those kind words, David. I shall travel to Bath then, and I shall paint to my heart's content without the Dragoness or Lady Fraidy to plague me. Do you think that your father will agree to assume my duties in my absence?"

"I am certain that he will. And I have no doubt that young Ned is quite capable of assuming my duties in the stable."

"You will do it then?" Harry's smile grew even wider.

David laughed at the delighted expression on Harry's countenance. "I did not intend to commit myself quite so hastily, but it appears that I have already done so. Yes, Harry. I shall take your place in London, but there are bound to be unpleasant consequences when I reveal my true identity."

"You shall not reveal your true identity, only that you are not me. And you shall disappear before anyone can discover exactly who you are. No one shall be able to place the fault at your door."

David frowned. "My own reputation is of little consequence to me, Harry. But what of you? It shall surely be discovered that you were a willing participant in this ruse."

"No, it will not." Harry began to smile. "I shall profess that when I was approached with the letter of intent, I declined to sign it and sent it back to the girl's grandmother straightaway, along with a note saying that I had no intention of marrying at this time. Believing that I had finished with that bit of business, I thought nothing further of the matter."

David nodded. "And you had no suspicion that the unsigned letter of intent had been intercepted and signed by another?"

"None whatsoever. I shall also maintain that I heard nothing of the wedding plans that had been so deviously made for me as I had traveled to Bath and was secluded in an artists' retreat, pursuing my painting."

David nodded quickly. "That should fadge. But I cannot shake my concern over the young lady's reputation once this fraud is revealed."

"I am convinced that the young lady's reputation will not suffer in the slightest." Harry made haste to reassure his friend. "It will be quite the opposite. She shall be seen as an unwitting victim and the honorable gentlemen of the *ton* will trip over themselves to rush to her rescue."

"Are you certain, Harry? I should not choose to deliberately harm an innocent young lady."

"In truth, I believe that you shall be performing a kindness for her." Harry began to smile. "We shall put our heads together and prepare a notice to be published in the *London Times*, on the day that you escape London. In it, you shall publicly apologize for your rash actions and assert that the young lady's great beauty and charm prompted you to masquerade as the Duke of Westbury and to forge my signature on the letter of intent."

David began to smile. "I see the path that you are traveling. I shall also state that I have fallen hopelessly in love with this lovely lady and find that I cannot continue in this deception and marry her under false pretenses."

"Precisely." Harry reached out to shake David's hand. "In view of this very public declaration of love by the bounder who had initially intended to deceive her, the young lady's popularity is certain to increase. All will wonder at the lengths to which this rake has gone to secure her affections."

David nodded. "You are correct, Harry. I wager to say that once this notice has been published, she will be regarded as an Incomparable."

"Even if she were an Antidote, which the Dragoness and Lady Fraidy have assured me she is not, Miss Olivia Tarrington shall receive scores of legitimate offers of marriage, many more than she should have had without our timely deception!"

Six

"You are the picture of perfection, Miss Samantha." Samantha's abigail smiled as she patted an errant curl in place. "And your gown is the finest I have ever seen."

Samantha smiled back. "It is all to your credit, Bettina. You have arranged my hair beautifully."

"Thank you, Miss Samantha." The young abigail blushed prettily at the compliment. "If there is nothing further that you require, I shall go to fetch the jewels that her Ladyship has set aside for you to wear."

"There is nothing further, Bettina. You may go."

The abigail dipped her head in a nod and hurried from Samantha's dressing room. The moment the door had closed behind her, Samantha moved closer to the mirror and turned so that she could see her reflection from various angles.

The gown was glorious, even more so than Samantha had envisioned. Madame LaFond had followed the procedure that she had suggested, and the modiste had exhibited a remarkable talent for painting lifelike flowers with the wax. A veritable garden of blooms graced the skirt of the gown, and she had dyed the background a most pleasing shade of brown. The hue was unusual, a brilliant bronze, and it matched the coloration of Samantha's hair precisely.

When she had delivered the gown, Madame LaFond had honored her promise to provide Samantha's wardrobe in exchange for the secret method of dyeing the gown. At

the same time, she had also made Lady Edna a gift of four
new gowns to be fashioned from materials that the dowager countess had chosen.

Samantha took a deep breath and practiced her smile.
Then she tipped up her chin, extended her hand in the
graceful manner that she had been taught, and gazed up
at an imaginary gentleman.

"I am pleased to meet you as well, Lord Westbury . . .
no, Lord Fielding." Samantha stopped suddenly and
sighed. She had got it wrong already! A duke was not a
lord. He enjoyed a special status. She seemed to remember
that one addressed a duke as *Your Grace*, but it was certainly
improper to say *Your Grace Fielding* as he would not use his
family name. Her duke was Harry Fielding, the Duke of
Westbury, but she certainly could not say, *I am pleased to
meet you as well, Harry Fielding, the Duke of Westbury*. If she
were foolish enough to do so, she would be repeating the
very words Lady Edna's butler would use to announce him!

Her brows knit together in a deep frown as Samantha
considered her options. Perhaps she should say *Your Grace
Westbury*, but that did not seem correct, either, and she
found herself at a complete loss. She knew full well that she
should not call him *Harry*. It was highly improper, almost
scandalous, to use his given name on their initial meeting.

What perverse fate had convinced Lady Edna to choose
a duke? Samantha sighed deeply. She had been taught
what to say if he'd been any of the other rankings. If he
had been an earl or a marquis she could have called him
Lord Westbury. And if he'd been a baron, she could have
addressed him as *Lord Fielding*. But Lady Edna had arranged for Olivia to marry a blasted duke and Samantha
was at a loss to know precisely how to address him!

Samantha scowled at her reflection as she considered
the differences that existed between the duke's position
and her own. He certainly had no need to suffer a moment's indecision. In light of his exalted ranking, he could
address her in any manner that happened to strike his
fancy. She could be *Miss Tarrington* or *Lady Olivia;* either

would suffice nicely. And if he cared to be less formal, he could address her *my dear,* or *my dear young lady,* or even *my lovely* with perfect impunity. In the unlikely event that he was so inclined as to call her *Olivia* at their first meeting, no one should dare to call him to task for his lack of propriety. He was a duke and as such, he was at the very pinnacle of the peerage. Only the royal family itself commanded more deference.

"Oh, bother!" Samantha favored her reflection with a frown. Then she hurried to the *escritoire* and pulled out a drawer. She had copied the proper forms of address from the book of etiquette that her instructor had shown to her. Her eyes raced to the line that concerned the rank of duke and she groaned as she realized her problem was not yet solved.

A duke is properly addressed as "Your Grace," if one is below the gentry. Samantha sighed as she read the words a second time. But she was not below the gentry. Olivia Samantha Tarrington was the daughter of a baron. And the following line did not assist her, either. It said, *A duke is properly addressed as "Duke" if one is a member of the nobility or gentry.*

Samantha sighed, praying that the answer would magically appear, but no such event took place. She supposed that she could say, *I am pleased to meet you as well, Duke,* but was that so abrupt as to be impolite? *Sir* was incorrect, as was *Lord,* and she truly had no other choices.

Suddenly the perfect solution occurred to Samantha and she erupted in peals of delighted laughter. What a silly goose she had been, worrying herself ragged over a problem so easily solved! Lady Edna would be the first to greet the duke and certainly a countess would know the proper way to address him. She would simply take her cue from Lady Edna and address her fiancé in like manner.

David scowled as the duke's London coachman pulled the carriage to a halt at the entrance of Tarrington Mansion. Cromley was an excellent whip and David was most pleased with his skills, but he did wish that he had felt free to take one of his own men to London with him.

Rather than risk trusting even the most loyal member of Harry's staff, David had taken the post chaise to London. The fewer who knew about the ruse, the better it should be for all concerned. A chance word here or there, no matter how innocently spoken, could set their plans awry.

Lodging had presented no problem. Harry had inherited a large town mansion from his father and the staff had been kept on to maintain it. Since none had met their new master, David's identity had not been questioned when he had presented himself at the door two days past. Harry had written to prepare the staff and they had welcomed David most cordially. It seemed that everyone employed at Harry's town mansion was doing his utmost to curry the young Duke of Westbury's favor.

The duke's housekeeper, Mrs. Fairweather, was a model of starched efficiency. The French chef, Pierre, was quick to inquire after His Grace's preferences. The butler, Mr. Hastings, was as proper and distinguished as a butler could possibly be. The valet, Mr. Billings, seemed well-versed in precisely which items of His Grace's clothing would best suit the current fashion and was remarkably versatile in styling David's hair so that it should not be out of mode. Indeed, David was certain that no other staff could be so excellent and he reminded himself to inform Harry of that fact when this ordeal in London was complete and he returned to his position at Harry's country estate.

David studied his reflection in the glass window of the carriage while he waited for Cromley to open the door. His blinding white neckcloth was tied in a perfect Mathematical, and his coat of navy blue superfine had been brushed to within an inch of its life. His new dress boots, which he had commissioned from Hoby within moments of setting foot in London, had been polished so highly that his reflection was mirrored in their shining surface. Mr. Billings had assured him that his appearance far outshone the finest *Pink of the Ton,* and that David should put even the famous Beau Brummell to shame.

In the sennight before David's departure, Harry had quizzed David in the proper mode of behavior for any occasion that could conceivably arise. As they had worked out various scenarios involving the duke and his intended bride, David's resolve had wavered. The ruse they had planned should take a great deal of skill on his part. He had never desired to be part of the glittering social life of the *ton.* Indeed, under his own auspices, he could not have been accepted, as he was neither a member of the peerage nor the gentry. It was true that he had been educated in the manner of the nobility. His years at Eton and Oxford with Harry had prepared him to assume a position of privilege. But all the while David had been learning the proper manner in which to bow before a lady, memorizing the polite phrases that should pass his lips, and practicing the figures that would be performed at grand balls, he had assumed that he should never be allowed the opportunity to employ these social skills. And now, despite that fact that he had in no way desired to rise above his station, he was about to be thrust into the midst of the *haute ton* in the guise of a duke!

Harry had laughed off David's concerns. In the unlikely event that he committed a social *faux pas,* no one should be so rude as to remind him of that fact. He was the Duke of Westbury and, as such, would set the standards of behavior for those who were of a lower ranking. Indeed, if David were to appear at a formal dinner wearing an improperly tied neckcloth, the other gentlemen in attendance would rush to arrange their own neckcloths in precisely the same manner to avoid offending him.

As the days before his departure had passed, all too swiftly to suit David, the sight of Harry's enthusiasm regarding his upcoming sojourn to Bath had given him new resolve. He was well aware that Harry was at his happiest when he was pursuing his passion for oils and canvas. It was quite apparent that Harry longed to meet his former

painting master's aunt and was eagerly anticipating his
long days of painting in congenial surroundings. This had
made it next to impossible for David to cry off from his
promise. Harry could not paint at Westbury Park. The
Dragoness and Lady Fraidy discouraged him at every turn.
Harry's dedication to the arts could not possibly survive
in such a climate of disapproval.

David had sighed and accepted his fate, resolving to do
his utmost to see that their ruse was successful. Poor Harry
was quite at the mercy of his mother's devious scheme to
see him leg-shackled to the young lady of her choice, and
David truly felt that it was his duty to rescue his friend
from her clutches.

It was on the eve of his departure that David had confessed his most pressing concern. What if he should fail to
respond when someone addressed him by Harry's name?
The two friends had considered the problem for long minutes and then Harry had devised the perfect solution. When
asked, David should simply state that he preferred to be
called "David." By sheer chance, it had been the original
Duke of Westbury's given name. David Fielding, the first
Duke of Westbury, had been known far and wide as a true
humanitarian. David should explain that he had begun to
use the name when he had first assumed his ducal duties,
as he wished to follow in his ancestor's footsteps.

Since Harry and David were of like size and build, the
required wardrobe had not presented a difficulty. Foot-
wear, however, had been an obstacle as David's feet were
larger and wider than Harry's. Harry had resourcefully
dispatched a messenger to the famous bootmaker, Hoby,
so that all should be in readiness for the creation of David's
boots the moment that he arrived in London.

Invitations had begun to arrive for David the moment
it was known that the Duke of Westbury was to take part
in the current Season. By the time that David arrived in
London, the silver salver on the piecrust table in the entrance hall of Harry's town mansion had been overflowing
with requests for his presence. David had turned them over

to Mr. Hastings and requested the loyal retainer's advice. Despite the butler's advanced years and frail appearance, he had kept abreast of the latest *on-dits* and knew precisely which invitations David should, and should not, accept.

This evening marked David's first venture into society. Mr. Hastings had informed him that he should accept no invitations prior to attending the countess's dinner party and making the acquaintance of his fiancée. Once that duty had been accomplished, David should be free to take part in the Season's entertainments.

"I should much prefer to be in the stable." David did not realize that he had spoken aloud until the door of the carriage opened and he observed the surprised expression on his coachman's face.

"What was that, Your Grace?" Cromley frowned slightly as he handed David down from the carriage. "I did not hear your words."

David knew he dared not admit to the actual words that had passed his lips. Cromley would find it quite shocking that the Duke of Westbury wished that he were in a stable. "I said I should much prefer to be at *table*. Perhaps I should have availed myself of the tea tray that Mrs. Fairweather offered, as I am frightfully empty. I assume it shall be an hour or more before I receive sustenance?"

"You have the right of it, Your Grace." Cromley nodded. "I have heard tell that these formal dinners are long and tedious with much ceremony to be observed before one is allowed to eat."

David sighed as he prepared to walk up the stone steps that led to the portals of Tarrington Mansion. Though his comment had been made in haste, entirely to cover his lapse of the tongue, there was indeed a void inside him that only food would fill. He had eaten lightly at breakfast, finding himself in a great rush to keep his appointment with Hoby and retrieve his new boots. Nuncheon had not been much to speak of, either, as he had availed himself of but a morsel, retiring to his study to write an account of his arrival in London for Harry's edification. When the letter had been completed, David had found he was reticent about franking the missive using Harry's name and title. It was strange that this small deception should bother him so excessively. In light of the huge deception that he was performing, it was virtually insignificant. But bother him it did, and if not for the fact that the servants should think it odd had he failed to frank it, David knew that he should have never accomplished the deed.

Despite his misgivings, David had posted his letter to Mr. Dawson's aunt. She would open it and, seeing Harry's given name on the inner envelope, hand it to him. As the true Duke of Westbury had been most anxious when David had departed from his country estate, the news of David's successful arrival should be certain to reassure him greatly.

And then there was the matter of the tea tray. David's belly growled as he thought of the hot buttered scones that Mrs. Fairweather had offered with the pot of delightful blackberry jam. How could he have refused such a tempting treat? But he had, and there was no way to reverse the course of his action at this late date. He should be forced to make the pretty to his hostess and his fiancée, endure the long interval that had surely been allocated for polite converse, and bide his time stoically until dinner was announced.

"Your Grace?" Cromley handed him a small packet wrapped in a square of clean linen. "One of the kitchen maids slipped this to me before we set out. It's a buttered scone with a bit of jam on it. It should serve to take the corner from your hunger."

David took the packet gratefully, unwrapping it with relish and taking a huge bite. "Well done, Cromley! You have just rescued me from committing a dreadful *faux pas.*"

"I have?" Cromley wore a bewildered expression. "How is that, Your Grace?"

David laughed as he finished the excellent scone and wiped the crumbs from his mouth. "You have thoughtfully provided the means to make certain that my belly does not do the conversing for me in Lady Tarrington's Drawing Room!"

Seven

Samantha's smile faltered briefly as Lady Edna's very proper butler announced the Duke of Westbury. Though she was firmly seated on a blue velvet sofa in Lady Edna's Drawing Room, Samantha's knees began to tremble and she had the horrid suspicion that she should not be able to rise to greet the duke properly when he entered the room.

"You shall do splendidly, Granddaughter." Lady Edna's voice was reassuring. "I am certain that the duke shall be more than pleased by your appearance and your comportment."

Samantha dipped her head in an obliging nod and prepared to rise to her feet. Her comportment would suffer, along with her appearance, if she were to fall flat on her face. Surprisingly, her trembling knees held fast and she managed to rise quite gracefully.

When the duke was ushered into Lady Edna's formal Drawing Room, Samantha kept her eyes on a level with his neckcloth, which was tied in a perfect Mathematical. She could not meet his eyes, for he should be certain to see the panic that lurked in their depths. He cut a dashing figure—tall, assured, and perfectly dressed. Samantha let out her breath in a soft sigh of relief. At least she would not have to be partnered at all the *ton* functions by a rotund gentleman who came no higher than her chin!

"I am delighted to make your acquaintance, Lady Edna." The duke crossed to the countess and received her hand in greeting. Samantha raised her eyes for a quick peek, but his back was turned toward her as he carried Lady Edna's hand to his lips in a formal salute.

"And I am most pleased to meet you at last." Lady Edna smiled charmingly.

Samantha willed the pleasant smile to remain on her face, though inwardly she was groaning. Lady Edna's greeting had been of no assistance for she had not addressed him as either "Lord" or "Duke." She should simply have to muddle through somehow and question Lady Edna on the proper manner of address when they were alone once again.

Lady Edna gestured toward Samantha. "I should like to introduce you to your fiancée, my granddaughter, Miss Olivia Samantha Tarrington."

Samantha drew a deep breath for courage and fixed her gaze firmly on his neckcloth as Lady Edna led him across the room. When the neckcloth was before her, Samantha dipped a graceful curtsy, precisely in the manner that she had been taught, and prayed that her voice should not falter when he addressed her.

"Miss Tarrington. It is indeed a delight to meet you. It is also a pleasant surprise to find that I have unwittingly declared for an Incomparable."

"It is exceedingly kind of you to say so." Samantha avoided a direct address quite neatly, she thought, as the duke received her extended hand. When he raised it to his lips, his features lowered into her line of vision and she uttered a small gasp of shock. Harry Fielding, the Duke of Westbury, was the rake that she had encountered at the Two Feathers Inn, the ill-mannered bounder who had kissed her most thoroughly and then declared that she still belonged in the schoolroom!

Covering her shock as best she could, Samantha quickly dropped her eyes again, to the exact center of Lady Edna's prized Aubusson rug. She should expire on the spot if he recognized her as the girl that he had mistaken for a light-skirt!

As if in answer to her unspoken plea, Lady Edna's butler returned at the exact moment to announce that several other guests had arrived. In the formality of greetings that ensued, Samantha was saved from the necessity of making a further reply to her fiancé. Lady Edna quickly bore the duke off to speak with Lord and Lady Halverson, while Samantha sat quite properly on the sofa, her smile fixed firmly in place, frantically hoping that the duke's memory was as faulty as his manners had been only three weeks past.

During the course of the polite converse that ensued in Lady Edna's Drawing Room, David found his eyes drawn to the lovely young lady who had been introduced as his fiancée. He was nearly certain that he had met her before, but the circumstances of that meeting eluded him. From information gleaned through Lady Halverson, David learned that she had come to London from a small estate in the country. Lord Paxton then mentioned that it was far to the north, at the very edge of the Scottish border, and David was even more puzzled for it was in an area that he had never had occasion to visit. He also learned, from Lady Danbury, that his fiancée preferred to be called by her second name, Samantha, and that this was the young lady's first trip to London—or anywhere else, for that matter. This ruled out the possibility that David had met her on holidays he had taken with Harry. From Lord Danbury, David discovered that Samantha had led a sheltered life with her maiden aunt. Since Samantha's aunt was unwell, she had not entertained, nor had she allowed Samantha to attend social functions alone. This precluded the possibility that David had made her acquaintance at a house party or a social gathering. Lord Danbury also remarked that it was unfortunate that Samantha's light had been hidden under a bushel for all these years, and that now that the charming young lady was in London at last, she was certain to take the *ton* by storm.

Lady Paxton offered more grist for the mill when she informed David that Samantha had made the acquaintance of Matthew Baillie, the esteemed London physician. According to Lord Paxton, who was listening to this conversation with interest, Dr. Baillie seemed quite taken with Samantha and had agreed to take her round to the Royal College when next he attended a lecture. This last comment prompted Lady Halverson to confide that she suspected simple kindness had prompted Samantha to indulge her grandmother's old friend, as it was certainly not fashionable for a well-bred young lady of Samantha's caliber to be truly interested in things scientific.

All the information David gleaned from this amiable converse failed to solve the riddle. He had met no young ladies who had come from the area of Samantha's former home, he could recall no introductions to anyone named Samantha or Olivia, and he had not made the acquaintance of any young lady who had claimed science as her interest.

As David studied his intended bride, he was aware that she appeared to be anxious and ill at ease. She covered it well with polite smiles and graceful gestures, but when she thought herself unobserved, an emotion approaching panic crossed her lovely face. Searching for a probable cause for her discomfort, David wondered whether Samantha held the same opinion of the betrothal as Harry did. He had learned from the letters that Lady Honoria, Samantha's aunt, had written to the Dragoness that Samantha had been given no choice in the matter. If she truly did not desire this marriage, perhaps Harry's problem would have a painless and expedient solution.

Dinner was a formal affair and David managed to observe Samantha closely. She consumed very little and appeared decidedly uncomfortable. On the occasions when her eyes met his, he was certain she wished to bolt from the table and escape to her chambers, never to set eyes on him again. He would have had to be blind not to see that something was dreadfully amiss and he vowed to get to the root of the problem as soon as he was allowed a private word with her.

The dessert had been served—a basket of the pastry chef's most delicious offerings, followed by a compote of fresh fruit in a sugary sauce. Samantha sighed with relief when the time came to rise at last and follow Lady Edna and the other ladies from the room. The gentlemen would enjoy aged port or fine brandy, with choice cigars, while the ladies retired to the Drawing Room to engage in pleasant female conversation until the gentlemen saw fit to rejoin them.

"What think you, Samantha dear?" Lady Halverson smiled at Samantha. "I must declare that I regard the duke as a pattern card of the perfect match."

Samantha nodded and smiled back politely, choosing her words with caution. Bettina, her dresser, had given Samantha warning that Lady Halverson was a notorious gossip. "Yes, indeed, Lady Halverson. He appeared to be perfect in all aspects."

"Appeared?" Lady Paxton smiled in amusement. "My dear girl! The Duke of Westbury is a superlative match! He is wickedly handsome and it is said that he is as rich as Golden Ball. What more could a young lady require?"

Samantha merely smiled and bit back the retort that threatened to fly from her lips. Love. A young lady could require love. A marriage should be merely a convenience without the presence of love.

"Love?" Lady Danbury voiced Samantha's thoughts and then favored her with a sympathetic glance when Samantha dipped her head in a nod. "Love grows with time, my dear. I must admit that I was not pleased when Phillip first declared for me. Ours was an arranged marriage, you see, and I had thought to choose better for myself. My father would have none of it and ordered me to accept Phillip's proposal. And look how famously it has turned out! Phillip and I rub along very nicely together."

"Yes indeed, Lady Danbury." Samantha nodded again. According to the latest *on-dit,* which Samantha had heard from Bettina, Lord Danbury had a young mistress that he visited regularly and showered with costly jewels.

"Why have we not seen the duke in London before?" Lady Halverson wondered aloud. "It seems quite odd that he has not favored us with his presence long before this current Season."

Lady Edna entered into the conversation. "It is quite easily explained, dear Sarah. The Fifth Duke of Westbury has been gone from this earth for only two brief years. I am certain that respect for his dear father's memory has kept the young duke from actively pursuing the entertainments of the *ton.* "

"Of course you are correct." Lady Halverson nodded quickly. "What a ninny I am not to have thought of it myself!"

Samantha's mind wandered as the discussion turned to the old duke and the extent of his holdings. At least one of her worries had been laid to rest during the lengthy dinner. The duke had not yet recognized her as the girl from the inn. Samantha was certain of that. And it was of little wonder, considering the fact that her hair had been styled in a far different manner and she was now clothed in the height of fashion.

A sigh escaped Samantha's lips as she thought about the consequences should the duke's memory return, and Lady Edna turned to her with concern. "Have you the headache, Granddaughter? Your complexion has gone quite pale."

"No, Grandmama. I am in perfect health," Samantha replied quickly. "Perhaps it is the late hour."

Lady Edna frowned. "But it is not late at all, my dear, for it is barely half-past nine!"

"It is undoubtedly the strain of meeting the duke for

the first time," Lady Paxton offered. "I myself had a similar experience when I first set eyes on Harlan."

"You are right, of course." Lady Edna nodded and turned to Samantha again. "Perhaps a bit of sherry would serve to bring back your color. We shall join you, Grand-daughter."

The sherry was poured from a crystal decanter and when the delicate stemmed glasses had been distributed, Lady Danbury raised hers in a toast. "We wish you happy, Samantha. May your marriage be as successful as ours have been."

Samantha did her best to stifle the bubble of laughter that attempted to escape her throat. Lady Danbury was wed to a philanderer who appeared to enjoy the company of his mistress much more than he did that of his own wife. And Lord Paxton was such an unlucky gambler that he was in danger of losing his estate. While Lady Halverson's husband was not a gambler or a rake, he was much too fond of the brandy bottle and rumor had it that footmen frequently carried him to his chambers quite senseless. Even Lady Edna had not escaped the ills of a less-than-perfect marriage. According to Bettina, the Earl of Foxworthy had criticized her constantly and embarrassed her socially whenever the whim came upon him.

They were waiting for her to acknowledge the toast and Samantha raised her glass to the assemblage. "It is most kind of you to wish me well. I am deeply appreciative."

All eyes were upon her as Samantha sipped her sherry and she succeeded in holding her amusement at bay. If the fate of the Duke of Westbury's bride should resemble those of the four ladies who sat so comfortably in the Drawing Room, it was no wonder that poor Olivia had begged Samantha to take her place!

David was greatly relieved when it came time to rejoin the ladies. He had received several invitations from his fellow gentlemen, all of which he firmly intended to decline. The first had come from Lord Danbury, who had congratulated him on his upcoming nuptials and claimed that he had never made the acquaintance of a young lady more deserving of the duke's attention than Samantha. Then, with a salacious wink, Lord Danbury had offered to introduce the duke to several young beauties from the ranks of the fashionably impure who might well serve his needs while he was residing in town. Lord Paxton had nodded his approval and said that he would be honored to sponsor the duke at White's, his gentlemen's club, where David would find a commodious environment in which to indulge in scrupulously honest games of chance. He had also offered to take the duke round to several other private establishments, if David were so inclined, in which the duke would find the stakes elevated and the gambling more enjoyable. Not to be left out of the action, Lord Halverson had offered to advise the duke as to the procurement of excellent spirits for his wine and brandy cellar. Indeed, Lord Halverson had almost begged to assist the duke, vowing that they should make the rounds of the clubs, tasting various vintages until they had found precisely those bottles that the duke must have to befit his exalted station.

As the gentlemen were ushered into the Drawing Room, David glanced at the ormolu clock atop the mantelpiece. It was nearly ten in the evening and he wondered how soon he could politely take his leave. Though the dinner had been of excellent quality and the company most congenial, David found himself eager to return to the duke's town mansion and garb himself in more comfortable clothing. Only in his private quarters could David wear the breeches and shirt of his choosing. It was a mystery how Harry could endure the uncomfortable clothing that was required of a formal evening.

As it was expected that he take a seat next to his fiancée, David joined Samantha on the sofa. She also looked ill at ease and he was curious as to the reason. Rather than speculate on the cause of her distress, he attempted to set her at ease and turned to her with a friendly smile. "Would you care for a glass of sherry, Miss Tarrington? I should be delighted to fetch it for you."

"Thank you, no." She answered his smile with one of her own. "I fear that my gown will not allow me to partake of another morsel or sip without splitting a seam. I simply do not understand how ladies can dress in this manner and claim to enjoy an evening of feasting."

David chuckled appreciatively. "You have stolen my thoughts exactly! I find myself eagerly anticipating the loose clothing I shall don the moment that I return to my quarters."

"Your clothing is also uncomfortable?"

An expression of surprise crossed Samantha's countenance when he nodded, and David laughed. "We have made an important discovery, Miss Tarrington. Fashion appears not to discriminate in the slightest betwixt the sexes. Shall we now enter an argument regarding which of us is the more uncomfortable?"

"I fear that should be most improper, for then we should be obliged to describe that which gives us the most discomfort. Why do they insist we wear these things?" She drew her perfectly shaped brows together and sighed charmingly. "It appears to me that the current fashions merely serve to keep one from enjoying oneself."

"But one must be in mode, mustn't one?" David waited for her answer eagerly. It was highly unusual for a properly bred young lady to speak her mind.

"Only if one cares about such things."

"And you do not?" David let a smile play over his lips.

"I care not a button, but I beg of you not to make this public knowledge. My dear grandmama should be quite disappointed in me as she has done her utmost to school me in the ways of a proper young lady."

David raised his brows. "You do not regard yourself as such?"

"As a lady? Of course I do, for I am certainly not a

gentleman. But as far as 'proper' is the correct term, I am much less certain. Propriety seems to demand attributes that I lack."

"What attributes might those be?" David found he was fascinated by the direction their converse had taken.

"I prefer to speak my mind and that is frowned upon in a lady. And I find I experience great difficulty when it comes to hiding my sense of humor. Indeed, I came very close to committing a social blunder only moments ago, when the ladies wished me happy and expressed their desire that my marriage should be as delightful as theirs."

David began to smile. "Then you have tumbled to the problems in their marriages?"

"Yes, indeed." Samantha lowered her voice and leaned closer. "If I tell you, you must promise never to speak of it to another. I should not like to spread tales."

David nodded. "I promise, but you have no need to tell me. In the short time I spent with the gentlemen, they made their foibles apparent to me. Ladies Danbury, Paxton, and Halverson are married to a philanderer, a gambler, and a tosspot respectively. Am I not correct?"

"You are!" Samantha's eyes grew wide with astonishment. "I compliment you, sir, on being most amazingly astute."

David grinned. "There was nothing astute about the conclusion I reached. It was readily apparent from the offers they made to me. Lord Danbury proposed to introduce me to a charming young lady of ill repute, Lord Paxton confided that he should enjoy escorting me to several nefarious gambling hells, and Lord Halverson begged to assist me in sampling wines and brandies for my cellar."

"I see." Samantha sighed. "If it is not too bold of me to ask, do you intend to accept any of their offers?"

For a moment David was thoroughly shocked. A young lady did not ask such a question of her fiancé. But then he remembered that Samantha had confessed that she often spoke her mind, and he laughed. "I think not. I am not a gambler and I prefer not to drink to excess. And as for Lord Danbury's offer . . ."

"I beg you to excuse my question and not to consider it further!" Samantha interrupted him quickly. "I should not have asked."

"But I wish to tell you." David noticed that his fiancée's color was high with embarrassment. "I have no need for additional female companionship when I am engaged to such a delightful young lady."

"Oh! Well . . . I am not certain what response should be proper, but I assume I should thank you nicely for your compliment."

His fiancée's countenance was still bright with color and David reached out for her hand. "You must promise never to hesitate to ask me a question, no matter how improper it may seem to be. I find I most thoroughly enjoy your honesty."

"I . . . I thank you again." Samantha nodded quickly. He was as personable as he was handsome, and Samantha wondered why he had offered for a young lady he had never met when he could have had any of his choosing. It was on the tip of her tongue to ask, but she found that even she did not have that much courage.

After another interval of scintillating conversation, David glanced at the clock and was surprised to see that it truly was time to take his leave. He turned to Samantha with real regret and took her hand in his again. "I fear I must take my leave. I go to Tattersall's early tomorrow to choose a matched pair for the phaeton."

"Tattersall's?" Samantha breathed the word. "How marvelous! Oh, I do so wish that I could go!"

David looked down at her in great surprise. "Perhaps you mistake the name for another, Miss Tarrington. One goes to Tattersall's to buy cattle."

"Yes, I know." Samantha nodded quickly. "Tattersall's prices can be extravagant, but I have heard it is still possible for one to make a good bargain if one is careful."

"How come you to know of Tattersall's?" David's eyes narrowed slightly.

"Why the squire bought one of his finest racehorses there, though it is most unusual to find cattle of that caliber at . . ." Samantha stopped in midsentence, aware that she had made a grievous blunder. Miss Olivia Samantha Tarrington would know nothing of racehorses or Tattersall's.

"The squire?"

David leaned forward, peering into her face, and Samantha took care not to groan. She must think of a way to cover her blunder immediately.

"But that was long ago, and of little consequence." Samantha gave David an anxious smile. "It was simply a story my father told me before he died. He went to Tattersall's as a young man, you see, with a neighboring squire, and I have . . . well . . . I have always desired to see the place."

David nodded. "I see. Unfortunately, I cannot oblige you. Females are seldom present at Tatt's, and when they are, one can assume that they are not ladies."

"Oh, dear!" Samantha looked properly abashed. "I did not know, nor did I think to ask Grandmama about it. I fear I have made yet another social blunder. I beg of you to please excuse my ignorance."

David smiled. "It is not only excused, it is forgotten. While it is true that I cannot take you with me to Tatt's, I should be glad to show you the pair I purchase and tell you everything I remember of the auction."

"Would you?" Samantha's eyes began to sparkle as he nodded. "Why, that should be almost the same as going there myself!"

"Then I shall ask your grandmother's permission and take you for a drive through the park tomorrow afternoon. Shall we say at four when we shall join the Promenade?"

"I am delighted to accept your kind invitation!" Samantha was beaming as she rose to her feet to accompany him to Lady Edna's chair. The duke's request was quickly made and just as quickly granted, and then Samantha accompanied him to the door where he took her hand and bid her a proper good evening.

When the door had closed behind him, Samantha stood there with a bemused smile on her face. The Duke of Westbury was the nicest, kindest, and most sensible of men. He had seemed to like her well enough; heated color stained Samantha's cheeks as she thought of the way his eyes had met hers throughout the interminably long dinner party, and the manner in which they had shared laughter and confidences in the Drawing Room. He was a perfect fiancé, and poor Olivia did not know what she was missing!

Less than an hour later, after all the guests had left, Samantha was alone in her room, preparing to blow out the candle. When the room was in darkness, she slid under the covers and stared up at the ceiling with a smile. She would see the duke again tomorrow, for a drive through the park. Though she had not asked or even hinted that she wished to see more of him, he had quite eagerly invited her to join the Promenade where they should be seen together. He did not seem to find her lacking in any of the aspects that had so concerned her. And he had claimed that he truly liked her outspoken honesty! Could anything be more wonderful than the glorious Season that she was about to experience as the fiancée of the most handsome and personable nobleman in all of London? Why, she was half in love with him already and she had only just met him tonight!

It was not until Samantha was nearly asleep that a most disturbing thought crossed her mind. Her lovely Season would disappear like smoke in a summer breeze if the duke ever recognized her as the girl he'd met at the Two Feathers Inn. Then he would know that she was not Miss Olivia Samantha Tarrington, and the ruse that Samantha had concocted with Olivia should be quickly exposed.

Samantha sighed, imagining the dire possibilities. If they were found out, Olivia's plans for her artistic career would be ruined and she should wind up penniless.

Samantha herself should be turned out from Lady Edna's house in disgrace and perhaps even prosecuted for her part in the deception. The duke should be so angry that he would never forgive either of them and they both should be outcasts for the rest of their lives.

Samantha gulped back her feelings of utter terror. It was too late to admit to the deception now and beg for forgiveness. Matters had gone too far to be set aright. She must somehow make certain that if the duke's memory of the girl he'd mistaken for a common wench resurfaced, it could not possibly be connected to her.

Eight

David smiled as he sat at Harry's desk in the library. He had spent an extremely enjoyable morning at Tattersall's, even though he had paid too dearly for the pair of matched greys that now drew Harry's high-perch phaeton. He had hoped to obtain a pair for less than two hundred pounds, but though this pair had gone for a considerably higher tariff, he had not been able to resist the spirited animals. David had no doubt that Harry would be pleased with his latest purchase. They were fine specimens indeed and they should be a credit to their owner. And Harry had previously agreed that since David would be in London anyway, he should accomplish the replenishment of their stables while he was there and had given him *carte blanche* to do so.

In a sense, David felt almost sorry for Harry. His friend was in Bath, with only Mr. Dawson's aunt for a companion, while David was enjoying the company of an extraordinary young lady. Indeed, David did not know when he had enjoyed himself more. Samantha was witty and charming, pretty enough in an unconventional way, and thoroughly delightful. He still held the notion that he had made her acquaintance previously, but perhaps it had been someone else who had resembled her closely in physical appearance.

There was only one fact about his fiancée that puzzled David and he intended to explore it further at the first opportunity. Though he could not have chosen a companion who had better suited him, she did not seem at all

similar to the description that her maiden aunt had offered in her letters to the Dragoness.

David glanced down at the letters again. There were a
whole sheaf of them, tied up with a ribbon, and he had
read only the first two. Lady Honoria, Samantha's aunt,
had described her niece's physical attributes and temperament in her first correspondence with Harry's mother. According to Lady Honoria, Samantha was tall and of slender
build, and David should agree with this assessment.
Though he was tall, Samantha came within only a few
inches of matching his height. But Lady Honoria had also
written that Samantha possessed a delicate constitution
and with this, David disagreed most heartily. There was
nothing delicate about Samantha. When he had taken her
arm to escort her to dinner, she had walked with purpose,
her strides almost equaling his. The pressure of her hand
upon his arm had been firm and when he had seated her
at table, she had surreptitiously lifted the heavy dining
chair when she had thought that no one should notice,
and moved herself a bit closer to her place setting. Samantha's slender form might give the outward appearance of
delicacy, but David suspected that she should be a match
in strength for any gentleman of a similar size.

Samantha's aunt had also stated that her hair was a
lovely golden color. Truth to tell, Samantha's hair was a
most unfashionable shade of red; perhaps Lady Honoria
had felt the necessity of describing it as a color that was
more in vogue. David found he did not mind this small
deception as he considered Samantha's hair color, coupled
with her lovely complexion, most attractive indeed.

In temperament, Lady Honoria's description had been
far from the mark. She had depicted Samantha as shy and
retiring, a most proper young miss, and David could testify
that the young lady he had met on the previous evening
was not the least bit reticent! Their discussion had turned
quite lively when they had discussed the subject of social
etiquette as it pertained to the sexes. Indeed, Samantha's
eyes had blazed with zeal as she had addressed the inequi-

ties. She felt it unfair that a widower should be allowed to wear a simple black armband in the military style, while a relict was required to dress in black bombazine for the first year following her husband's death, and in half-mourning for a second year. Indeed, his fiancée had pronounced quite firmly that most of society's rules appeared to favor the gentleman over the lady. A gentleman could go where he pleased, when he pleased, and no one would call him to task. A lady's actions were severely restricted, requiring the presence of a maid, another female friend, or a gentleman whenever she ventured out in public. According to Samantha, riding was another area where society's rules were unfair. While a gentleman rode astride, dressed in comfortable riding breeches, a lady was required to dress in full skirts and ride sidesaddle. This was uncomfortable, forcing her to twist her body in order to see the direction in which she was headed, and it was also dangerous as it was far more likely that she should be thrown.

David smiled as he remembered the other examples that his fiancée had cited. It appeared she had compiled a lengthy list during her time in London. A lady was discouraged from having strong views on any subject, deferring to a gentleman in all such matters, regardless of how misinformed he might be. A lady was required to wear silly bonnets, decorated with idiotish flowers, birds, and fruit, while a gentleman was allowed to go bareheaded if he so wished. A lady was required to wait for a gentleman to hand her down from a carriage, even if she was quite capable of disembarking by herself, and she was never allowed to call on a gentleman alone, except on matters of a business or professional nature. She could not wear pearls or diamonds in the morning, dance more than three times of an evening with the same partner, or set foot in a gentlemen's club. When she married, her wealth became her husband's, and she could not spend a penny of what was rightfully hers without first asking his permission. She was not allowed to take part in the exciting

amusements permitted a gentleman, such as riding to the
hounds, stalking the wild stag, or riding a thoroughbred
in a race. She was expected to content herself with needlework, practicing musical pieces on the pianoforte, and
sketching the idiotish subjects deemed suitable for the
gentler sex.

When Samantha had drawn a breath, David had asked
her which of these inequities had discomforted her the
greatest. Samantha had confessed that she particularly ab-
horred the rules that governed manners of address. She
had remarked that David could address her in any way he
pleased. He was a duke, and because of his status and title,
it was not possible for him to commit a social infraction.
She, on the other hand, must be entirely correct in her
address of him. At that point, she had readily admitted
that she had no clue as to what she should properly call
him.

David had laughed and admitted that he did not know,
either. "Duke" should be too cold, and "Your Grace" too
servile. He had suggested that she call him David. It was
his name, after all. And since they were formally engaged,
there was no reason why they must be on formal terms.

Samantha had nodded quickly, spoken his name once
in trial, and announced that she was quite pleased with
the sound of it. And then she had quickly invited him to
call her "Samantha." They had been "David" and
"Samantha" for the remainder of the evening, and David
felt that they had established a most friendly footing. Perhaps this afternoon, if the fates presented the perfect opportunity, he would broach the subject of their betrothal
and learn the degree to which she approved of the match
that had been arranged for them.

Though he was smiling as he turned to the letter in his
hand again, the next few words made David frown. According to Lady Honoria, Samantha was fond of sketching,
had an abiding interest in birds, possessed an admirable
singing voice, and was accomplished on the pianoforte.
The only negative in the letter was the surprising fact that

Samantha did not ride. Lady Honoria reported that
Samantha had been thrown by a horse when she was a
child and had subsequently developed an abject fear of
the beasts.

How very odd, David thought as he reread the words
to make certain that he had not mistaken the meaning.
But there it was, spelled out in Lady Honoria's precise
hand. If Samantha was so fearful of horses, why had she
expressed a desire to see an auction at Tattersall's?

For the space of a heartbeat, David actually thought he
might ask her about it, but he quickly discarded that notion. Samantha might regard his query as confrontational
and David certainly did not desire to alienate her. It was
best if he waited until more facts about Harry's fascinating
fiancée came to light. He would gather them carefully and
perhaps he could be able to use them in discouraging this
ill-fated match.

Samantha grimaced at her reflection in the glass as Bettina tied on her bonnet. It was a silly confection with the
prerequisite flowers and bows that were an anathema to
her. Her sprigged muslin gown, however, was much to
Samantha's liking as it contained her favorite hues of
green and blue. Gloves and a matching parasol completed
her ensemble and Samantha marched down the stairs,
back straight and head held high, to seek Lady Edna's
approval.

"It is exquisite!" Lady Edna nodded as Samantha entered the Drawing Room. "You shall be quite the crack,
my dear. Oh, to be young again and able to wear that
ridiculous bonnet to perfection as you do!"

Samantha burst into laughter and crossed the room to
hug Lady Edna. "So you agree that it is ridiculous, Grandmama?"

"Certainly." Lady Edna smiled as she patted a stray curl
in place. "But it is the perfect afternoon to put on a silly

confection and go for a drive with your handsome young duke. I will assure you, Granddaughter, that within a sennight's time, every young lady of consequence will be wearing a bonnet exactly like yours."

Samantha noticed the gleam of amusement in Lady Edna's eyes and asked the question, "And what shall I do then, Grandmama?"

"Why, you shall never wear it again, of course! You shall say that you have come to regard bonnets with bows and flowers as passé. Then you shall place something equally ridiculous on your head and watch them scramble to emulate you again."

"Perhaps you should consider the purchase of several millinery shops, Grandmama." Samantha raised her brows. "You could order inexpensive bonnets made up, I could be seen wearing a sample, and you could inflate the prices and sell every one."

Lady Edna laughed. "Do not tempt me, Granddaughter. My investments are quite comfortably placed at the 'Change, thank you very much! And it is not considered polite for a lady to speak of investments and profits. See that you remember that, Samantha."

"You are correct, of course, Grandmama." Samantha bobbed a quick curtsy. "By the by, how fare the tea crops this year?"

Lady Edna's eyes began to sparkle. "Very well, indeed! The weather has been most commodious—an adequate amount of rainfall with the proper intervals of heat and sunlight. Some even speculate that this will be one of the most profitable . . ."

Lady Edna stopped her recital as she realized that Samantha was bubbling with laughter. "Whatever is amiss, Granddaughter?"

"Only moments ago, you warned me that a lady must never speak of investments and profits."

Lady Edna gave her a withering glance. "Of course I did, child! And take care that you heed my advice! Only when you reach my advanced years may you also disregard those rules of society that you do not wish to obey. In the meantime, do not tease me so or I shall purchase those millinery shops we spoke of and force you to wear clusters of huge purple grapes on your bonnet!"

"You would not!" Samantha gasped in pretended fright.

"I would so!" Lady Edna nodded severely. "And if you continue to plague me, I shall add several gilded oranges to the mix."

Samantha laughed gaily. "Gilded oranges? Surely you can do better than that, Grandmama! If I were you, I should settle for nothing less impressive than pineapples!"

"Pineapples it is then." Lady Edna nodded. "With a large bunch of bananas thrown in. Perhaps a bird or two for good measure."

Samantha laughed gaily. "Have you a preference for the type of bird?"

"Of course." Lady Edna nodded gravely. "It shall be an albatross. I have always thought that an albatross should look lovely on a bonnet."

Both ladies turned at the sound of a stifled chortle, and Samantha gasped as she saw David standing in the open doorway. "You! I mean, . . . Duke! I beg your pardon, Your . . . Your Grace?"

"David." He corrected her gently. "I hope I'm not interrupting, but your butler told me to come directly here. Good afternoon, Lady Edna."

"It is, isn't it?" Lady Edna gave a most unladylike giggle. "What think you of my granddaughter's bonnet?"

A smile played around the corners of David's mouth as he silently surveyed the ribbon-and-straw confection that sat slightly askew on his fiancée's head. "It is most decorative."

"And you are most politic." Lady Edna favored the duke with a nod of approval before she turned to Samantha. "Run along, Granddaughter, and enjoy your afternoon. I shall order that refreshments be waiting when you return."

"What was that all about?" David questioned her the

moment they had gained the relative privacy of the hall-way.

Samantha laughed and reached out quite naturally to take his arm. "Nothing of consequence. Grandmama and I were merely discussing the possibility of going into the millinery business."

"Really?" David's brows raised in a question. "You propose to decorate bonnets with albatrosses?"

Samantha shook her head quite solemnly. "No, David. Grandmama and I were merely teasing. I am certain she should prefer to choose a bird that is even larger."

"Which bird would that be?" David handed Samantha up and took his seat on the high perch.

Samantha shrugged. "I am certain I do not know."

"But I thought . . . that is, I had heard that you had an abiding interest in birds."

Color rose to Samantha's cheeks as she remembered the part that she had agreed to play. Olivia was quite knowledgeable, while she knew very little about birds.

"It is not so much an interest as an . . . an avocation." Samantha did her utmost to cover her blunder. "I am not so much interested in the habits and classification of the birds themselves, but in the accurate rendering of their coloring and likenesses. The truth of the matter is that I could have chosen to depict *any* species. Birds were just there, and . . . and that is why I chose them."

"I see." David nodded as he picked up the reins. "Which would you say is your favorite among the birds?"

"That is a difficult question." Samantha's mind spun in circles as she attempted to come up with the proper one. "I would say . . . the peacock. Yes, I am extraordinarily fond of the peacock. Such divine coloring, and . . . and such a lovely song."

David did his best not to burst into laughter. It was abundantly clear that Samantha had never heard a peacock's raucous call. He did not believe that one who painted various species of birds could fail to know the pertinent facts about them. Why had Samantha deceived him when she had claimed to paint likenesses of birds?

"This is the pair you purchased at Tattersall's?" Samantha neatly steered the conversation in another direction.

"Yes. Do you like them?"

Samantha nodded quickly. "They seem sound and quite spirited. Are they from the same dam and sire?"

"Yes." David risked a glance at his fiancée, but she did not seem to realize that most proper young ladies would not use those particular words.

"They are well matched." Samantha studied the horses with interest. "The filly appears older than the colt. Were they trained together or separately?"

"Together. And you are correct. The filly is older."

Samantha nodded. "If you switch their places, they will do much better. See how he favors his right?"

"Correct again!" David frowned slightly as he glanced over at Samantha. He had been thinking the very same thing! "How do you come to know so much about cattle?"

Samantha winced. She must take care to guard her tongue for she had almost given herself away again. "I was raised on a country estate, and I spent much time at the stables. It was my favorite place."

David made no comment, storing this new information about Samantha in a corner of his mind for further perusal. He thought that the stables should be an odd choice for anyone fearful of horses, but perhaps she had been speaking of a time prior to her mishap.

"This is my very first ride in a high-perch phaeton." Samantha smiled as they turned into the entrance of the park and joined the Promenade on Ladies' Row. "How perfectly delightful it is to ride up so high and look down on everyone and everything! It puts me in mind of the steep hill I used to climb as a child. I stood at the top and surveyed the land for miles around, pretending that I was king of all I could see."

"You pretended that you were a king instead of a beautiful queen?" David raised his brows.

Samantha laughed lightly. "Yes, indeed. I never wished to be a queen, for then my only purpose should be to produce heirs to the throne. I was much more enamored of the adventures and intrigue a young king should enjoy."

"You should prefer to be Prinny?"

"Oh, no! Prinny is not a good example at all! But I should prefer to go to my grave rather than be Prinny's wife!" There was the sound of rapidly approaching hoof-beats and Samantha turned to look behind her. "David? Is there a rider on that horse?"

David swiveled around and a frown quickly replaced his smile. "No, but there is a saddle. Some poor fellow must have been thrown."

"When he comes abreast of us, try to pace him and I shall attempt to seize his reins."

Before David could voice his objection to this risky en-deavor, Samantha grabbed his arm to anchor herself and leaned out as far as she could. As the stallion approached, David veered to the side so that the beast should be forced to pass on Samantha's side of the carriage.

"Pace him, David." Samantha shouted out, extending her hand for the reins. She wound them once around her hand and hung halfway out of the conveyance as she at-tempted to calm him. "There's a good fellow. I have you now. What is a magnificent boy like you doing all alone? How handsome you are, and such a fine pacer. It is clear to me that your rider did not appreciate you in the least, and you undoubtedly landed the unlucky pink in the bushes, just as he deserved. And now, my fine fellow, we shall slow our team and you shall join us for a well-deserved rest."

David was amazed as he expertly slowed his pair. He was not quite certain how Samantha had managed to accom-plish the deed, but she had managed to calm the stallion to the point where he was now walking quite docilely by the side of the phaeton. The moment they came to a halt, Samantha jumped down from her perch to soothe the frightened animal and rub him down with her shawl.

Samantha was still crooning to the stallion when David hopped down to join her. "Poor fellow. He was terribly frightened, finding himself all alone in a strange place. He has obviously been well trained, and he looks to be of excellent temperament. I wonder what could have happened to cause him to bolt."

"I say there!" A dusty gentleman came into view, limping slightly and shaking his head. "Thank you for catching my mount."

"What happened?" David turned to the gentleman with a frown.

"The devil if I know!" The young gentleman winced and turned to Samantha. "Begging your pardon, Miss. Orion just bolted at the first turn and threw me off like a bushel of grain. I've had him for two years and he's never done anything like this before."

"Then there is a good reason for his behavior." Samantha nodded quickly. "Would you please remove his saddle and blanket for me?"

Both David and the stranger stared at her as if she had asked them for the moon, but when she moved to do it herself, they quickly obliged her. Then they watched, nonplused, as Samantha ran her hands expertly over Orion's back.

Orion reared up suddenly, but Samantha was ready, catching him expertly by his bridle and calming him once again. Then she turned to the stranger with a sigh. "Orion has two problems, sir. He has a saddle sore that is just forming, and from its position, I would suspect that it was caused by a cinch that was pulled too tightly. Take care in future when Orion is saddled, or you will wind up in the bushes again."

"I shall. How long will Orion's sore take to heal?" The young gentleman addressed Samantha directly, unconsciously recognizing her expertise.

"He should be rested for at least three weeks. Tell your groom to make a salve of pounded sassafras bark, soda, and hot water and apply it to the area twice a day. When it is no longer sensitive to the touch, you may ride him again."

David nodded. It was precisely what he would have told the young gentleman. "You mentioned two problems, Samantha. What is the second?"

"Orion's left rear shoe should be carefully examined. He is limping a bit and he may very well have picked up a pebble." Samantha turned to the young gentleman with a smile. "Orion is a magnificent stallion, sir. You should feel proud to be his owner."

The young gentleman smiled as he rubbed the side of Orion's neck. "He is my prized possession and we have been inseparable. This is the very reason that I was so shocked when he deposited me in the bushes."

Samantha nodded and watched the stallion nuzzle the young gentleman's arm. It was apparent that gentleman and beast were equally fond of each other.

"We should be pleased to offer assistance in returning him to his stable." David spoke up. "He did well walking with my pair."

"Thank you." The young gentleman accepted with a smile.

On the journey back to the gentleman's stable, David learned that he was Ned Barclay, the second son of a baron, and he was in London for the Season. Ned seemed quite impressed at meeting a duke in such odd circumstances, and even more impressed with Samantha.

"But you know so much about cattle, Miss Tarrington!" Ned stared at her in amazement as they shared the narrow seat of the phaeton. "However did you learn so much?"

Samantha smiled, quite unaware that David's eyes had narrowed perceptibly. "I was raised in a rural setting and one of my favorite haunts was the stable. I much preferred the company of the grooms and the cattle to any other."

David's mind was busy storing new information about Samantha as the three exchanged pleasantries on their journey to the Barclay stable. Lady Honoria had been in error when she had claimed that Samantha was afraid of horses. She was not only comfortable in the presence of cattle, she knew every bit as much about them as David did. That much had been made abundantly clear to him by their experience today. David wondered what other errors he would discover in Lady Honoria's letters, and which additional facts had been entirely misrepresented concerning Harry's fiancée.

Nine

David turned to Samantha with great amusement. "A crow with a worm stuck in its throat? Or the squealing of a pig led to the slaughter?"

"Two cats, I should think, fighting over their lady love," Samantha promptly replied.

Samantha and David were exchanging confidences in Lady Ralston's Music Room after an interminably lengthy series of performances. The latest had featured their hostess herself, who had favored them with a rendition of German lieder that had left Samantha's ears ringing painfully. Thankfully, it was time for the intermission. The others who had surrounded them, held captive on the small, uncomfortable chairs that Lady Ralston had provided, had departed like rats deserting a sinking ship, to enjoy the delights of tea and pastries. The room was now empty, save for Samantha and David.

"Do you perform this afternoon?" David raised an inquisitive eyebrow.

Samantha shook her head. "Heaven forfend! I most politely declined, claiming a weakness of the throat. I suppose I shall be required to do so eventually, but I am delaying that dubious pleasure for as long as is possible."

"But you *do* play?"

Samantha nodded her assent a trifle reluctantly. "I have been trained to do so, yes, but I do not enjoy it much. There are so many livelier things to do, and I confess that I often spent the hours that had been set aside for my practice on other, more enjoyable pursuits."

"If you will play but one short piece for me now, I shall promise to contrive a way to elude this crush."

Samantha's eyes sparkled with the joy of anticipated freedom. "I should desire to avoid the rest of these performances above all else!"

David laughed. "Then play for me now and I promise that I shall make good our escape."

After a hasty glance round the room to make certain that they were unobserved, Samantha hurried to the pocket door to close it. Then she took up her position at the pianoforte and turned to him with an anxious expression. "Give me your promise that you will not laugh."

"I promise." David nodded gravely. "Proceed, Samantha, and when you have finished, I shall spirit you away."

Samantha dutifully struck a soft chord and proceeded to sing a short ballad. She had a pleasing voice and an adequate skill, but none should call her a master of either keyboard or song. As she struck the final chord, she smiled up at him and David smiled back. Samantha most certainly did not possess the talent that Lady Honoria had described in her letters to the Dragoness, but she had pleased him greatly by her ready compliance with his wishes.

"You must tell me how we shall make our escape." Samantha's eyes were twinkling. "Shall I claim the headache?"

David shook his head. "That will not be necessary. Are you inordinately fond of the gown you are wearing?"

"This gown?" Samantha looked down at the yellow muslin that Bettina had chosen for her to wear to the musicale, and shrugged. "Not particularly. Why do you ask?"

"Because I plan to spill a glass of orgeat on it."

"How clumsy of you, and how very clever!" Samantha nodded quickly. "And then we shall have to take our leave so that I may change my gown?"

David nodded, pleased with her rapid grasp of his plan. "Precisely. Do you have any objections, Samantha?"

"Not a one! I shall gladly sacrifice this gown for our freedom as I am not at all fond of it. Bettina chose it for me and it is part of Olivia's . . ." Samantha stopped suddenly, appalled at the blunder she had committed. "I meant to say, this gown belonged to the *old* Olivia, before I decided to call myself Samantha."

"I see." David nodded gravely and stored away another piece of the puzzle to examine later. "When, exactly, did you decide to call yourself Samantha?"

"Only a month or so ago. Of course, some people have always called me Samantha. It is just that I did not think of myself by that name until quite recently. Perhaps it is because my . . . my aunt always referred to me as Olivia and continued to do so until the day she died. Let us go and find the orgeat, David. I find that I am most anxious to leave Lady Ralston's musicale behind."

"Of course." David nodded. The explanation that Samantha had given him might satisfy others, but it did not entirely convince him. There were simply too many puzzling facts about her that contradicted the description that Lady Honoria had given the Dragoness in her letters. Olivia was afraid of horses and Samantha was not. Olivia had an interest in birds and Samantha knew next to nothing about them. Olivia was touted to possess a marvelous talent for the pianoforte and an incomparable singing voice, while Samantha was adequate at best. And now, Samantha referred to her old dresses as belonging to Olivia instead of to her. Could it be possible that Samantha was not Olivia at all? It was a shocking suspicion that David was not prepared to voice until he had gathered more facts to either substantiate or repudiate the theory. But David did admit that the possibility existed, albeit slim, that he was not the sole pretender in this arranged match.

"I should think a jot more cerulean blue might better match that feather." Harry pointed to the sketch that Olivia was coloring.

Olivia nodded and added a bit more pigment to the

area. "You have a marvelous eye for color, Harry. And I have never seen the like of your landscapes."

"Does this mean that you like them? Or are you merely attempting to be tactful?"

"Tactful? Me?" Olivia burst into laughter. "I shall never win a prize for tact as I seldom think before speaking. But I speak the truth, Harry, and I should have to be the silliest of gooses not to recognize your talent! If I could paint half as well as you, Harry, I should devote my life to nothing else!"

Harry smiled at the lovely young student who had joined him on his retreat. She was Mr. Dawson's newest prodigy and her paintings of birds were exquisite. "But you *do* paint as well as I do, Jane."

"Never! But perhaps, with further instruction, I shall. In the meantime, you are the master and I shall be your willing pupil."

Harry laughed, but he was quite pleased at her words. "You flatter me, Jane, and I warn you that I shall become quite swelled in the head."

"No, you shall not. You are the most modest of fellows, Harry. Perhaps it is due to that perfectly awful mother of yours, who seems to regard it her life's work to belittle your genius. Or your idiotish aunt who never says a word to contradict her. And you could not overestimate your talent, Harry, even if you set out to do so. Why, I should be completely full of myself if one of my paintings had been chosen to hang in the Lower Rooms where all of the elite should admire it! And I certainly should not content myself to sign only my initials!"

"There is a reason for that, Jane." Harry sighed deeply. "I told you that I am here incognito, and must needs avoid recognition. If I signed my full name, my mother should surely hear of it and hasten to collect me like an errant schoolboy."

Olivia laughed. "I do wish that she would attempt it, for I should put a stop to her, I can tell you that! I have quite a temper, you know, especially when someone dear to me is being threatened."

Harry raised his brows in a question. "Am I dear to you, Jane?"

"Of course you are! In the past few weeks, I have come to like you much more than I have ever liked any other gentleman. You are handsome and kind, and you understand my passion for painting. I shall regard you as my friend for life!"

Harry nodded and wished again that he could speak his mind. He had fallen quite under Jane's spell during the short time that they had spent together. If he had been free, he might very well have offered for her. But Harry was not free. He was engaged to another and until David's ruse had been exposed, he could not speak of it to a single soul.

"You are very dear to me also, Jane." Harry permitted his hand to rest lightly on hers for a moment, and then he withdrew it to gesture toward the large cage that contained her specimen. "When will you release this fine fellow?"

"This afternoon. Would you like to come along, Harry, and watch him fly free? It is a most wondrous sight!"

"I should enjoy that immensely." Harry nodded quickly. "I shall see that the horses are saddled for us."

Olivia's face blanched of color and she swallowed anxiously. "No! You know that I do not care for horses, Harry. I explained it all to you. They are so . . . so large, and they frighten me dreadfully."

"I should not permit you to be thrown again, Jane." Harry smiled at her kindly. "Some day soon, you must promise that you will ride with me on my stallion. I shall hold you and see that no harm comes to you and then you shall no longer be afraid."

Olivia nodded. "Perhaps. But not quite yet, Harry. I am not ready for such an excursion. Let us walk today. It is such a delightful afternoon. I . . . I shall think about riding tomorrow."

"The longer you wait, the more difficult it will be,"

Harry warned her gently. "I should like to see you cured of this affliction, Jane, so that we could ride of an afternoon."

Olivia sighed and squared her shoulders. "Tomorrow then. I shall ride with you tomorrow. But you must promise to stop if I tell you that I am too frightened to go on."

"I promise." Harry nodded solemnly. "Shall I ask Agnes to pack a hamper for us so that we can spend the afternoon in the woods after we have released your handsome fellow?"

Olivia nodded quickly. "That should be delightful, Harry."

As Harry left the studio, Olivia sank down on a bench and sighed deeply. She had come to Bath without the slightest intention of becoming romantically involved. Indeed, she had made a point of avoiding the possibility of such entanglements in the past. To her aunt's chagrin, Olivia had refused to attend the few parties and assemblies to which she had been invited. And once she had politely declined those invitations, further invitations had decreased in number until they had finally ceased altogether.

Her shyness was one reason Olivia had avoided the social life that existed in the country. What she had told Samantha was true. Olivia had always harbored the fear that strangers should judge her and find her wanting, precisely as her parents had done.

Olivia sighed, remembering her mother's constant criticism of her appearance and conduct. Lady Tarrington had been an Incomparable and some had rumored that Byron had once written an ode to her beauty. Olivia remembered how attractive her mother had been with her perfectly rounded figure and midnight-black hair. Her complexion had been faultless, and her long, dark lashes had swept down like a curtain over her sparkling brown eyes. Her features had been strong but utterly feminine, and she had possessed the type of classic beauty that had inspired great sculptors and artists throughout the ages. She had been vivacious, her eyes flashing with a delicious excitement whenever she had been pleased, her laughter ringing out with the delight of silvery bells.

During her first Season in London, Olivia's mother had met Gerald Tarrington and made the perfect match. When she had married Olivia's father, a handsome gentleman with hair of gold and eyes the color of a summer sky, all had admired the image of perfect opposites that they had presented. Their house parties at Tarrington Mansion had been legendary and invitations to their affairs highly prized by members of the *beau monde*. Olivia remembered the sounds of such parties, the laughter and the gaiety that had floated up the stairs, all the way to the nursery on the third floor.

Olivia knew that she had been a great disappointment to her mother. She had not been pretty, inheriting her father's golden hair and her mother's dark eyes. She had also been thin, with sharp features, and had lacked the cherubic roundness of a pretty child. Quiet by nature, she had preferred her books and her solitary pursuits to the raucous entertainments that her parents and their constant stream of guests had enjoyed.

Once Olivia's parents had thought her old enough to take some part in their festivities, she had suffered dreadfully. She had been a timid rider at best, though her father had hired the best groom to teach her, and once she had been thrown, she had never dared to ride again. She had also failed miserably in conversation, afraid that she might utter some comment that would bring ridicule crashing down upon her head. She had thought of herself as an insignificant brown wren amongst a flock of exotic birds with brightly colored plumage.

There were only two areas in which Olivia had excelled and she had been far too shy to exhibit these skills to her parents. Her drawings had been lovely, astounding her drawing master with their intricacy and attention to detail. And her music instructor had claimed that she had a wondrous skill on the pianoforte, coupled with a lovely voice. Unfortunately, Olivia had been too timid to perform for her parents' guests or to show her drawings to them, and her talents had gone completely unnoticed.

In Olivia's eleventh year, her parents had planned a gala Christmas party. Her governess had announced her intention to leave for the holidays and Olivia's parents, unwilling to be bothered with the sole care of her, had agreed that she should accompany her governess on the holiday. Before the gala party could commence, an epidemic had swept the countryside and both of Olivia's parents had been fatally stricken. Olivia had received the sad tidings on Christmas Day and she had been sent to live with her mother's maiden sister.

In her Aunt Honoria's home, Olivia had been relatively isolated. She had not been truly unhappy, since she still possessed the means to amuse herself with her drawings and her music, but she had not been exposed to any guests as her aunt did not choose to indulge in the expense of entertaining. After the glittering social life that her parents had enjoyed, it was no wonder that Olivia had shied away from accepting any invitations that came her way. She had not met any eligible young men during her stay in her aunt's home, and she had not sought them out.

By her aunt's example, Olivia had learned that it was quite possible for one to live by oneself without a mate. She had come to the conclusion that such a life was less complicated and, indeed, preferable to the wedded state. She had regarded romance as an unwelcome intrusion in her ordered life and she had convinced herself that she much preferred the life of a dedicated, unencumbered artist to that of a wife and mother. But all that was before she had met Harry.

Olivia smiled a trifle ruefully. When she had first met Harry upon her arrival at Mrs. Dawson's country home, she had experienced a moment of panic. The man her grandmother had arranged for her to wed had borne the very same name! But Harry had quickly put her fears to rest when he had explained that he was also a student of Mr. Dawson's, a fellow artist who had come on holiday to pursue the painting of landscapes. He had also confessed that his family did not approve of his artistic endeavors and for this reason, he had kept his destination a secret from them.

At first, Olivia had been shy around Harry. He was a gentleman, after all, and gentlemen had held no particular interest for her. But Harry was also an artist and a friendship had developed despite Olivia's shyness. She had found herself seeking Harry out to ask his opinion on a number of subjects involving art and she had been delighted when he had come to find her to ask for her opinion of his work.

As the days had passed, Olivia's fond regard for Harry had grown. He had been the first young gentleman of her acquaintance, and she had found herself wondering whether she had unwittingly deprived herself of similarly pleasurable acquaintances in the past. To Olivia's surprise, she had discovered that she did not suffer from her usual shyness with Harry. She had even been quite bold, on several occasions, and inquired about his past and his family. When she had learned that Harry had also been ignored by his father and ridiculed by his mother, she had felt a kinship with him. And when he had admitted that he experienced bouts of painful shyness around members of the opposite sex, she had confessed that she also suffered from this affliction. Their friendship had grown into an even deeper affection that caused Olivia to suspect that she was experiencing the first blush of love.

Olivia sighed and then she smiled. There was no doubt about it. She had formed a genuine *tendre* for Harry. He was the perfect gentleman, kind and wise, and most breathtakingly handsome. Olivia knew that if she had not been embroiled in this distressing tangle, she should have encouraged him openly and prayed that he should eventually come to offer for her. Olivia was certain that she should be supremely happy as Harry's wife, but of course, that could never be. She was promised to another, and if Harry ever learned of the ruse that she had perpetuated

with Samantha, he should quickly lose all respect for her.
She could never tell him what she had done, for her actions were too terrible to forgive. But she could enjoy this
interlude with him, and hold the memory of what might
have been close to her heart for the rest of her life.

Samantha was laughing as they walked up the steps to
Lady Edna's town mansion. Olivia's frock was soaked with
orgeat, but that did not disturb her in the slightest. Even
if Bettina could not manage to remove the stain, Olivia
should not mind the loss of an afternoon frock. She should
have all the new gowns in Samantha's wardrobe and that
should more than compensate for the one that she had
lost.

"Good afternoon, Miss Samantha, Your Grace." Lady
Edna's butler greeted them most properly at the door.

"Good afternoon, Spencer." Samantha smiled at the
staid, elderly gentleman. "Shall we find my grandmother
in the Drawing Room?"

The butler shook his head. "No, Miss Samantha. My
Lady has gone out on an errand. I daresay she did not
expect you to return this early."

"We had a slight mishap, Spencer." Samantha gestured
toward her gown. "Will you escort the duke to the Drawing
Room and ring for refreshments? I shall make myself more
presentable and rejoin him there."

The butler nodded." Of course, Miss Samantha."

Samantha waited until David had left with Spencer and
then she rushed up the staircase to her quarters. Once
Bettina had assisted her to dress in a clean gown and had
taken the stained frock off to be cleaned, Samantha sat
down at her dressing table and patted her curls in place.
It was most unusual for Lady Edna to leave on an errand.
She had always sent one of the footmen to do her bidding
in the past. Perhaps the remedies that Samantha had given
Lady Edna had worked so well that now that good lady

felt recovered enough to resume an active life. If this was truly the case, Samantha was well pleased. She had come to love Lady Edna in the time that she had spent here, and she desired to repay her, in some small measure, for her kindness.

A frown furrowed Samantha's brow as she thought of the blow that Lady Edna should suffer when her ruse was revealed and she discovered that Samantha was not her granddaughter. Samantha was dreading that moment of truth and the consequences it should have, not only for Lady Edna but also for herself. She prayed that she might think of a way to make the dear lady understand and forgive her, but Samantha was living a lie and with each hour that ticked by, there was more to forgive.

Perhaps Lady Edna would remember her own youth and be charitable. Samantha desperately hoped that that should be the case. But even if Lady Edna forgave Samantha's part in the ruse, there was another person to consider. David should not be in the least bit tolerant when he learned that Samantha had deceived him. Merely thinking of the angry words that David should surely utter when he discovered that she was not Olivia made tears gather in Samantha's eyes.

"What have I done?" Samantha spoke the words softly to her reflection in the glass. "I never meant to fall in love with him and now I have complicated everything!"

"Excuse me, Miss?" Bettina came back into the room at the sound of her mistress's voice.

"It was nothing, Bettina." Samantha fixed a smile on her face and sat very still as Bettina put the finishing touches on her toilette. But though she could dismiss Bettina's question with a wave of her hand, it was not so easy to dismiss the tender feelings she had begun to harbor for David.

It had come about so gradually, so naturally, that Samantha had not truly noticed until it was far too late. The signs had been small and easily mistaken for simple friendship. Of course Samantha had noticed that her breath seemed to quicken when David entered a room. And she was well aware that her heart pounded faster when his eyes met hers. She was even cognizant of the fact that her knees grew weak when David took her hand. But she had not added all the small signs together until this very day and reached the distressing conclusion that she had most willingly given her heart to Olivia's fiancé.

Bettina stepped back and nodded at Samantha's reflection in the glass. "You look lovely, Miss."

"Thank you, Bettina." Samantha smiled at her dresser. Then she walked slowly from the room and down the staircase, wishing that she could confess her ruse to the man she had come to love, and beg his forgiveness for her deceit.

David closed the sketchbook on the table with a frown. He had seen Samantha's standard drawings of bowls of fruit and bouquets of flowers. Though they were competent, they had shown no true artistic talent and it was clear to him that Samantha had been merely following the instructions of a drawing master. Even more surprisingly, there had been no drawings of birds on the pages of the sketchbook, and Lady Honoria had written that birds were Olivia's favorite subject. Their omission was startling and David vowed to ask Samantha about it.

Samantha entered the Drawing Room several minutes later. She was dressed in a fetching, sea-green gown and she smiled as she walked over to the table to join him.

"I am glad you are here, Samantha." David was frowning as he turned to her. "I have been perusing your sketchbook and I was surprised to find no drawings of birds."

Samantha sighed. Birds again. Olivia's passion was becoming a thorn in her side. "You are correct, David. There are no birds in my sketchbook."

"Why is this, Samantha?"

"Because I did not wish to spend my entire time in London at work." Samantha gave what she hoped was a convincing smile. "You see, painting birds is my passion and if I allowed myself to become involved in that pursuit, it should quickly claim all of my attention."

David nodded. "I see. Then you did not bring your nature portfolio or any of your sketches?"

"I brought nothing." Samantha smiled again. "My painting master has my work, and will keep it secure for me. These sketches are merely to satisfy Grandmama's opinion that a lady should spend a small portion of her time in artistic pursuits. I also do needlework, though it bores me dreadfully, because it pleases her."

"What pleases *you*, Samantha?" David's voice was kind.

"Spending time with you," Samantha answered quite honestly. "But I should prefer it to be in a rural setting. In spite of all the excitements to be found in the city, I find I miss riding through the dawn to meet the sun and hearing the rustling of wild creatures stirring in the wood. I miss the way the pines sigh as the wind blows through their branches and . . . and I miss the greetings of neighbors as they hail me from their fields and wave their straw hats in greeting. Some complain that life in the country is lonely, but I have never found it so."

David nodded. Samantha had voiced his thoughts exactly. "How could one be lonely, surrounded by such a multitude of life?"

"You must love the country almost as much as I do." Samantha turned to him in amazement.

"Perhaps even more so." David reached out to touch the velvety softness of her cheek. He traced the path a tear of longing had made, and then he smiled at her. "You are homesick, Samantha. And I must confess that I also long for the country."

Samantha nodded. "It is true. I had thought that the excitement of London would cause me to forget the pleasures of a rustic life, but it has not. Perhaps the difference has caused me to appreciate it even more."

"I am glad that you have told me of your sentiments,

Samantha." David smiled kindly at her. "And I have just thought of a perfect place to take you on our next outing."

"Where?"

David congratulated himself on the excitement that now gleamed in Samantha's eyes. He had successfully shaken her from her brown study. "It shall be my secret. I should like to collect you at midday tomorrow and take you to my favorite spot in London. But first I must make the arrangements. Would it distress you greatly if we did not stay until the conclusion of tonight's ball?"

"That should be most agreeable to me." Samantha smiled at him. "I must confess that I am not anticipating this evening's entertainment with any degree of pleasure."

"You do not care for balls?"

"It is not that." Samantha sighed. "I do not know whether I care for them or not, for this is the first ball that I shall attend."

David laughed. "Do not look so glum. Perhaps you will enjoy it. Most young ladies appear to take great pleasure in dancing."

"But I am not like most young ladies. I . . . I find I cannot, for the life of me, remember the figures of the dance! Mr. Pauley, my dancing instructor, has quite given up on me. And he is reputed to be the most patient of teachers. Even dear Grandmama declares that I put her in mind of a clumsy bear!"

David's eyes twinkled in amusement. "And you are concerned that you shall trod on my toes if you dance with me?"

"That is it, precisely. So you see, I should not mind at all if we do not attend. I am simply not capable of dancing with grace."

"I am certain that you are quite capable." David smiled at her reassuringly. Samantha's honesty was most refreshing and he was certain that no other young lady should have admitted her shortcomings so readily. "I would even wager to say that the problem lies entirely with the partner that you have enjoyed. Are you and Mr. Pauley of equal height?"

Samantha shook her head. "No, Mr. Pauley is far shorter than I am, and he declares that my unfashionable height is at the root of my problem. He has stated that it is quite impossible for someone of my height to be graceful."

"He is mistaken." David sighed and wished that he could box the famed Mr. Pauley's ears for embarrassing Samantha regarding her lovely, tall figure. "Shall we practice so that you need not feel so anxious."

Samantha's face lit up in a smile. "That should be most helpful, indeed! But we have no music. We cannot dance without music, can we?"

"It should be much more difficult." David looked about the Drawing Room, and spied a gold music box on a pie-crust table near the windows. "Is that not a music box on the table?"

"Why . . . yes!" Samantha crossed the room with eager steps to fetch it. She wound it up and her expression turned to one of dismay as she listened to the tune it played. "A waltz! And I have not yet received permission for the waltz. Even if you succeed in teaching me this dance, I shall not be allowed to partner you. It should be seen as a terrible scandal!"

David chuckled. "You forget my position, Samantha. I shall ask for permission to partner you in the waltz and it will be granted immediately."

"Of course." Samantha nodded quickly. "But I am not certain it is wise of you to ask me to partner you. Though I am able to perform the steps without fault, I am most dreadfully awkward. Mr. Pauley has decided that I shall never be proficient in the waltz."

David wished again that he could plant Mr. Pauley a facer. The man had caused Samantha to doubt herself and it was little wonder that she was anxious. "Mr. Pauley is quite wrong and I shall prove it. May I have the pleasure of this waltz, my dear Miss Tarrington?"

"Most certainly. It is most kind of you to ask." Samantha

smiled as she gave the expected response, but she trembled when she took David's arm and they walked to the center of the Aubusson carpet. She took a deep breath for courage as he took her hand in his and they assumed the correct position.

"This will not be an ordeal, Samantha." David's laugh rumbled from his throat. "Smile and close your eyes."

"Close my eyes?" Samantha's eyes opened even wider at his instruction. "But . . . why should I do that?"

"So that you shall be able to hear the music more clearly. And do not worry about trodding on my toes, for I shall simply move them out of the way if you miss a step."

Samantha nodded and dutifully closed her eyes. She did not understand how David's method could assist her, but she was quite willing to follow his directions.

"Do you feel the pressure of my fingers on the side of your waist?"

Samantha nodded, her eyes tightly closed. "Of course I do. You are pushing me."

"I am not pushing you. I am guiding you," David corrected her. "All you must do is listen to the music and allow me to guide you in the patterns of the waltz. It is so simple, even I can do it. And so shall you."

"But you do not know how very clumsy I am."

"You may have been clumsy with Mr. Pauley as a partner, but you shall not be so with me. Be assured that if you trip, I shall steady you. And if you fall, I shall catch you. Now let us move to the music."

Samantha moved as David's hand exerted pressure and after a few, faltering steps, she was soon moving about the room with a modicum of assurance. As yet, she had not trod on David's toes and this gave her new confidence.

After another few moments passed, free of mishap, Samantha drew a sigh of relief. The waltz was not difficult at all! A smile replaced her frown and she found she was enjoying a heady, sweeping sensation as she glided over the carpet in David's arms. She felt light as a feather, tethered to the earth only by his warm fingers on her waist. If all dancing could be like this, she would love to do it above all things!

Gradually, inevitably, the music box wound down, its tinkling notes playing slower and slower until they stopped altogether. Samantha opened her eyes, the magic of her first successful waltz still upon her, and gazed up into David's dark blue eyes. She wanted to tell him how marvelous their dance had been, how enthralled she had felt in his arms. But Samantha was speechless, her lips slightly parted, the color high on her face. And then his lips lowered to hers and she sighed as he softly kissed her.

"Samantha." He whispered her name and she moved more firmly into his embrace, fitting her trembling body to his. She had one fleeting moment of panic as his lips claimed hers once again. Would he thrust her away, as he'd done when he'd first kissed her at the Two Feathers Inn, and declare that she belonged in the schoolroom? But he did not utter a single word as he was far too intent on exploring her mouth with his.

Samantha's mind whirled in confusion. She felt heat and cold simultaneously, and she shivered with perfect delight. He was so strong and yet so gentle, a contrast that she found remarkable in the extreme. Her lips parted of their own accord as she tasted the sweet heat of his mouth, and she sighed in sublime bliss. She would have fallen if not for his strong arms around her, for she felt as if every bone in her body had dissolved in the fire of their embrace. Indeed, there was no sensation of being held to the earth at all. She was soaring on a cloud of delightful pleasure and she felt quite wondrously weightless.

Only one thought ran through Samantha's mind at this delightful juncture, a notion that was exceedingly improper for a decorous young miss. If this was how a gentleman made love to a lady, she desired to experience it to the fullest degree!

When he broke their embrace, after long moments, there was a bemused expression on his face. "Indeed, Miss Tarrington! If the waltz has such an amazing effect upon your sensibilities, I would suggest that you refuse all other partners save me."

"Oh, I shall!" Her color was high, heating her cheeks, and Samantha was aware of the slight catch in her voice as she answered him. "I should not wish to waltz with anyone else."

He nodded and gave her a smile of approval, and then he led her back to the sofa. "Let us have the tea that your butler kindly provided, and await your grandmother."

"Yes. That is what we should do, of course." Samantha's hands trembled slightly as she poured out the tea. "Grandmama should be well pleased with me, for I now see the need for all those rules of etiquette that have taken me forever to learn!"

"Which rules would those be?"

Samantha laughed, her composure returning. "The rules that concern a young lady and her fiancé. It is considered quite improper for them to dance more than three waltzes of an evening together and you have taught me precisely why this is so."

"What do you think might happen if there were no such rule?"

"Why, she should be firmly compromised, of course. And if my initial experience in this subject is of any weight, I daresay she should enjoy it most thoroughly!"

It was David's turn to laugh and he did so with true abandon. And it was at this point, precisely, that Lady Edna entered the room.

"It is good to see you two young people enjoying yourselves." Lady Edna crossed quite spryly to her chair and helped herself to a chocolate biscuit on the way. "Such an afternoon I have had! It is not to be believed!"

"What has happened, Grandmama?" Samantha was immediately concerned.

"Nothing that need concern you, my dear. It is merely that I found myself in the position of having to give my solicitor of forty years a dreadfully harsh dressing-down. I fear that the poor man has gone quite over the bend."

"Is there some way that I can be of assistance, Lady Edna?" David crossed the room to her side.

"No, dear boy. I have resolved the matter. I should have gone to see him sooner, if I'd had the slightest suspicion that he should invest the bulk of my estate in the manufacture of hot air balloons!"

Samantha rushed over with a cup of tea. "Hot air balloons? Oh, dear, Grandmama! Please tell me that you are not penniless!"

"Not at all, my dear." Lady Edna took a sip of her tea and smiled at Samantha. "Quite the opposite is true. His investment proved to be extremely profitable."

David frowned. "But yet you dressed him down?"

"Yes, indeed." Lady Edna nodded firmly. "He failed to secure my approval, and that was a cardinal error on his part. He assumed that by virtue of being a lady, I should find the process of investing quite tedious. Most of his female clients, you see, are concerned only with profits and do not care to be bothered with the particulars. I assured him that this was not accurate in my case, and I took him to task for assuming too much and depriving me of all the fun."

Samantha stared at Lady Edna in shock. "If you had known his intentions, should you have allowed this investment?"

"Of course! And what fun it should have been for me! I should have traveled to France to observe their manufacture, and I might even have agreed to be carried aloft. It is most distressing to think of the enjoyment that I have missed."

David smiled at Samantha and then he turned to Lady Edna. "I know very little about this invention, Madame. It would please me greatly if you should enlighten me."

"I should be delighted." Lady Edna took another sip of her tea as David and Samantha took seats near her. "The first hot air balloon was flown in 1783 by two French brothers, the Montgolfiers. That same year marked a successful manned flight, and the invention has reached unexpected heights of popularity in Paris where the populace regards this device as the greatest novelty. Now it seems that these contraptions have other uses as well."

"What would those be, Grandmama?" Samantha was clearly enthralled.

"Our own military has ordered as many as my small manufactory can produce." Lady Edna smiled in delight. "They have paid in advance and are eagerly awaiting delivery."

Samantha was puzzled. "For what purpose? Surely they do not wish to entertain the troops!"

"Observation." David began to smile as he hit upon the answer. "They should be able to observe much more from the air than they could at ground level."

Lady Edna nodded. "Precisely! Until man can grow wings like a bird, the balloon will suffice. I have made such a lovely profit on this contraption that I shall treat your entire wedding party to a balloon ascension, Samantha!"

Samantha smiled and her eyes met David's briefly. Then she remembered her promise to Olivia and dropped her gaze quickly, lest David should notice the tears that were gathering in her eyes. They would not have a wedding day. She should be forced to take leave of David on the day before their nuptials took place. They could never marry, even if he forgave her ruse and declared that he loved her for herself. A duke simply did not marry below the gentry, and Samantha Jane Bennings was well below the gentry. As the daughter of an adulterous mother who had deserted her at birth and a father whose identity should forever remain uncertain, Samantha was the most unsuitable match that David could possibly make!

"What is it, Granddaughter?" Lady Edna noticed the expression of dismay that flickered across Samantha's countenance.

Samantha was about to deny her sudden discomfiture when she realized that Lady Edna had presented her with a perfect opportunity. She had promised Olivia that she should delay the wedding and she had not yet found the proper time to introduce the subject. "It is only that Miss Fairchild has told me that it usually rains on the week that we have chosen for the wedding. It is a pity that we cannot delay our nuptials to increase the chances of dry weather."

"There is no reason why we cannot delay the wedding." A thoughtful expression crossed Lady Edna's face as she turned to David. "Do you have any objection to the delay?"

David cast a quick, teasing glance at Samantha as he shook his head. "None but the usual bridegroom's wish to be wed as soon as possible."

"Then we are in agreement." Lady Edna smiled at the color that flooded Samantha's face. "What date would you choose, Samantha?"

Samantha smiled. "The day after my birthday, Grandmama. The grand ball that you have planned on our wedding eve can also serve as my birthday celebration. Since my birthday and our wedding follow one another so closely, David should have no difficulty remembering the anniversary of our nuptials in the years to come."

"Well done, Granddaughter!" Lady Edna laughed. "It shall be exactly as you wish."

Samantha drew a deep breath of relief. Olivia would be pleased that she had managed so adroitly to delay the wedding. But something in Lady Edna's searching gaze made Samantha avert her eyes and turn the conversation to other, more mundane matters. Perhaps it was due to her guilty conscience, but Samantha was almost certain she had seen a glimmer of suspicion in Lady Edna's eye when she had suggested that they delay the wedding until the day *after* Olivia's birthday.

Ten

David watched as Samantha joined the couples on the dance floor on the arm of Viscount Struthersford. If he had known of the gentleman's reputation as a rake before Samantha had accepted his invitation to dance, David should have warned her to be cautious around him. David did his best to keep his expression pleasant and contented himself with the fact that there could be little danger to Samantha while she was engaged in a country dance. The most the viscount could do was press her hand as he encountered her in the figures or swing her a bit too close to him. There should be no opportunity for any further contact so long as the viscount and Samantha remained on the dance floor.

An expression of pride crossed David's handsome face. Samantha was performing the intricate steps of the dance perfectly. It appeared that his lesson in the waltz had given her new confidence. After she had displayed her new skill as his partner for the first waltz of the evening, Samantha had been approached by a half-dozen young swains seeking permission to dance with her. During it all, her steps had been faultless. David had observed her closely as she had moved across the floor. And the uncharitable urge to confront her dancing master, Mr. Pauley, to inform that man of the disservice that he had done to Samantha had grown ever greater.

"If you continue to glower, all will suspect you are con-

sumed with jealousy at your dear fiancée's choice of partners."

David turned and smiled politely as he found his hostess
at his side. Lady Fairchild's gown was most elegant and it
came very near to concealing the bulky figure beneath it.
Her face, however, had faults that no amount of cosmetics,
however expertly applied, could correct. Mr. Billings,
David's valet, had told him that Lady Fairchild had survived an epidemic that had left her complexion permanently scarred. All who knew Lady Fairchild had accepted
this disfigurement and had come to ignore it, as she had
a lively and pleasing personality. But her husband, the earl,
was rumored to have left her bed for that of his mistress,
never to return.

"You are most astute, Lady Fairchild." David acknowl-
edged the truth of the lady's words. "I must try to maintain
a pleasant expression, though I admit I do not like to watch
my fiancée partner such a man. If I had known of his
reputation earlier, I should have counseled her to decline
his invitation."

"Your concern does you credit, but no harm shall come
to her on the dance floor. Perhaps you should attempt to
amuse yourself while your dear fiancée is engaged. There
are several young debutantes who are without partners."

David glanced quickly at the young ladies who were sitting with their chaperones. Lady Fairchild's own daughter,
Elizabeth, was among them, and Samantha had remarked
what a pity it was that the young gentlemen seemed inca-
pable of looking past Elizabeth's rather short and bulky
figure to the lovely young lady beneath. "There is only
one young lady that I should care to partner, Lady
Fairchild."

"Who might that be?" Lady Fairchild's expression was
carefully guarded.

"Why, your daughter, of course. My fiancée has told me
that she is a most delightful companion."

Lady Fairchild seemed most grateful for his kind words
and she smiled her approval. "I am certain that Elizabeth

should be most pleased to partner you. You need do no more than ask her."

"Then I shall do so straightaway. And would you, Lady Fairchild, do me the honor of partnering me in the following dance?"

"I shall be delighted!" Lady Fairchild's smile grew wider and the color rose to her cheeks. It was an amazing transformation, causing her lips to look less pinched and her complexion to glow quite pleasingly. "And you must not be so anxious about your fiancée. I have spoken with her on several occasions, and your dear Samantha seems quite capable of managing any social occasion that should arise."

Smiling, David joined the group surrounding Miss Elizabeth Fairchild. As he made polite conversation and waited for the opportunity to ask her to partner him, his thoughts again turned to Samantha. Though he had solemnly vowed not to kiss her again, keeping his vow should be difficult. Samantha was the embodiment of every aspect he had imagined in a wife. She was not in the least bit missish, she was highly intelligent, and she had the courage of her convictions. Samantha was lovely, both in manner and appearance, and kind to those who were less fortunate than she was. She loved animals and appeared to have an amazing affinity with them, and though she did very well in London and was treated with favor by the members of the *ton*, she also appreciated the pleasures of a rustic life. David was firmly smitten, completely in the grips of a powerful love for Miss Samantha Bennings. But the object of his affections was a Lady, and as such, she could not marry below the gentry. She was, however, a perfect match for Harry.

Though he was not aware of it, David began to frown. For the first time in his life, he felt a stab of pure jealousy and he found that he did not appreciate that baser emotion in the slightest. By virtue of his birth, Harry had been given the necessary qualifications to marry Miss Samantha Bennings, while David could not. And Harry, the utter fool that he was, did not wish to wed her. Could anything be more ironic?

One of the group surrounding Miss Fairchild had turned to gaze at him curiously. David forced his lips to turn up in a polite smile and moved forward, to Miss Fairchild's side. Though he could not marry Samantha, David could make a difference in Miss Fairchild's life. He would take pleasure in partnering her and perhaps his deception would serve some small good.

Samantha glanced around her as the dance ended and she saw that David was conversing with Miss Fairchild. Samantha's lips turned up in a delighted smile and she altered her course so that she should not disturb them. It would please her greatly if David should ask Elizabeth to partner him. She was genuinely fond of Elizabeth and perhaps if David expressed an interest in her and invited her to dance, other young gentlemen might fall in line behind him. Samantha was certain that if even one gentleman took the trouble to seek out Elizabeth's company, her charms should soon be recognized.

"Should you care to partner me in the next dance, Miss Tarrington?" Viscount Struthersford turned to her eagerly. "Your fiancé seems occupied with Miss Fairchild."

Samantha sighed. The viscount was an excellent dancer, but there was something about him that did not please her and she could not decide what it was. He had been unfailingly courteous and his converse had been entirely proper.

"Thank you, but I must decline." Samantha smiled as she shook her head. "I find that I am quite exhausted and desire nothing more than a bit of rest."

"Your exhaustion is due to the crush, no doubt. These balls are often overcrowded, and I notice that the air has grown quite close."

"You are right, of course." Samantha nodded. "I am

amazed that they do not think to open the windows to let in the fresh breeze from the garden."

The viscount laughed. "And risk disturbing the ladies' coiffures? I think not, Miss Tarrington. But I do agree that a breath of fresh air should be quite the thing."

Samantha was surprised as he took her arm and led her toward the windows. Did he intend to open them himself? But then she observed that a set of French doors had been left ajar and she sighed in relief as a gentle breeze cooled her flushed cheeks. "How delightful! If we stand here, we shall catch a hint of the breeze!"

"You are not anxious that your coiffure should be ruined?"

The viscount was obviously teasing her and Samantha laughed. "I have not the slightest concern for my coiffure, I assure you."

"Then we must take full advantage of the opportunity that has presented itself." The viscount pushed the doors open a bit wider and moved out to the terrace with Samantha in tow. Then he dropped her arm, moved a step to the side, and sighed in contentment. "There! Is that not better?"

"It is." Samantha nodded in agreement. They were only three steps from the door and still in full sight of the assembly inside. There could be nothing improper in merely standing here, several steps apart, to enjoy the fresh air.

"Would you care to stroll through the garden, Miss Tarrington? I have heard that Lady Fairchild's roses are the talk of the *ton*."

"Thank you, no." Samantha turned to him, the surprise clearly evident on her face. "You must know, sir, that I cannot walk with you unescorted."

The viscount nodded. "Quite right. Please forgive me for making such an improper suggestion. I was only thinking of how delightful it should be and I neglected to consider . . . did you hear that?"

"Did I hear what?"

"It was . . . a cry, as if someone had fallen far off in the distance. I heard it quite clearly a moment ago, but all is silent now. Perhaps it was merely the wind blowing through the . . . oh, dear!''

"You heard it again?'' Samantha was concerned.

"Not the cry, no. It was more of a . . . a splashing. Do you suppose that someone could have fallen into Lady Fairchild's lily pond?''

Samantha listened intently, but she heard nothing unusual. "I hear nothing.''

"Nor do I.'' The viscount breathed an audible sigh of relief. "I merely thought, that since that section of the garden is not well lighted, someone might have . . . there it is again! I must go to see if someone needs my assistance!''

Samantha hesitated as the viscount started down the steep steps that led to the garden below. Should she go back into the ballroom and ask for assistance? Or should she take action as the viscount was doing? She cast one panicked glance behind her and reached a decision. There was no time to waste. As she hesitated here, someone could very well be drowning in the depths of Lady Fairchild's lily pond.

"Wait!'' Samantha called out for the viscount, who had reached the bottom of the steps. "I am coming with you!''

The viscount stopped and waited as Samantha picked up her skirts and ran down the steps. He took her arm and they set off at a run down the garden path.

"Where is the lily pond?'' Samantha struggled to keep up with the viscount's long strides.

"Down this path and only a few feet ahead.'' The viscount pulled her down a darkened path. "It is here. And . . . I do not see anyone, do you?''

Samantha shook her head, her eyes peering into the depths of the pool. "But it is not deep at all! If someone had fallen, they could have easily stepped out.''

"Very true. How silly of me not to have thought of it.'' The viscount smiled. "Take care you do not trip, my dear. Here . . . I shall hold you.''

Samantha's eyes narrowed as she caught sight of the viscount's face in the moonlight. His smile was predatory and here she was, alone with him . . .

The dance had ended, and David smiled as he escorted Elizabeth back to her chair. "Thank you, Miss Fairchild, for a most enjoyable interlude. Could I presume to invite you to join me in another dance a bit later in the evening?"

"Why, yes! I should be most delighted!" Elizabeth smiled at him. Then she leaned a bit closer so that her lips were on a level with his ear. "Thank you for asking me. I know that it is dear Samantha's doing, and I am most grateful."

David nodded. "Our first dance was Samantha's doing, but the second dance will be mine. You are every bit as charming as my fiancée told me you should be."

Elizabeth was glowing as he left her, and as David walked away, he noticed another young gentleman approach her. Perhaps he had served his purpose tonight if Elizabeth should become more popular than she had been before their dance.

"Oh, dear! I am so glad I have found you!" Lady Fairchild approached David and took his arm.

"Of course, Lady Fairchild. I was about to seek out your company. The next dance is ours, I believe?"

"It would have been." Lady Fairchild pulled him off to the side, where no one could overhear their conversation. "I think you had rather seek out your fiancée. She was standing on the terrace with Viscount Struthersford. It was all quite proper, you understand. They were in full view of the assemblage and several steps apart. But now that I look again, they have both disappeared!"

David nodded quickly. "Thank you for your warning, Lady Fairchild. I shall locate Samantha immediately."

"Yes, you must hurry." Lady Fairchild looked extremely anxious. "As you are no doubt aware, the viscount is not to be trusted. At least you need not be anxious about your dear fiancée's reputation. No one saw them leave and I shall never mention it to anyone!"

Seemingly in no great hurry, David slipped through the crowd and approached the open doors to the terrace. He wished to break into a run, but appearances must be maintained. He did not suspect that Samantha had gone off with Viscount Struthersford willingly. The scoundrel had somehow tricked her, and he had to rescue her before it was too late . . .

Samantha stepped back until she was on the very lip of the pond. She could not retreat any further without taking a tumble into the water. She took a step to the side, but the viscount quickly countered her movement with a step of his own. For long moments, it seemed they would feint and evade, neither achieving their purpose.

Samantha's thoughts were of escape. If the viscount would but drop his guard for an instant, she should whirl and cut around him to race for the safety of the path. But he did not take his eyes from hers and he seemed able to read her intentions.

Weight centered firmly on both feet, Samantha dipped and bobbed, eluding his grasp as he continued to reach for her. To an observer, it would have appeared that Samantha and the viscount were performing a strange new dance, one in which neither partner came into contact with the other. But despite Samantha's quickness, the viscount had the advantage of stronger, lengthier arms. It was only a matter of time before Samantha was firmly caught and pulled into the vise of his arms.

"Unhand me, sir!" Samantha pretended to struggle to set herself free. It was what the viscount expected and to do otherwise should be suspect. But as she struggled she turned slightly, pulling the viscount in the arc of a circle.

The viscount laughed and captured her fist in his hand.

"You fight to preserve your virtue, my dear, and this is a grave mistake on your part. I shall show you that losing it shall be most pleasurable."

"You are the one who is wrong, sir!" Samantha maneuvered him further in the arc. "Admit that you have deceived me!"

"Deceived you? How did I do that, my dear?"

"When you told me you heard a call for help, it was merely a trick. You heard nothing at all!"

The viscount laughed and turned further, so that he was facing Samantha. "That is simply not true, my dear. I heard your heart calling out to me. It said, *Take me into the garden and claim me for your own, for I wish to be loved by none other than you.* How could a mere mortal resist such a delightful summons from his goddess?"

Though it was difficult, Samantha managed a coquettish smile. "Sir! Your eloquence leaves me quite . . . quite speechless!"

The viscount smiled back, certain that he had convinced her to surrender to his advances. As he pulled her close, Samantha glanced over his shoulder and gave a relieved sigh. His back was directly to the pond, exactly as she had intended. She tipped up her face, inviting his kiss, and waited.

In the brief moment before his lips were about to claim hers, the viscount relaxed his hold. This was the opportunity that Samantha had sought and she took full advantage. She lifted her skirts and with one well-placed thrust, hooked her slippered foot round the viscount's ankle. This action rendered him quite off balance; as he struggled to regain his equilibrium, Samantha placed both her hands against his chest and shoved with all her strength. The push was every bit as effective as she had hoped it should be for the viscount toppled backward, straight into the lily pond.

* * *

From his vantage point behind a tree, David barely managed to stifle his chortle of amusement. The viscount was a large man, well muscled and strong. Yet Samantha, who was barely half his weight, had felled him like a properly axed oak. David wished to applaud her adroit maneuver, but it should only embarrass her if she knew that he had chanced to witness the scene.

With his hand clamped tightly over his mouth to hold in his laugher, David watched his fiancée straighten her clothing and pat her curls back into place. She completely ignored the splashing and sputtering the viscount made as he attempted to climb the slippery bank of Lady Fairchild's lily pond. Indeed, she did not spare a single glance in his direction.

When Samantha was convinced that her appearance had been set to rights and would pass the scrutiny of the guests in the ballroom, she turned to face the viscount. He had, by this time, achieved dry ground and was vainly attempting to dry his clothing with a soggy square of linen from his pocket.

"I would advise you to take your leave from the ball, lest you take a chill." Samantha's voice was steady. "The evening air is frigid and you seem to have gotten yourself thoroughly drenched with pond water and algae."

The viscount made as if to speak, but Samantha silenced him with a glance. "Go now, sir. I am certain that there is a gate that leads from the garden to the street. You have only to find it to save what remains of your dignity. Do not be concerned that others may wonder why you have left. Rest assured that your presence shall not be missed in the slightest."

Without even waiting to see if the viscount did as she had bid him, Samantha turned on her heel and marched back the way she had come. Though David could see that her color was high as she passed beneath one of the torches that lit the garden path, she wore a serene expression and her lips were formed in a perfect smile.

David again felt the urge to applaud as he watched the

dignity of his fiancée's retreating form. He had no doubt that Samantha could carry off her re-entrance to the ballroom with equanimity. She appeared to be surprisingly resilient. When she had disappeared round a bend in the path, David turned to investigate the whereabouts of the viscount and chuckled softly to himself. That rake was beating a hasty retreat toward the garden gate that Samantha had indicated, his clothing dripping water and his head bowed low in defeat.

Rather than follow Samantha, David took another path toward the ballroom. As he walked past blooming flowers and lush green plants, he thought about the scene he had witnessed. Samantha had not required his assistance in dealing with the viscount, and had bested that scoundrel with seemingly little effort. It was most unusual for a gentleborn young lady to prove capable of such physicality, and David was curious to learn exactly how she had become so proficient in the art of defending herself. Of course, he could not ask her without admitting that he had witnessed her moment of triumph, but David vowed to broach the subject in a roundabout manner to see what facts he could glean. His fiancée was a most unusual young lady. As the daughter of a baron and the granddaughter of a countess, David wondered how, under heaven, Samantha had learned to wrestle in the manner of a common farm boy.

When he entered the ballroom once again, David located Samantha immediately. She was speaking to Lady Fairchild and David hurried to join them.

"Why there you are, David!" Samantha gave him a perfectly innocent smile. "I have just come from the terrace. Someone told me that you had stepped out for a breath of fresh air, but when I did not see you, I returned to speak with Lady Fairchild."

David nodded, silently pleased at the ingenious manner in which she had covered her action. "We must have just missed each other, for I was there until but a moment ago. The breeze was most welcome."

"Yes, indeed." Samantha smiled at him serenely. "It is such a lovely evening."

At that moment a young gentleman approached to request that Samantha partner him in the next dance. She turned to David, as if to ask his permission, and David smiled at her indulgently. "Do dance with him, my dear. Our hostess has kindly agreed to partner me in the next dance and perhaps we may find another two couples to make up our own square."

"There's my brother," the young gentleman offered eagerly. "He has engaged Miss Fairchild for this dance."

Lady Fairchild's eyes twinkled merrily as she turned to the young gentleman. "I do believe my daughter's friend, Miss Wheeling, has just accepted an invitation to dance. Let us go and ask them if they would care to join us."

"I do hope I will not step on his toes." Samantha turned to David with a smile as Lady Fairchild and the young gentleman left them.

"After all that I have witnessed this evening, I believe you need have no fear of that." David grinned at her. "I would say that your feet are most talented."

Samantha tipped her head to the side and favored him with a curious glance. "What an odd thing to say! And you are smiling as if you are highly amused. Do permit me to share in the joke."

"But there is no joke." David took her hand and pressed it. "I am simply enjoying the evening in your company."

Samantha smiled, but she was not entirely satisfied at David's answer. And his turn of phrase when he had praised her *talented feet* gave her pause. Was it possible that David had witnessed her encounter with the viscount in the garden?

"I have heard that Lady Fairchild's garden is lovely." Samantha hoped that her expression was completely guileless. "Have you seen it?"

"Only in passing, but I have been told that her lily pond is spectacular. Should you care to take a stroll after this dance is finished?"

"I . . . I think not." Samantha dropped her eyes. The last place she wanted to visit again was Lady Fairchild's lily pond! "I should prefer to take our leave so you will have ample time to prepare for our outing. I am eagerly anticipating your surprise."

David nodded, the ghost of a smile on his face. "Of course. We shall depart unfashionably early tomorrow afternoon, the moment your morning callers have left."

"But I have not invited anyone to call." Samantha frowned slightly.

"Nevertheless, I suspect that you shall have many callers." David did his best not to laugh. Samantha's actions may very well have been unobserved, but word of the viscount's dunking in the lily pond was bound to surface. A groom was certain to speak of the guest who had come to collect his conveyance in clothing that was doused with pond water. And a gardener was certain to speculate about the fact that Lady Fairchild's lilies had been disturbed on the night of the ball. Rumors would fly amongst the servants and be repeated to other servants who would then inform their masters and mistresses. At that juncture, some guests would remember that Samantha had appeared on the terrace in the viscount's company and they would come to quiz her on what she knew of the matter. He would be in attendance, of course, and his presence would aid Samantha in countering the rumors, but Viscount Struthersford's ignominious dunking in the lily pond should be the subject of many an *on-dit* for the remainder of the Season.

Eleven

Olivia was trembling as she approached Harry's magnificent stallion. He was a most handsome specimen and she attempted to concentrate on the strong lines of his form, rather than on the activity that should soon take place. Despite her best efforts, Olivia's breath came in short, fearful gasps as Harry helped her up into the saddle. She was feeling quite light-headed by the time he mounted and took his seat behind her. As he gathered her firmly into his arms, Olivia glanced down at the ground. From her high perch on Harry's big stallion, the ground appeared very far beneath her. She was aware that she was quivering in terror, but she did not seem to be able to control her emotions. All she could think of was the horrid fall that she had taken.

The day had been bright and sunny, much as this day was, and Olivia had been practicing with her riding instructor. Though she had been far from an accomplished rider, her parents had demanded that young Olivia be taught to take the jump.

Olivia had been terrified of the jump. The sight of the low fence that she and her horse were to hurdle had filled her heart with terror. But the thought of her parents' disapproval if she refused to attempt the jump had filled her with an even greater dread.

Though Olivia had been quaking with fright, she had determined to master this feat. In her young mind, it was the single barrier that prevented her from enjoying her parents' love. She had raced her mount toward the fence with no little courage and closed her eyes tightly as she had approached the barrier. If she could but accomplish just one successful jump, she should prove herself worthy in her parents' eyes.

To this very day, Olivia was not certain what had gone amiss, but the moment her mount had taken the fence, she had been thrown from the saddle. She had landed awkwardly, striking her head against a rock and breaking a bone in her leg. Mercifully, she had lost consciousness and had been carried to her chambers to await the surgeon.

When Olivia had regained consciousness a full week later, the broken bone had been set and was already beginning to heal. It had been a clean break and the surgeon had assured her parents that it should not leave a lasting infirmity if it were given time to heal thoroughly. Though her young body would mend, the effect on Olivia's mind, however, had been devastating. She had found herself terrified of horses and she had trembled in dread at the thought of being forced to ride again.

The surgeon had told Olivia's parents that she could not ride for at least six months, explaining that if her leg were to be re-broken, she could be left permanently lame. Even Olivia's father, who was of the opinion that once thrown, a rider should mount again immediately to vanquish any residual fear he might have of the incident, had agreed that his daughter should follow the surgeon's caveat. And since Olivia's parents had died less than four months later, she was spared the necessity of ever attempting to conquer her fear.

"You shall not fall, Jane. I promise."

Harry's comforting voice brought her back to the present and Olivia nodded. "I know, but the ground seems so very distant."

"It is actually only a few feet and I shall hold you tightly. You have nothing to fear."

Gradually, Olivia's trembling abated and she began to

relax in Harry's warm embrace. A proper young lady was not allowed to ride in this manner, but since there was no one here to observe them, she need not have a care for the opinions of others. And riding with Harry behind her on the saddle was certainly less frightening than riding alone.

"We shall move forward now, Jane." Harry held her a bit closer. "You must tell me if you are too frightened to proceed."

As Olivia nodded, her fear returned, and her voice was shaking as she answered him. "I am as ready as I shall ever be."

Harry picked up the reins with one hand and kept his other arm around her waist. Then he clucked softly to his stallion and they began to move slowly down the path.

Olivia shut her eyes tightly at first, concentrating on the protection of Harry's embrace. After a moment or two of gentle swaying, she began to relax slightly. Harry's solid presence was a comfort and the motion of his stallion was very like the sensation of being rocked to and fro in loving arms. As she became accustomed to the motion and discovered that she no longer feared that she should lose her balance, Olivia breathed a sigh of relief.

"Are you comfortable, Jane?"

Olivia nodded and opened her eyes. She glanced down at the ground passing beneath them, and gave a timid smile. It still seemed a very long distance below her, but she was no longer as frightened as she had been at first.

"Is the pace too rapid?"

There was a note of concern in Harry's voice and Olivia quickly shook her head. "No, it is perfect. This is not as difficult as I had expected, Harry. It is actually quite pleasant."

"I had hoped you would find it so." Harry sounded pleased. "Let us step up the pace a bit and see how you fare."

"I am ready." Olivia nodded her assent. The stallion was a fine animal and it was a pity to force him to walk so very slowly. She had no doubt that he should like to run like the wind and she should like to see him do so if she were not on his back. She had always been partial to horses. They were such noble animals. At one time she had thought that she should like to paint them, but that was before she had fallen.

Under Harry's direction, the stallion gradually increased his speed until he had broken into a canter. Olivia smiled as she realized that she was not in the least bit fearful.

"Shall I slow him, Jane?" Harry's voice was anxious.

"Please do not rein him in for my sake." Olivia began to enjoy the scenery about her and the lovely path that Harry had chosen for their ride. The stallion's motion was powerful, but Harry seemed in perfect control. "I find his pace quite pleasing, Harry, and I do not think I should mind it if he were to go a bit faster."

Harry smiled as he urged his mount on. David had trained this stallion for him and Romulus was entirely reliable. The gentlest of Harry's saddle horses, he had chosen the stallion expressly for this purpose.

Olivia sat up a bit straighter and relaxed her grip on Harry's arm. She no longer felt as if she would tumble to the ground below and she quite enjoyed the sensation of the breeze as it rushed past her face.

"Let us step up the pace a bit, Harry." Olivia turned her head to smile at him. She was impressed with the manner in which the stallion obeyed Harry's every command. He was a fine horse and Harry was an excellent rider.

Harry gave Romulus a bit more head and the stallion broke into a run. Olivia was startled at first and gasped, renewing her grip on Harry's arm. But she soon became accustomed to the pace and was exhilarated at the speed the stallion garnered. In a very short time she was laughing in pure delight as they sped across the fields.

When they stopped, at last, near a lovely wooded knoll, Harry helped her down from the saddle. Olivia approached the stallion with no fear and patted his velvety nose. Then she took Harry's arm and smiled up at him, inordinately pleased with herself and the ride she had just accomplished. "It was marvelous, Harry! I had forgotten how enjoyable riding could be and without your urging, I doubt that I should ever have gathered the necessary courage to brave the saddle again. Only think of what I should have missed!"

"Congratulations, Jane. You have conquered your fear." Pride for her accomplishment gleamed in Harry's eyes.

"Thank you, Harry." Olivia felt a rush of gratitude for the gentleman who had been so patient with her. "You have done a great service for me. Not only can I now enjoy riding again, but you have also allowed me to understand the reason why I was so frightened."

"Then it is not because you were thrown?"

"Not entirely." Olivia shook her head. "It is because I despaired of ever learning to ride as well as my father or my mother. In my heart, I felt that regardless of my effort, I should fall short of their expectations. It was easier for me to find a reason not to make the attempt."

"You chose to fall deliberately?" Harry's expression mirrored his surprise.

"I do not precisely remember. I was but a young child at the time. But I should not be surprised to find that I did. I do remember that I desperately desired my parents' approval. Now that they are dead, it has eluded me forever."

"There are some people who are impossible to please." Harry draped a comforting arm around her shoulder. "I am certain that your parents loved you, in their fashion. Now that I consider it, this is the exact same manner in which my mother loves me. Perhaps both of us should cease seeking other peoples' approval so desperately and strive only to please ourselves."

Olivia thought about it for a moment, and then she nodded. "That should be marvelous, Harry. Shall we make a pact?"

Harry reached out, intending to shake her hand, but found himself gathering her into his arms instead. She raised her face to his and Harry placed a light kiss upon her lips. "The pact is sealed. What shall you do first, now that you must only please yourself?"

"I shall resume my riding lessons, if you will agree to teach me."

"I agree." Harry smiled at her. The trust he saw in her eyes made him feel strong and powerful, quite willing to slay dragons for her. "Shall we have our first lesson tomorrow morning?"

Olivia laughed. "That would be delightful! Do you think that you could teach me to ride Romulus? He is such a magnificent fellow."

"Romulus should be honored." Harry spoke for his mount. "He has been trained to the sidesaddle and it will present no difficulty for him."

"Then a woman has ridden him before?" Olivia's eyes narrowed slightly. She did not enjoy the thought that Harry had permitted another lady to ride his horse. Their previous discussions had not been of such a personal nature that either of them had mentioned affairs of the heart.

"Romulus has had but one female rider. She is the sister of a groom, and a bruising rider in her own right. She broke him to the sidesaddle, and claimed that she had never ridden a more biddable horse."

Olivia's lips turned up in a smile. It was idiotish of her to be so relieved, but she was delighted that Romulus had been ridden only by the groom's sister and not another young lady of Harry's acquaintance. She still did not know if Harry had formed a *tendre* for another, but she suspected that if he had, he would have offered to let her ride Romulus. Rather than open such a discussion now, Olivia turned their conversation to less personal matters. "Have you many cattle, Harry?"

Harry was about to tell her that his stables were extensive when he remembered that he had represented himself as a modest fellow of little means. The urge to confess his true identity was strong, but he could not admit that he was the Duke of Westbury. The banns had been published and it was possible that she had heard of his engagement. He dared not tell her the details of the deception that he had arranged with David lest he jeopardize the success of the ruse.

"I have an interest in thoroughbreds." Harry settled for only part of the truth. "My father bred them and raised them."

Olivia clapped her hands in delight. "How wonderful! I should have guessed as much, as you are such an excellent rider."

"You also have an interest in thoroughbreds?" Harry was surprised at her enthusiastic response.

"Yes, indeed! I have always regarded the thoroughbred as a beautiful and perfect creature. I think that I should have chosen to paint them if only I had not developed my fear of horses. There is such perfect symmetry between horse and rider. I am amazed that you have not attempted to capture such beauty on canvas."

"I have." Harry gave a rueful smile. "But I have had little success. My painting of Romulus, as a colt, resembled nothing so much as the Trojan Horse."

Olivia burst into laughter. "Surely you are bamming me, Harry!"

"No, I am not. My talent lies solely in landscapes, I fear. Living creatures quite elude my canvas. But perhaps you should try to paint thoroughbreds, Jane. You appear to have a true appreciation of them."

Olivia's face lit up in a smile. "I should enjoy the attempt most certainly! Perhaps I should endeavor to paint Romulus when my nature portfolio is completed. I have only one specimen left to portray and then my work is finished."

"How would you proceed in such a venture?" Harry smiled at the delight he saw in her expression.

"I would first need to study the bone structure of the horse, of course. And the manner in which the muscles relate to movement. I should need time to observe the thoroughbred in a natural setting and complete a series of sketches."

"I should be delighted to assist you!" Harry offered his services eagerly. "Perhaps you could visit my country estate and sketch the thoroughbreds there."

"Your country estate?"

"The estate where I am employed." Harry quickly corrected his slip of the tongue. He did not like to mislead her, but he could not tell her the truth of the matter until his difficulty was settled.

"But what of your mother, Harry?" Olivia frowned as she remembered the manner in which Harry had described his mother. "You have told me that she does not favor artistic pursuits. Surely she should not approve of my visit!"

Harry laughed, dismissing her concerns with a wave of his hand. "I have received a message from my mother. She travels with her sister and shall not return for some months."

"Then I cannot visit you, Harry." Olivia's disappointment was mirrored clearly on her face. "It would not be proper for I am neither married nor chaperoned."

"This will present no problem. There are several small cottages which are currently unoccupied and it should be a simple matter for me to secure one for your use. And we shall observe the proprieties, Jane. The groom's sister is also unmarried and she shall serve as your chaperone."

Olivia considered it for a moment and then her eyes began to sparkle with excitement. "I should enjoy that above all things! What a marvelous suggestion, Harry! But do you think that the owner would object? The cottages belong to him, after all."

"I am certain that he will not." Harry did his best to hide a smile. "He is a most understanding gentleman who possesses a true appreciation of the arts."

"How fortunate for you to be employed by such a gentleman! If not for your mother's disapproval, you should be in a perfect climate for artistic pursuits. I had thought to secure a small cottage and paint flowers, but I should much rather sketch your thoroughbreds. Now that I am no longer afraid of horses, it is much more to my liking."

"And to mine." Harry wore a bemused expression as he gazed at the young lady he had come to love. He should be required to tell her the truth before he took her to Westbury Park, but her speedy acceptance of his invitation left no doubt in his mind that she had become quite fond of him. His only hope was that this affection on her part should enable her to forgive the manner in which he had initially deceived her.

Samantha's eyes widened as Lady Edna's butler announced her first group of morning callers. There were eleven in all, and Samantha could not for the life of her understand why she was suddenly so popular.

"Did I not tell you it would be like this?" David, who was sitting by her side, wore an expression that bordered upon the smug. "They have come to observe your demeanor on this day. Choose your words cautiously, my dear."

Samantha turned to him with a puzzled look, but the arrival of Lady Edna silenced the question on her lips. The next to enter were her guests; the ensuing minutes were filled with greetings to her friends and acquaintances and the required exchange of pleasantries. Tea and lemonade were served, cakes were passed, and still Samantha was puzzled. Why had all these callers come to see her on this particular day?

"Samantha, dear." Lady Truesblood claimed her attention. "Have you heard the news of the viscount?"

Samantha shook her head. "No, Lady Truesblood. To which viscount are you referring?"

"Viscount Struthersford, of course." Lord Evingston spoke up. "It appears that he has departed London quite suddenly, supposedly bound for his country estate."

Samantha nodded politely. "I had not heard. Is there a crisis with the viscount's family?"

"Perhaps not yet, but there most certainly will be when he arrives." Miss Rothham giggled quite fetchingly. "I hear tell his dear mother has a friend in London who is quick to inform her of the latest scandal."

Samantha frowned slightly and attempted to look merely curious. "Is Viscount Struthersford involved in a scandal?"

"One could come to that conclusion, my dear." Lord Evingston chuckled. "Lady Fairchild's head groom has an eye for one of my maids and you know how the servants gossip."

Samantha nodded. It seemed to her that they were indulging in the very same sort of thing, but this was not the opportune time to mention that fact.

"It seems that the viscount came round to the stable last night to collect his carriage, long before the ball was over. The groom thought that odd. It is usual that when a guest takes his leave, a footman is sent to the stables to ready his carriage and order it brought round to the entrance."

"Yes." Samantha nodded. She had seen this occur at every party that she had attended. "I would think it strange that a guest fetch his own carriage."

"Precisely. And when Viscount Struthersford stepped into the light of the torches, the groom observed that his clothing was dripping with water!"

There was silence in the Drawing Room and Samantha had the uncomfortable sensation that all eyes were upon her. She raised her brows and assumed a surprised expression. "Water? But that *is* very odd. It did not rain last evening that I recall."

"You are correct, my dear." David entered the conversation. "Is it possible that someone upended the punch bowl over Viscount Struthersford's head? From what I hear of the man, it would not surprise me."

Lady Edna laughed. "Nor would it surprise me. From

what I hear, several young ladies have had cause to flee from the viscount's unwelcome attentions."

"It was not the punch bowl." Miss Pierpont spoke up. "I noticed that as I was leaving, it was still quite full."

"A glass of liquid refreshment perhaps?" Samantha's question was suitably innocent. "It should not be unusual for such an unfortunate accident to occur in a crowded ballroom."

Lord Evingston shook his head. "It could have been none of those things. The groom reported that it had a fearfully stale odor, reminiscent of pond water."

"Pond water." Samantha repeated the words. Then she turned to David with a guileless expression. "Did you not tell me that Lady Fairchild had a pond in her garden?"

"Yes. When I partnered Miss Fairchild she mentioned that her mother's lily pond is quite lovely."

Lady Edna began to shake with laughter. "Oh, my! You do not suppose that someone . . ."

"Yes, indeed!" Lord Evingston reached out to pat her hand. "I *do* suppose! The likely scenario is that some young lady, as yet unknown to us, was lured into the garden by Viscount Struthersford. And when his attentions became, too . . . er . . . personal, this same young miss pushed the viscount into Lady Fairchild's lily pond."

Lady Edna dissolved with laughter. When that good lady could speak again, she wiped her eyes and declared, "If that is indeed what happened, I should like to shake that young lady's hand!"

"As would I." Samantha nodded quickly. Then she assumed a thoughtful expression and frowned slightly. "I wonder who could have accomplished such a noble deed. I partnered Viscount Struthersford myself, and even stepped out on the terrace with him, in an attempt to find David. During our brief interlude together, he made no mention of a particular young lady in whom he was interested."

Lord Evingston laughed. "Your innocence is charming, my dear. Viscount Struthersford is interested in any young lady that draws breath, regardless of her charms. He is a rake of the first order!"

"I had no idea!" Samantha managed to look perfectly surprised. "But he made no improper overtures to me."

"You are engaged, and the viscount undoubtedly feared the duke's wrath." Miss Rothham gave David a flirtatious glance before she again turned her attention to Samantha. "Though I must say that such considerations have not brought him to heel in the past."

Samantha contrived to look a bit anxious. "I am most grateful that I did not take his fancy, for whatever reason. If I had known that he was such a rake, I should not have stepped onto the terrace with him!"

"To quote the bard, *All's well that ends well.*" Lady Edna laughed lightly, but Samantha noticed that the dowager countess was regarding her with some amusement. "Do ring for more cakes, Samantha dear. The chocolate biscuits I asked Cook to make for Lady Malbury should be ready."

Lady Malbury, a plump woman well past the first blush of youth, turned to Lady Edna in delight. "How thoughtful of you! Your cook's chocolate biscuits are my very favorite sweet!"

The conversation turned quite naturally to cakes and confections, and Samantha breathed a sigh of relief. Lady Edna had neatly steered the subject away from Viscount Struthersford and she was very grateful.

The remainder of the visit passed quite uneventfully with Miss Rothham's discussion of the wonders she had found at the Pantheon Bazaar and Lord Cadbury's explanation of the window tax to Lady Thalinger and Miss Douglass. No further mention of the viscount's scandal was made and, at last, Samantha's guests took their leave.

When all had departed and the Drawing Room had been tidied for future callers, Lady Edna turned to Samantha. "You handled the situation admirably, Granddaughter. If I am not mistaken, you may have convinced all but the most suspicious."

"Convinced them of what, Grandmama?" Samantha assumed her most innocent expression.

Lady Edna gave a most unladylike snort. "You know very well to what I refer, but I shall say no more. You may leave on your outing and I shall stay here to quash any further rumors."

Samantha was about to protest her innocence a second time, but David pressed her hand in a warning as he guided her to her feet.

"We are in your debt, Lady Edna." There was a smile on David's face as he addressed the dowager countess. "You may depend on me. I shall return your granddaughter safe and sound before the sun sets."

Lady Edna nodded, a ghost of a smile hovering about her lips. "I am certain that you shall. But take care that you do not carry my granddaughter in the vicinity of Drury Lane."

"Certainly not!" David could not suppress his laughter as he faced Lady Edna. The dowager countess had a fine sense of humor.

"You do catch my meaning, do you not?" Lady Edna's eyes were twinkling.

"Yes, indeed." David nodded quickly. "It would not do for the aficionados of Drury Lane to see how well suited your granddaughter is for a life on the boards."

Lady Edna's laugh rang out, coupled with David's amused chuckle, and Samantha did her best to retain what was left of her composure as she took David's arm and exited the Drawing Room. She was not at all certain how she had given it away, but there was no doubt that both Lady Edna and David knew that she was the young lady who had pushed the amorous viscount in the lily pond.

Twelve

Laughter bubbled from Samantha's throat as she urged her mount forward. David had taken her to a secluded area in southern Hyde Park where fashionably dressed ladies and gentlemen were permitted to ride. They had arrived at the unfashionable hour of three in the afternoon and the horse paths had been deserted. David had informed her that they had missed the crowd that usually rode between noon and two, and the late-afternoon riders should not appear until five. Until that time, they had the lovely wooded area to themselves and they planned to take full advantage.

Samantha had been amazed when David told her that he had purchased their mounts that very morning. He had arrived at Tattersall's quite early and employed the privilege of his ranking to gain entrance. The two fine beasts had been scheduled for auction that very afternoon, but David had purchased them outright, paying what he claimed had been a fair price. Since he had refused to meet her eyes when he had told her of his purchase, Samantha suspected that the price he had paid had been much too dear.

Samantha's mount was a high-spirited chestnut mare. Her name was Chloe and Samantha had found her a challenge indeed. While Chloe was biddable, under firm hands, she was not the sort of mount a fainthearted rider should enjoy. Chloe was a goer, pure and simple, and

Samantha knew that the mare's long legs fairly itched to stretch out in a gallop.

David had chosen a magnificent black stallion for his mount. The horse was called Lucifer and once Samantha had observed the wild glint in his eye, she had agreed that Lucifer had been aptly named. She had no doubt that David could handle the beast. He had proven himself to be a bruising rider and Samantha had regarded him with real envy when he had placed his foot in the stirrup and mounted with a grace born of long and frequent practice. She, of course, had been assisted into the sidesaddle by a groom and was continuing to regret that she was not permitted to ride astride.

"You ride well." There was admiration in David's voice as he reined Lucifer in beside her.

Samantha nodded. She *did* ride well and there was no point in denying the obvious. Uncle Charles had trained her himself, when she was no more than four years old. Aunt Phoebe had objected, claiming that there was no need for Samantha to learn to ride at so early an age, but Uncle Charles had ignored his wife in this as in so many other matters.

"Who taught you to ride?"

"My uncle," Samantha replied without thinking. "We had no pony so he trained me on the gentlest mare in his stable."

"How old were you then?"

"I had just celebrated my fourth birthday. I wished to ride earlier, but he made me wait until then."

"Your *uncle?*" David frowned slightly as he thought about the information that Samantha had just given him. "But I thought you told me that your aunt was unmarried."

Samantha took care to keep the pleasant smile on her face though inwardly, she winced. She had forgotten that Olivia's aunt was a spinster. "He was no true relation. I called him 'Uncle' as a term of affection. The gentleman was a dear friend of my aunt's and lived on a neighboring estate."

"I see."

David did not look convinced and Samantha sighed. She must learn to watch her tongue more carefully. In an effort to channel the conversation away from her mistake, she glanced down at her saddle and laughed. "I should ride much better if not for this ridiculous sidesaddle!"

"Your uncle did not require you to use a sidesaddle?"

There was a gleam of amusement in David's eye and Samantha knew she was in for further questioning. "No, he did not. Uncle Charles had no children of his own and it did not occur to him to obtain a sidesaddle. He taught me to ride on the same saddle he had used as a child."

"Astride?"

David's brows shot up with the question and Samantha giggled. "Yes. I must hasten to add that Aunt Phoebe knew nothing of my riding lessons until they were a *fait accompli*. At that time, she purchased a sidesaddle and insisted that I use it."

"No doubt she did." David laughed. "And did you use it, Samantha?"

"Of course I did, on every occasion when she was there to observe me. But I must admit that I found it a nuisance. It is much easier to control a spirited horse when one rides astride."

"But how on earth do you manage your skirts when you . . ." David stopped without completing his question. He wondered whether he had overstepped the bounds of propriety by referring to an article of feminine attire.

"I do not wear skirts when I ride astride." Samantha favored him with an impish grin. "I altered a pair of my uncle's breeches to fit me."

"And you wear those?"

Samantha nodded, wishing now that she had not embarked upon this particular subject. "You must promise not to tell anyone, David. Grandmama should think me a complete hoyden if she knew that I was used to riding in breeches."

"Your secret is safe with me." David gave her a conspiratorial grin. "After we are married, I think I shall order a daring new riding *ensemble* for you, a green velvet jacket with trousers to match."

Samantha's mouth opened in surprise and she stared at David in disbelief. When she saw that he was indeed serious, she laughed with pure delight. "What a grand idea! Perhaps the trousers could be cut very full and appear as a skirt when I walk. It would be great fun, David. Just think of the astonishment my actions should generate when I mounted to ride! Why, everyone who saw me should be perfectly outraged!"

"Perhaps you could become a trendsetter, Samantha. I am certain there are other ladies who should enjoy wearing what appeared to the observer as a skirt, but actually had the freedom of trousers."

Samantha nodded. "It does sound practical. I can think of several young ladies who should desire to wear such a creation."

"Precisely! Such an *ensemble* could be all the crack if it were done in the pinnacle of style. You are just the person to wear it!"

Samantha smiled. "Do you truly think so?"

"I do."

"But I should be criticized roundly for my daring." Samantha sighed. "It is unfair, David. If you were to appear in a daring new style, none would dare to criticize you. As a duke, you can do precisely as you please."

David nodded. "You have the right of it. And as my duchess, you can also do precisely whatever you please."

"Oh!" Samantha gasped and the color rose to her cheeks. She had forgotten that if she married David, she should be his duchess. But as much as the prospect pleased her, she could not marry him for she was not the lady he thought her to be.

"What is wrong, Samantha?" David saw the distress that

was clearly written on her lovely face. "Is the thought of marrying me so repulsive to you?"

Samantha shook her head quickly. "Oh, no! That is not it at all! It is just that I . . ."

At that exact moment, Samantha's horse shied. She struggled to maintain her balance and reined her horse in before she could bolt. When she turned to discover what had frightened her mount, she gasped. "Stop, David! There is something in those bushes, just ahead!"

David quickly reined in his mount and leaped from the saddle. He helped Samantha to the ground and both of them hurried to the bushes.

Samantha knelt down to examine the unfortunate creature that was lying there. It was a small brown dog and it whimpered as she touched it. When she looked up at David, her expression was grave. "She is still alive, but her pulse is weak. I think she's been beaten within an inch of her life. I can feel nothing broken, but we must take her to a secure place and see to her injuries."

"Of course." David nodded, removing his coat. "Wrap her in this and I shall carry her."

"But your coat will be ruined. She is bleeding." Samantha frowned slightly.

"That does not signify." David wrapped his coat around the injured pup and picked her up. "Can you hand her up to me and manage to mount by yourself?"

Samantha nodded, handing the bundle to David when he had mounted. She hoisted herself up into her saddle and picked up the reins. "Shall we take her to Grandmama's town house?"

"My place is closer." David shook his head. "Follow me."

Samantha followed as David rode toward his town mansion, cradling the pup gently in his arms. Her mind was on the injured dog and she did not waste a single thought to propriety and how the gossipmongers should relish the tale of how she had accompanied her fiancé to his home without a suitable escort.

In very little time, they were ensconced in the kitchen in front of a cheery fire. Further examination revealed that the pup was suffering from prolonged exposure to the elements and a lack of nourishing food. Samantha cleansed the pup's injuries and applied a healing salve that David's groom brought her from the stable. She bound up the pup's foot, which had a nasty cut on the pad, and looked up at David with a smile.

"She will live?" David reached out to pet the little pup.

"She will recover nicely with the proper care." Samantha smiled up at him. "You see how she follows you with her eyes? She could not do that if she had a concussion."

David nodded. "Her eyes are focused. I had noticed that. And the salve you applied to her pad will prevent infection. Why is it that you did not stitch such a deep cut?"

"Stitching the cut closed should do more harm than good." Samantha explained. "The pad will stretch as she walks and the stitches will pull out, causing further injury. I bound it firmly, so that she will be unable to step down with her full weight and spread the pad, but she will have to be carefully watched to make certain that she does not chew off her bandage."

"That can be easily arranged." David glanced at the scullery maid, who was hovering nearby, making small cooing sounds to the pup. David was certain the girl should be delighted to be relieved of her usual duties and assigned the care of the pup.

"I do wish I could think of a way to keep her from chewing off the bandage." Samantha shook her head. "I have tried all manner of bandages in the past and none has survived the onslaught of the canine incisor. I even thought to brew a bitter tea to paint on the outside of the bandage, but that did not serve, either."

David looked thoughtful. "It is possible that you may be going about this the wrong way. A horse being shod is put into a position where he cannot kick. Perhaps the dog should be put into a position where he cannot chew."

"I know of no such position." Samantha frowned slightly. "Do you?"

"Perhaps I do. The object should be to place an impediment between the dog's mouth and the bandage."

"A muzzle?" Samantha began to frown. "I should use that only as a last resort. A muzzle also prevents a dog from eating and drinking, and its use may cause other problems."

David shook his head. "No, not a muzzle. I do not approve of them, either. What about a stiff collar, such as the pinks of the *ton* often wear. If it were all of a piece and wide enough, it should serve to block the pup from raising her paw to her mouth."

"A collar?" Samantha thought about the concept for a moment. "Perhaps that might do the trick. If it were properly formed, it should still allow her to lower her head for eating and drinking. I shall experiment with the design tonight and see what I can fashion."

David nodded. "I will assist you. How do you come to know so much about caring for these types of injuries, Samantha?"

"Uncle Charles was a veterinarian." Samantha answered quite honestly. "He taught me to assist him when I was but a child."

"This is the uncle who was not truly an uncle?"

"Yes." Samantha nodded and took comfort in the fact that what she had told David was quite true. If Aunt Phoebe's brother was not her father, then Uncle Charles was not her uncle.

"And this is why you knew the ailments of the horse we captured in the park?"

Samantha nodded her assent. "Yes, David. Uncle Charles tended to the squire's cattle. As his assistant, I learned much about horses."

"Come, Samantha." David motioned for her. "I must carry you home. It is growing late and I promised your grandmother to have you back before nightfall."

Samantha waited until David had spoken to the scullery

maid about the care of the pup. The young girl seemed delighted at her new duties and promised to give the pup a bowl of meat broth every hour to nourish her. When they exited the kitchen, Samantha looked back to see the pup cradled tenderly in the young girl's arms.

"Could it be our lucky pup has found a mistress?" Samantha's eyes gleamed with amusement.

"I should think that would be the likely outcome." David's arm quite naturally settled around Samantha's shoulders. "Do you have any objections?"

Samantha shook her head. "Not a one. It is good of you to take the pup into your home. Do you have other dogs, David?"

"Not here." David shook his head. "But there is old Meg at Westbury Park. I've had her since she was a pup and her mother before her. Then there's Bruno, my father's dog. He is a remarkably intelligent beast and has the run of the stables. My father adores him."

"But . . . your father is dead, is he not?" Samantha frowned slightly. David could not hold the title of duke if his father were still alive.

David winced at her question. For a brief moment, he had quite forgotten that he was playing the part of the duke. "Yes, my father is dead. There are times, when I am not actually in residence at Westbury Park, that I expect to find him still there, waiting for me to come home. Perhaps it is because I did not have the opportunity to bid him farewell. His life was taken in a carriage accident. He was traveling to Oxford to attend my graduation when it occurred."

"That is very sad, David. Perhaps you might take comfort in the fact that he did not suffer from some dreadful lingering illness."

"Yes." David turned to smile at her. "Your words are a comfort, Samantha."

Samantha sighed as they approached David's curricle and he made ready to hand her up. She reached out to touch his face in a gesture that was intended to comfort him and somehow she wound up in his arms. There was a moment of indecision and then his arms tightened around her. They stood there for a moment, embracing warmly as the sun faded over the horizon, and Samantha sighed in true regret. She loved David. She could no longer deny the emotion that colored every moment of her daily existence. And her heart was breaking with the knowledge that she should soon have to give him up.

"I love you, Samantha."

David's voice was low, as if the words were forced from his throat despite his best intentions, and Samantha spoke past the lump in her own throat. "I love you, too, David."

And then their lips met in a sweet kiss that promised further delights once they were wed, and tears filled Samantha's eyes. She had spoken the truth. She did love David, but she would never be permitted to marry him once the truth became known. If only she were truly Olivia Samantha Tarrington, the real fiancée of the Duke of Westbury, she should be the happiest young lady on the face of the earth,

Thirteen

David frowned as he looked down at the letters that Harry had given him. After he had taken Samantha back to her grandmother's home, something she had said in their earlier conversation had nagged at him. There had seemed, at the time, to be an inaccuracy, but he had not been able to remember what it was. He had decided to read the letters again, hoping to discover the source of his unease, but one glance at the envelope had provided him with the answer. The letter had been sent by Lady Honoria at Newbridge Manor while Samantha had referred to her Aunt Phoebe and her former home as Hawthorne Cottage.

Just as David had begun to ponder the meaning of this discrepancy, Mr. Hastings tapped on the library door to announce that three unexpected guests had arrived. David glanced down at the calling cards, properly turned down at the corners to signify that their owners had arrived in person, and gave a deep sigh. There was no choice but to let them in.

After calling for brandy and a light refreshment, David took a chair by the fire to await his guests. This was the one evening of the past two sennights when there were no scheduled entertainments. Samantha had been previously engaged for the evening as she had arranged to attend a lecture with Dr. Matthew Baillie. David had been invited to accompany them, but he had cried off. He enjoyed Dr. Baillie's society, and the lectures they had attended together in the past had been most engaging, but he had been anticipating a quiet night of relaxation in which he could pen a letter to Harry, telling him of the events that had transpired. Unfortunately, his plans were now interrupted. Fate had intervened in the form of Lords Danbury, Paxton, and Halverson. David had no doubt that they had called for the express purpose of inviting him to share in an evening of revelry, a prospect that did not suit him in the slightest.

As he waited for Hastings to show his guests to the library, David wished that it were possible to turn back the clock and accept Dr. Baillie's invitation. He would have much preferred a scientific lecture to the company of Danbury, Paxton, and Halverson. Even if the subject of the lecture had not intrigued him, he should have enjoyed seeing Samantha's rapt expression as she listened to the speaker. She had told him that she was deeply interested in medicine, especially as it related to the care and treatment of animals. The care she had taken with the pup that they had found in the park gave testament to the depth of that interest.

David glanced down at the letters again, frowning slightly. He must read them once more to make certain, but he was convinced that Lady Honoria had made no mention of the fact that her niece had an interest in veterinary medicine and had assisted the gentleman she called "Uncle Charles" in his work. It seemed unlikely that this fact about Samantha had been revealed, for Lady Honoria had made a special point of noting Samantha's crippling fear of horses. This puzzled David deeply as it was patently untrue. Samantha loved horses and she was a bruising rider. It was possible that Samantha herself was responsible for her aunt's glaring untruth. If Samantha had feared that Lady Honoria might forbid her from accompanying "Uncle Charles" on his calls, she might have hidden these interests from her aunt.

There were other discrepancies and David had kept careful note of them all. The young miss that Lady Honoria had described in her letters bore little resemblance to the Samantha he knew. The list of differences between the two accounts was growing longer with each day that passed. Either Lady Honoria had been a most unreliable correspondent, or Samantha had hidden her true character from her aunt. There was also a third possibility, one that David intended to explore to the fullest degree. If Lady Honoria's account of her niece was accurate, and if Olivia had not deceived her aunt as to her true character, then the young lady that David loved was not Miss Olivia Tarrington.

David smiled at that prospect. It should be delightful indeed if Samantha was not Harry's fiancée, for then he should be free to admit that he was not Harry. David had been dreading the moment when he should have to expose their ruse to Samantha. He wished to tell her now and beg her forgiveness for his part in the deception. If he could only be certain that Samantha was not Olivia, he should greet that moment of truth with supreme delight. Once their mutual ruse had been revealed, he should ask her to truly be his wife.

This possible turn of events was so appealing that David wished to dwell further on the happy prospect. He had no doubt that he should be supremely happy, wedded to Samantha, and she had given him cause to believe that she should share in that delight. His enjoyable contemplation of wedded bliss was interrupted quite rudely by the sound of approaching footsteps. His guests were about to arrive. David stuffed the packet of letters into a drawer, placed the appropriate expression of welcome on his face, and rose to greet his callers.

"So kind of you to receive us." Lord Paxton observed the proprieties. "We were just passing by and decided to stop in to see you on a lark."

"You are most welcome. Please sit down, gentlemen." David formed a smile he did not feel and gestured toward the grouping of chairs near the fire. He noticed that Lord Halverson was eyeing the brandy decanter with no little expectation and he motioned for the glasses to be filled.

"Hope you don't mind us barging in like this." Lord Halverson took a large sip of his brandy. "Excellent brandy! I see that you do not require my advice in stocking your cellar."

David smiled. "My father laid in a good supply many years ago. Since he did not often visit London, it is nearly untouched."

"How long ago was that?"

It was clear by the expression of interest on Lord Halverson's face that the man was intrigued. David smiled and told him what he had learned from Harry's staff. "Before I was born, I should think. If memory serves me, my father once mentioned that he had procured a shipload of the stuff."

"My word!" Lord Halverson appeared thunderstruck as he gazed down at his glass. "It is of this excellent quality?"

"The very same, I should imagine. No gentleman ever accused my father of cheeseparing and I must assume he purchased a premium vintage. My steward tells me that cases of it have been carefully stored in the cellar all these years and that only one or two bottles have been opened."

Lord Halverson raised the glass to his lips once again. He seemed at a complete loss for words; a beatific expression crossed his face as he sipped the amber liquid.

Lord Paxton glanced at his friend in amusement and then turned to David. "We've lost Halverson, I fear. And now you shall have to contend with him laying siege to your cellar. I have never seen him in such a blissful state."

"Nor I," Lord Danbury chuckled. "Though I am not the connoisseur Halverson claims to be, I must admit that it is uncommonly fine brandy. But we did not come here to raid your cellar."

Lord Paxton nodded. "Quite right. We came to offer an invitation to join us in a bit of fun. Our wives put us up to it, you see, as a favor to Lady Edna."

"Your wives?" David frowned slightly. "For what reason?"

Lord Danbury had the grace to appear slightly uncomfortable. "The ladies insist that since your lovely fiancée has no male relatives, we must serve in their stead. They have set us the task of proving that you are a regular fellow, worthy of her attentions."

"Ah-ha!" David chuckled at the thought of being trotted out for Lords Danbury, Paxton, and Halverson's approval. "Have I passed muster?"

"You have with Halverson, that is for certain!" Lord Paxton gestured toward his bemused friend who was holding his glass with reverence.

"And with us, also," Lord Danbury hastened to add. "But if we return to our wives at this early hour, they will accuse us of not thoroughly researching your character. What say you to a game or two at White's? We must do something to while away the time until we may safely return to our spouses."

David thought to offer an excuse, but the identical expressions of anxiety on their faces made his refusal impossible. It was quite obvious that all three gentlemen were loath to displease their respective wives.

"Are we to return home in defeat?" Lord Paxton asked the question.

"No, gentlemen, you are not." David rose to his feet and gestured toward the tray of refreshments and the brandy decanter. "Please feel free to partake of whatever you wish while I dress in the clothing appropriate to our evening together."

Samantha took a deep breath as she prepared to enter the Drawing Room. This evening's lecture had not been lengthy and she had returned home even sooner than she had anticipated. When she had learned that Lady Edna was still ensconced in the Drawing Room, Samantha had decided that it was the perfect time to approach her. There was a matter of business that Samantha had yet to discuss with Lady Edna, and she had delayed it as long as possible.

She raised her arm to knock on the partially open door and hesitated. Samantha truly did not desire this audience, for it should mean the telling of yet another untruth. She had grown extremely fond of Olivia's grandmother in the weeks that she had spent under her roof. The prospect of once again deceiving that good lady filled Samantha with genuine regret.

Was there any way of extricating herself from this unfortunate tangle? Samantha sighed, knowing that such hopes were futile. If not for Olivia's distressing predicament, Samantha might well have confessed all and thrown herself upon Lady Edna's mercy. She had come to realize that the dowager countess was not the sort of harsh disciplinarian that Olivia had believed her to be. Hidden under Lady Edna's stern and unbending countenance was a wise and compassionate lady who was capable of enjoying a good joke.

Not for the first time, Samantha wondered what would occur if she told the story of the ruse that she had concocted with Olivia in the meanly appointed room at the Two Feathers Inn. She suspected that Lady Edna should have been touched by her actual granddaughter's predicament and highly amused at the lengths to which they had gone to secure Olivia's inheritance. But Samantha could not take such a risk without Olivia's prior approval. She had given her word that she should continue in this deception until Olivia had received her inheritance.

"Come in, Granddaughter." Lady Edna's amused voice carried out to the hallway. "I have watched you stand there for the better part of ten minutes. Even if you have some failing to confess to me, it cannot be as bad as that!"

The color was high on Samantha's cheeks as she pushed open the door and walked swiftly to Lady Edna's side. "No, Grandmama. Though I am certain I have many failings, it was not one in particular that gave me pause to stand there."

"What then?" Lady Edna's smile was slightly risqué.

"Were you thinking fond thoughts of your intended groom?"

Samantha laughed as she dropped a kiss upon Lady Edna's cheek and quickly settled herself in a nearby chair. "That is it, precisely. I freely admit that I was thinking of David, and my thoughts of him are always fond. You have arranged a splendid match for me, Grandmama, and I am very grateful to you."

"Yes, it is working out even better than I had dared to hope." Lady Edna nodded. "Though I suspect that David is not the gentleman that I had been led to expect, I believe that the two of you are admirably suited."

Samantha experienced a moment of anxiety. Lady Edna's comment was exceedingly strange. "What had you been led to expect, Grandmama? And who led you to expect it?"

"That does not signify." Lady Edna waved Samantha's questions aside. "I have eyes in my own head and I trust my own judgment. David is the best of all possible matches for you."

"Yes, David is perfection!" Samantha nodded quickly, a smile lighting up her face. Then she remembered her initial purpose for seeking Lady Edna's company and a slight frown replaced her smile. "But I find that I do not know him as well as I had thought, for I cannot decide upon a suitable bridal gift for him. I had hoped that you might have a suggestion, Grandmama."

Lady Edna considered the subject for a moment and then she shook her head. "I can think of nothing at the moment. Let us consider his interests and perhaps we shall light upon the perfect thing."

"He is an excellent whip and a superb rider. I should say that he is the finest judge of cattle that I have ever had occasion to meet." Samantha spoke quickly, without considering her words.

"How can you adequately judge this matter, Granddaughter?" Lady Edna peered closely at Samantha. "In

Lady Honoria's correspondence with me, she mentioned that she did not keep a stable."

Samantha came close to groaning aloud. She had forgotten what Olivia had told her of her life in the country. "This is true, Grandmama. But I was acquainted with the neighboring squire and I observed his cattle on numerous occasions. They were not nearly so fine as the beasts that David purchased at Tattersall's."

"Enough about cattle." A smile turned up the corners of Lady Edna's lips. "Tell me of David's other interests."

"He has told me that he loves to fish in the streams that run through his lands. He does not ride to the hounds. He sees no point in chasing and killing an animal that does not provide food for the table. But he does hunt occasionally, as all gentlemen of his station do."

"This information shall not help us in our quest, my child." Lady Edna shook her head. "I do not think either of us has the necessary knowledge to select the appropriate rod for fishing or rifle for hunting."

Samantha nodded. What Lady Edna said was true.

"I have it!" Lady Edna began to smile. "You shall purchase a fine set of monogrammed markers for his gaming table. I am certain that he must have a room set aside for that purpose."

Samantha shook her head. "Oh, no, Grandmama. That shall not do at all. David has told me that he no longer indulges in games of chance. He admitted to me, quite candidly, that he was not at all proficient at the practice."

"Then we must think of something else." Lady Edna nodded quickly. "Perhaps several cases of choice brandy should make an excellent gift."

Samantha shook her head once again. "I fear that shall not serve, either, for David does not drink strong spirits. He has told me that they quite muddle his head and cause him to be most foolish."

"Are you quite certain that he did not say this just to impress you?"

"Yes, Grandmama. I admit that I also suspected he was

doing it up much too brown. But I have observed him closely and I have never seen him take more than one glass of wine of an evening."

Lady Edna sighed. "Then I am quite out of suggestions. Have you none of your own?"

"Only one." Samantha took a deep breath, hoping that the suggestion she was about to make should serve her true purpose. "I do know that David takes great joy in driving his own equipage and I had thought to purchase one of the new French cabriolets that Lady Mansfield mentioned to me. Of course, it must be ordered immediately so that it shall be ready in time, but it should be such a grand bridal present."

Lady Edna sighed. "It should be far too grand, Granddaughter. I am certain that David would not expect such a costly gift."

"I know! And that is why it is perfection itself! Don't you see, Grandmama? David shall never suspect that I have ordered it for him and when he receives it, he shall be thrilled beyond measure!"

Lady Edna smiled. "I am certain that you are right. It is the perfect gift, Samantha, and I have no doubt that David should be exceedingly impressed. Have you given thought to how you should pay for such a lavish equipage?"

"Oh, yes, Grandmama!" Samantha smiled in a manner she hoped would appear guileless. "I shall use my inheritance. I will have no other need of it, once I am David's wife."

Lady Edna frowned. "But the funds cannot be released prior to your birthday. It is written so, in your father's will. Are you asking me for the loan of this money until your own funds are released?"

"Oh, no, Grandmama! I should never presume to do that! I shall go directly to the carriage maker and tell him that the funds will be available on my birthday. I am certain that once he speaks with the solicitor and is told that the proper papers have already been signed, he will start work on the carriage straightaway. I shall also elicit his promise that it shall be delivered the moment that we return from our wedding trip."

"Yes, I am certain that he shall be able to meet your request." Lady Edna nodded. "I daresay it should be his top priority. You plan to tour the continent on your wedding trip, do you not?"

"Yes, Grandmama. David has told me that we shall be gone for at least three months, perhaps four. We shall visit his mother in Vienna, as she is unable to return for our wedding. From there, we shall go on to Italy and Spain."

"Since you shall be gone for such a lengthy time, the completion of your carriage should present no problem." Lady Edna began to smile. "And I find that I completely agree with you, Samantha. It is a thoughtful and lovely gift."

"Thank you, Grandmama." Samantha breathed a sigh of relief. Her Banbury tale regarding the carriage had served her well. "Shall I send round a message to the solicitor, telling him to expect you tomorrow?"

"Not tomorrow, my dear. I shall send him an invitation to the wedding and tell him to bring along the necessary papers. Rest assured I shall sign them the very moment your wedding ceremony has taken place."

Samantha's eyes widened. "But Grandmama! I had thought I should be able to collect the funds on the day of my birthday!"

"Yes, this was the original plan." Lady Edna nodded. "But you forget that you were to be married by that time. It was your choice, my dear, to delay your wedding."

"But what difference should it make whether I receive the funds on the day before my marriage, or on the actual day of the ceremony?"

"I fear it makes a great deal of difference." Lady Edna sighed deeply. "This is not my doing, Samantha. I should be delighted to sign the release immediately if I had not promised your dear father that I should do so only *after* you were wed."

Samantha felt the tears well up in her eyes. Her carefully structured plan had failed.

"You must not be overset, my dear." Lady Edna reached out to pat her hand. "Your carriage shall be ready in time, never fear. You may order it now, exactly as you planned. If you tell the carriage maker that you are engaged to the Duke of Westbury and it is to be your wedding present to him, I doubt that he will ask you for any deposit. If he does, you need only tell him to contact me and I shall make haste to assure him that his bill shall be paid."

"Thank you, Grandmama." Samantha did her best to smile.

"And now it is growing late and we must be off to bed." Lady Edna stood and waited for Samantha to rise to her feet. "All will be well, my dear child. I will make certain that your lovely present shall be waiting for David, precisely as you have planned."

Fourteen

Olivia closed her sketchbook with a sigh and turned to Harry, who had been sitting in companionable silence, watching her work. "It is late, is it not?"

"I believe that it is." Harry glanced at the handsome gold timepiece that had belonged to his father and nodded. He was in a rare form indeed, as this date marked the eve of his scheduled wedding. If all had gone according to the original plans that had been arranged by the Dragoness and Lady Edna Tarrington, Harry would soon be a free man. By this time tomorrow, the ruse he had arranged with David would be complete and he should be at liberty to tell Jane his true identity. "It is nearly midnight, my dear, and you have been sketching the entire day."

"Then it is no wonder that I am so fatigued! I am so glad that I have finished my drawings at last, Harry."

Harry smiled at the small caged bird that she had used as her subject. "Then this little fellow is no longer needed. Shall we release him tonight?"

"No. We must wait until tomorrow, when the sun is high and the hawks and owls have finished their hunting. I would not wish him to come to any harm after he has served me so well."

Harry turned to her, remembering her promise to visit Westbury Park when her folio was complete. Perhaps, if she should agree to marry him quickly, her first visit to

Westbury Park would be accomplished as his bride. "When will you complete your final painting?

"Within a week, I should think. Then I must pay a quick visit to London to settle a small matter of business there."

Harry nodded. She had told him that her folio was to be published and he assumed that she was to meet with the publisher to make the necessary arrangements. "How long will you stay in London, Jane?"

"For one night only. I plan to leave of an evening and arrive in London the following day. My business should be concluded on the second day and I shall return immediately to Bath."

Harry began to frown. The thought that his intended bride planned to travel at night filled him with dread. The roads were treacherous at best, and danger lurked in the form of highwaymen who could waylay the unwary traveler. "Surely you do not plan to travel alone?"

"Yes, but you must not be anxious on my account. I have heard tell that the post chaise is quite safe."

"It is not safe enough." Harry's frown grew deeper. "I will take you to London myself. It is the only way to be certain that you will come to no harm."

"Oh, Harry! Traveling together should be such fun!" Olivia began to smile in delight, but her expression quickly turned to one of dismay. "But I fear it is quite impossible. We must consider your mother's sensibilities."

Harry was completely at a loss by this reference to the Dragoness. "My *mother?* What has she to do with this subject?"

"It is not proper for us to travel together. Indeed, it should be quite scandalous. From what you have told me of your mother, Harry, I am certain that she should disapprove."

"Bother my mother!" Harry dismissed the objection out of hand. "I am well past my majority, Jane. I no longer need have a caution for what my mother does and does not approve."

"But Harry . . . it would be truly improper. If others

learned of our disregard for convention, they should assume the worst. I do not care for my own sake, but we
would most certainly be the subject of gossip."

"Bother gossip, too!" Harry began to grin. "I seem to
remember a pact that we made, a promise to please only
ourselves."

Olivia began to waver in her resolve. Her concern had
not been for her own reputation. She did not care whether
others gossiped about her or not. Her only goal had been
to protect Harry from his mother's censure. "You truly do
not care if there is gossip, Harry?"

"Not in the slightest." Harry hastened to set her at ease
on that particular score. "Now that we fully understand
each other, will you permit me to carry you to London?"

Harry wore such a pleading look that Olivia began to
laugh. "Only if you cease regarding me in that particular
manner."

"What manner?" Harry was clearly puzzled.

Olivia giggled and reached out to touch his face. "You
have the look of a starving child who gazes into a ginger-
bread stall! It is extremely flattering if I am the ginger-
bread, but there is no need for you to go hungry. I shall
be delighted with your company and your coach, Harry,
for I am certain that it is exceedingly more comfortable
than the post chaise."

"It is one of my employer's best coaches." Harry im-
provised quickly, grateful that David had reminded him to
have the telltale crests removed from his favorite equipage.
He should keep his secret for just a bit longer, until Jane
was safely ensconced in his coach. Then he would tell her
the whole of it, in a place where she had no choice but to
listen to him. "When shall we leave on our journey, Jane?"

Olivia quickly counted the days that remained until her
birthday and turned to him with a smile. "I must arrive
in London no later than Thursday next. And I shall leave
at the conclusion of business on the following day. Will
that be acceptable to you, Harry?"

"Perfectly acceptable." Harry nodded quickly. "What

say you we take in the sights while we are in London? I have never been there before and I should like to view the city. As artists, it should be truly unfortunate if we departed London without thoroughly perusing the museums and galleries—there is a collection of Sir Joshua Reynolds's paintings at the British Institute in Pall Mall that I should especially care to see. I have heard that there are over one hundred and thirty of his performances to view. And we must not fail to take in the Great Exhibition at Somerset Place."

Olivia nodded, excitement glittering in her eyes. "There is also the Society of Painters Exhibition in Spring Gardens. I should like to see them all, Harry! But I do not think that we should be able to accomplish all that in two short days, especially since a portion of my time shall be taken up with matters of business."

"Then we shall stay longer. I propose that we spend at least three nights in London. Think of the fun we shall have, Jane!"

"It should be wonderful, indeed." Olivia sighed regretfully. "But I fear that I cannot stay as long as that. Our hostess has made arrangements for me to spend the night with an acquaintance of hers, but she expects houseguests the very next day. Her London residence is quite small and I am permitted to avail myself of her hospitality for one night only."

"This is not a problem, Jane. I will secure lodging for us at one of the fine hotels." Harry stopped speaking as soon as he saw the distressed expression that crossed his love's face. "What is wrong, Jane?"

"I . . . I am not certain that we should do that, Harry."

"But why?" Harry took her hand, but she refused to meet his eyes. Her color was high and she appeared distressingly embarrassed. Harry was at a loss for a moment, wondering what he had said to overset her so dreadfully. Then he realized the reason for her distress and made quick to reassure her. "We shall have separate rooms, of course. I may be forced to claim that we are brother and sister to satisfy the owner's sense of propriety, but that shall not disturb you, shall it, Jane?"

"Oh, no! Not in the slightest!" Olivia breathed a sigh of relief. She should have known that Harry was trustworthy and had never meant to imply that they should be involved in an illicit situation.

Harry reached out to press her hand. "I find that I am most anxious to depart on our journey."

"As am I." Olivia smiled as she rose from her chair. "Until tomorrow, Harry. I shall dream of the wondrous sights we shall enjoy together in London."

It was not until Harry was alone in his room that he thought to read the last account that David had sent him concerning their ruse. He had only favored it with a cursory glance when it had arrived, and once he had ascertained that all was going according to plan, he had put it aside to read later. Near the end of the letter, David had included a list of events that preceded his wedding, along with the dates that those events should occur. Harry's face turned pale as he perused the schedule. This could not be correct! According to the list that David had sent, his wedding would occur at the very time that Harry had planned to be in London with Jane!

Harry checked again to make certain that he had not confused the numbers, but it was written out clearly, in David's firm hand. Olivia's grandmother was to host a grand ball on Thursday, attended by all the notables of the *ton*. On the following day, at precisely two in the afternoon, the Duke of Westbury and Miss Olivia Tarrington should formally speak their vows!

This could not be accurate! Harry drew out the letter he had copied from his mother's sheaf of correspondence. The wedding was to have been held the week *preceding* the schedule that David had penned.

Frantically, Harry read the remainder of David's letter and a loud groan of dismay escaped his lips. Miss Tarrington had requested that the wedding be delayed for one full week so that the Grand Ball, on the eve of the nuptials, should also be her birthday celebration.

Harry stood up to pace the floor. Though he had no acquaintances in that city, chance encounters occurred more frequently than the term implied. He had been part of the artisan groups at both Eton and Oxford, and it was possible that one of his old schoolmates should journey to London to view Sir Joshua Reynolds's exhibition. This fact had not concerned him when he had proposed this tour to Jane for he had planned to tell her of his true identity long before they reached London. Now everything had changed. He dared not tell Jane the truth before David had made good his escape.

The tempo of Harry's pacing increased as he explored his options. If he journeyed to London with Jane, he should be putting David in danger. Tempers would flare if their ruse were discovered prematurely and David could be in actual danger from those who sought to protect Olivia from such an obvious bounder. At the same time, Harry could not allow Jane to travel to London alone. It was simply too dangerous for a young lady to travel unescorted at night in a public conveyance. He must find a third alternative, one that should satisfy both of his concerns.

Harry paced for upwards of an hour, but no such solution occurred to him. He was caught firmly on the horns of a dilemma and there seemed no way out of his difficulty. David had performed a great service for him and he could not, in all conscience, risk placing his dear friend in danger. On the other hand, Jane was his love and, as such, it was his duty to protect her from the perils she might encounter on her journey. It seemed he must choose one over the other: his dear boyhood friend who had risked all on his behalf, or the young lady he had come to love with all his heart.

When he was so tired that he could no longer think, Harry climbed into bed and closed his eyes. He had not thought of a solution and he was far too exhausted to dwell on his dilemma any further. As he slipped into a troubled sleep, one thought ran through Harry's mind. The fates had conspired to place him in a perfectly untenable position and he could not have chosen a worse time to journey to London with Jane.

Alone in her room, Olivia opened the letter that had come for her in the morning post. It was quite correctly addressed to Miss Jane Bennings and Olivia knew immediately that it had come from Samantha. As she read the words that Samantha had penned, she let out a soft cry of dismay. Samantha had quite correctly contrived to delay the wedding, but only for a week. This meant that the nuptials were scheduled to take place at the very time that Olivia was to be in London with Harry.

Olivia shivered. This new scheduling was a bit too close for comfort. All should be well, however, as their original plan would still suffice.

When she had parted ways with Samantha at the Two Feathers Inn, they had agreed to a plan. When Olivia went to collect her inheritance, she had promised to leave an envelope for Samantha at her solicitor's office, containing the funds that were necessary for Samantha to make good her escape. On the day following Olivia's birthday, Samantha was to slip away from Lady Edna's residence and make her way to the solicitor's office. Once she had collected the envelope, she was to exit from a rear door and hire a conveyance to spirit her away from London before anyone came to realize that she was missing.

Olivia sighed with relief. Though the scheduling should now be critical, Samantha could still be successful in her escape. In the hustle and bustle of her wedding morn, Samantha could slip away to the solicitor's office, collect the envelope that Olivia had left for her, and quit London well before the time of the wedding.

But there was another page to the letter and Olivia's

eyes widened as she read on. Though Samantha had done her utmost, Lady Edna had refused her request for an early release of the funds. It seemed that she had made a promise to Olivia's father not to sign the release paper until Olivia was safely wed. Lady Edna had invited the solicitor to the wedding and had assured Samantha, most sincerely, that she should sign the release the moment her vows had been spoken.

Samantha's next sentence gave Olivia pause as it begged for a speedy answer.

> *You must advise me of precisely what you wish me to do. The date of the wedding draws ever near and I am at a loss to know your wishes. I shall speak my vows if that is necessary to secure your grandmother's signature. I know how desperately you need your inheritance and I shall assist you in this endeavor. But you must make some arrangement to collect me before my wedding day is out. The festivities shall conclude before midnight at which time we take our leave in the duke's coach. I do not know our destination. He has told me that it is a surprise. I do know, however, that we set sail to join his mother in Vienna on the following Monday.*

Olivia gave a cry of distress as she realized the full meaning of Samantha's words. What they had thought was a perfect scheme had been neatly foiled by Lady Edna's refusal to release the funds. Though Samantha had offered, Olivia could not ask her to go on with the wedding, pretending to be someone she was not. Olivia was not certain of the consequences of such an act, but she was convinced that there should be some illegality involved. When Samantha was found out, as certainly she would be, she should be penalized for her part in their ruse.

The thought of dear Samantha being tried and sentenced to prison, or perhaps even worse, caused Olivia to break down in tears. She had placed Samantha in grave

danger and she must devise a way to rescue her before
this ill-fated wedding could take place

Lady Edna paced the floor in her room, her lips occasionally twitching up in a smile. The pieces were beginning
to form a pattern and a complicated one it was. Though
some of the players were still absent, others had taken their
places. Samantha and David were in place, along with Lady
Edna herself. And soon the others would come to play
their chosen parts. Lady Edna had no doubt of that. The
stakes were far too high to keep them away.

This complicated farce was worthy of the bard himself.
Indeed, Lady Edna felt as if she were a character in one
of his plays, strutting and fretting across the stage with the
best of them. Even now, as she strode back and forth, her
stiff joints loosened very nicely by dear Samantha's remedy,
she could not decide if this more closely resembled a play
or a game of chess with living, breathing pieces. If chess
was the game, she was the white queen, and she had sent
her knights on a quest this very evening.

Lady Edna smiled in great amusement as she contemplated the gentlemen she had chosen for her knights.
They were an unlikely trio, but their very ineptitude should
serve to disguise her true purpose. Lords Paxton, Danbury,
and Halverson believed that they were performing a service for Samantha, making certain that her future husband
was a regular fellow who was worthy of her love. They had
no idea that they were also gathering evidence to either
confirm or deny Lady Edna's contention that the gentleman who had presented himself as the Duke of Westbury
was an out and out impostor.

A smile turned up the corners of Lady Edna's mouth
as she thought of the number of impostors in this game.
Though she did not know for certain, she should put the
number at four. David was not Harry Fielding. The information she expected to receive this very evening should

support that fact. The real duke was in hiding and Lady Edna suspected that he might have assumed his impostor's identity. And then there was the matter of her granddaughter's whereabouts with which to contend.

Lady Edna sighed. As much as she wished that dear Samantha were truly her granddaughter, she knew otherwise. Samantha had played her part well, deceiving all who had met her with the exception of Lady Edna. The dowager countess had known from the very beginning that the lovely young lady who had presented herself so charmingly was not her granddaughter. It was a simple matter of comparing Samantha's features to that of a miniature Lady Edna had requested of Olivia's painting master only last year, a miniature that had been accomplished without Olivia's knowledge. Mr. Dawson had been delighted to paint the portrait for Lady Edna and had presented it as a gift to the patron who had paid so handsomely for all of Olivia's lessons in the past.

Lady Edna sighed. Perhaps it had been unfair of her to permit this ruse to continue, but it had afforded her a great deal of pleasure. Samantha had proven to be a thoroughly delightful addition to her household and Dr. Baillie had pronounced her to be of remarkable intelligence though he had not succeeded in discovering her true identity. It was also true that Samantha had fallen desperately in love with the gentleman that she assumed was the Duke of Westbury. It would be interesting indeed to discover David's true identity for Lady Edna suspected that he was every bit as smitten with the lovely Samantha as she was with him.

A chuckle escaped Lady Edna's throat as she thought of Olivia, hiding away at Mrs. Dawson's artistic retreat. According to the painting master's aunt, dear Olivia had met a fellow artist and she seemed quite enamored of him. His name was Harry, a former student of Mr. Dawson's, and Lady Edna was almost certain that he was the true Duke of Westbury. Though Olivia and the duke had not met in London as Lady Edna and the duke's mother had planned, fate had contrived to place them together even as they thought to escape each other.

Olivia and Samantha were in communication. Though she had not opened them, Lady Edna had seen the letters that Samantha had posted to her "friend" in Bath. Soon Olivia would come to rescue Samantha from her marriage to the Duke of Westbury and Lady Edna suspected that Harry should accompany her, also planning to save his impostor friend. The convoluted machinations were too delicious for words and Lady Edna was smiling as she pulled the bell rope to summon her dresser and friend, Michele. There would be time for a small glass of sherry and then they must take their places for another act of this intriguing drama in which no one was quite the person they appeared to be.

Fifteen

David was well aware of the scowls that he was receiving from the other gentlemen at the gaming table. Even though he had attempted to bungle the last few hands, he could not seem to lose.

They were in a gaming hell that Lord Danbury had recommended, a well-appointed place that seemed frequented by scoundrels as well as gentlemen of the *ton* who desired higher stakes than they could achieve at Boodle's or White's. Names were not divulged, and David could readily appreciate why a climate of anonymity was maintained. Some of these men were not gentlemen, but professional gamblers. As such, they were dangerous and ruthless.

Lord Danbury, who was observing the play, also seemed keenly aware of the chilly reception that David was now receiving. He tapped David on the shoulder and cleared his throat. "It is growing late. We must soon take our leave."

"Yes. We must." David rose to his feet despite the protests of the other players, who had apparently hoped to win back some of their losses by further play. "I thank you for the game, gentlemen. It was a most welcome diversion. But I have made it a practice never to play for profit."

The most dangerous in appearance of the group round the table, a tall gentleman with a coal black beard, spoke up in his gravelly voice. "You never play for profit?"

"Never." David separated his original stake from his pile

of winnings and slipped it into his pocket. Then he pushed the rest to the center of the table. "I depend on you, sir, to distribute these winnings fairly. And I thank you, gentlemen, for a most enjoyable and diverting evening."

Lord Danbury turned to David in shock. "But you have won a fortune! Why do you . . ."

"Come." David gripped his arm and propelled him toward the door while Paxton and Halverson followed closely in their wake. It was not until they were in the carriage and had achieved a distance of several city blocks that David spoke again. "The gentleman with the black beard had a pistol at the ready and his friend was armed with a dagger. I thought it prudent to give up my winnings rather than lose our lives."

Lord Halverson's eyes widened. "Good heavens! Do you suspect that they might have killed us?"

"It was a distinct possibility." David nodded. "I departed with my life and my original stake, and I consider myself well ahead of the game. Which should you rather have, gentlemen, your winnings or your life?"

Lord Paxton chuckled. "I should rather have my life and I wager to say that Halverson shares my sentiment. But Danbury, here, shall have to ponder that one for a bit."

David threw back his head and laughed. He had not thought that Lord Paxton was such a wit.

"I should prefer my life, I assure you." Lord Danbury's face had bleached of color and his voice trembled as he spoke. "But I have frequented this particular establishment many times in the past and I have never experienced difficulty in taking my leave."

"Did you depart with winnings?" Lord Paxton asked the question.

"No. I had cursedly bad luck on every occasion that I played there. But surely you do not think that . . ."

"I observed the black-bearded gentleman exchange a signal with the group round the door," Lord Halverson interrupted. "I have no doubt that the duke is correct in his assessment. If he had attempted to take his winnings, we should have been set upon the moment we reached the street."

Lord Danbury's expression was solemn and he shuddered slightly. "Perhaps it should not be wise of me to play there again."

"Perhaps it should not be wise of you to play anywhere!" Lord Paxton chuckled. "From your own admissions, you have lost a fortune at the tables."

"Yes . . . well . . . I shall consider that advice."

David recognized Lord Danbury's discomfort at the turn their conversation had taken and thought to steer it in another direction. "It is past midnight, gentlemen. Have I passed the test your wives set for me?"

"Tests." Lord Halverson corrected him. "As far as I am concerned, you have. We enjoyed several snifters of brandy at White's and you have shown no ill effects."

David laughed. "You thought that I should become regrettably foxed and make a cake of myself?"

"I did not, but we were required to make the attempt." Lord Halverson chuckled. "My wife devised that test and you may well guess the reason that she was concerned over this particular subject."

David gave Lord Halverson a quick smile. It was apparent that the gentleman was aware of his own weakness. "I have received little enjoyment from evenings that I do not clearly remember. I find myself wondering what pleasures I have experienced and cannot recall."

Lord Halverson raised his brows at the comment and then he nodded. "Yes. I have not considered it in exactly that manner, but there is something to be said for your position. I shall have to devote more thought to this matter."

David smiled and then he turned to Lord Danbury. "I assume that we have just recently departed the scene of Lady Danbury's test?"

"Yes, indeed. I am happy to say that you have passed

with honors. There is but one test remaining and that is Lady Paxton's."

Lord Paxton chuckled as David turned to him. "Dammed if I know why the lady devised this particular test, but she asked me to take you to the Cyprians' Ball. Can you imagine my gentle wife requesting such a thing? I felt certain that she was completely unaware of such goings-on."

"Perhaps you would be well advised to step down a bit, Paxton." Lord Halverson grinned at his friend. "Your wife may suspect much more than you think."

"Yes. I shall take care to practice a goodly amount of discretion in future." Lord Paxton sighed deeply. "Though I claimed that I did not know where such an event should take place and I should have to ask round the club, I fear she has found me out."

"We go to the Cyprians' Ball then?" David chuckled slightly.

"Yes." Lord Paxton nodded. "Have you attended such an event in the past?"

David shook his head. "Never. But I must admit that the concept is intriguing. I should like to observe it, but I have no intention of becoming . . . er . . . actively involved."

"Why is that?" Lord Paxton asked the question. "You shall find yourself surrounded by ladies who are both beautiful and skilled in the art of pleasing a gentleman. Do not forget that you are not yet married."

David nodded. "I am certain that you are correct, but I shall soon possess all the beauty that I desire. And skill is the product of frequent practice under excellent tutelage, is it not? I plan to spend many happy hours as an instructor."

"Well said!" Lord Danbury's eyes were twinkling as he turned to his philandering friend. "Perhaps if you followed the duke's plan, Paxton, you might have little need for diversions."

Lord Paxton's eyes flashed with anger for a brief moment and David thought that he should give Danbury a scathing reply. But his anger abated quickly and a thoughtful expression spread over his countenance. "An interesting theory. Perhaps I shall put it into practice when I return to my country estate."

"Think of the blunt you'd save on maids!" Lord Halverson's laugh rang out. "You should not have to replace them nearly so often."

Lord Paxton's amusement overrode his discomfort at having his foibles so rudely exposed and he laughed with genuine good humor. "S'truth. And I should not be forced to spend my time shopping for baubles and silk. There is *congé* to consider also. My coffers should be overflowing if I did not have that particular expense!"

All four shared a good laugh and David's opinion of his three companions improved considerably. They were not bad fellows and they readily admitted their faults.

"We have arrived." Lord Paxton pulled back the curtain to glance out as the carriage slowed and came to a stop. "Let us make our final appearance of the evening, gentlemen. Perhaps I am experiencing the full weight of my years, but I find that I am most anxious to complete this test and return home."

Lady Edna sighed as the Drawing Room door closed behind her recently departed guests. The ormolu clock on the mantelpiece showed the time as half past two. It was most unusual for her to receive guests in the wee hours of the morning, but she had requested, indeed demanded, this audience. She had not wished to wait until morning to hear Lords Halverson, Danbury, and Paxton's account of the evening that they had spent with the Duke of Westbury.

"You may come out now, Michele." Lady Edna called to her dresser; a moment later, Michele appeared in the doorway of an adjoining chamber. "Were you able to hear them clearly?"

"Well enough, My Lady."

Lady Edna laughed and patted the seat next to her. "We are quite alone, Michele. There is no further need of formality between us."

"You are right, of course." Michele smiled. "Would you care for a glass of sherry, Edna?"

"Most definitely. Pour one for yourself as well. It has been an exceedingly tiresome evening."

"But an extremely productive one." Michele poured out two glasses of sherry and handed one to Lady Edna. Then she took a seat and sighed deeply. "What think you of their account, Edna?"

A bemused expression spread over Lady Edna's face. "It was precisely as I had suspected. Did you come to a similar conclusion?"

"Most definitely. In light of the report the three gentleman offered, David cannot be the Duke of Westbury."

"But have you any notion of his true identity?" Lady Edna watched her dresser carefully. Michele had proven to be an excellent judge of character in the past.

"I have no notion whatsoever." Michele frowned. "I do know that he is not a worthless fribble. Of that I am certain."

Lady Edna nodded. "Quite true. David has been educated as a gentleman. I have spoken to him at length on several subjects and he has proven himself to be well informed. And he has the demeanor of a gentleman."

"Yes." Michele smiled in agreement. "But I do not think that he is a member of the peerage."

Lady Edna's eyes narrowed. "Could he be an actor playing the role of a gentleman?"

"I do not think so." Michele took a sip of her sherry. "I have observed him closely and he is most comfortable in genteel society. His responses are spontaneous, while an actor's responses should be much more slowly calculated. This is why I am in complete agreement with your assessment that he has been educated as a gentleman."

"But you are also certain that he is not the duke?"

Michele nodded. "Very certain. You have read the description that my cousin sent to me, and his information comes directly from a member of the duke's staff at Westbury Park."

"Let us go over the differences once again." Lady Edna sighed wearily. "Your cousin wrote that the duke cannot drink strong spirits without becoming quite muddleheaded."

"That is correct. And Lord Halverson reported that although David enjoyed several snifters of the finest brandy that White's had to offer, he appeared to be completely unimpaired."

"There is also the gambling." Lady Edna nodded. "Lord Danbury reported that David won a tidy sum and appeared to be highly skilled at the art of wagering."

"And the real duke is an extremely foolish gambler. My cousin reported that he often lost large sums while he was at Oxford and was forced to appeal for advances on his quarterly allowances from his father."

"As far as I am concerned, the incident that occurred at the Cyprians' Ball leaves little doubt." Lady Edna's eyes crinkled with amusement. "Poor Paxton appeared quite overset that the loveliest offering in that establishment greeted David by name!"

Michele's eyes widened. "By name? I had missed that part. Which name did she use to greet him?"

"David. Lord Halverson gave a detailed account. He said that a stunningly beautiful young girl, clothed in an ensemble of brilliant red satin, rushed up to kiss David most intimately on the lips."

Michele's brows raised. "And what did this young girl say to him?"

"She uttered the words, *Coo, David. Wherever have you been hiding for so long?* Then, as she was about to kiss him again, David whispered in her ear and she made a hasty departure."

"He is known, then, in these circles. And we may assume that his name is truly David."

Lady Edna nodded. "Yes, indeed. We may also assume that he is personally acquainted with the duke."

"However did you reach that conclusion?" Michele frowned slightly.

"I queried Lady Appleton this very morning when I paid a call upon her. I had asked David to describe Westbury Park to me, knowing full well that Lady Appleton had been a frequent guest of the former duke and duchess. Her description of the mansion and the grounds matched perfectly with David's description."

Michele began to smile. "Then it should be a simple matter to find out who David really is. I shall write to my cousin immediately to ask if the duke has a friend of that name."

"Thank you, Michele." Lady Edna nodded. "At least we have gleaned one fact from this exhausting evening. David is not the Duke of Westbury. I only wish that our other problem were so simple."

"Our other problem?" Michele frowned slightly.

"Yes, indeed. In the past few weeks, I have observed Samantha carefully. What a dear child she is!"

Michele nodded. "She is most certainly! You are indeed fortunate to have such a loving granddaughter."

"That is the other problem." Lady Edna gave a humorless chuckle. "Samantha is not my granddaughter, Olivia!"

Michele raised the glass to her lips and took a much larger than ladylike sip. "If Samantha is not Olivia, who is she?"

"I do not know. I am certain, however, that Samantha does not know that David is not the duke. And I am also certain that David assumes Samantha to be Olivia. It is delicious, Michele!" Lady Edna looked highly amused. "They are both of them practicing a subterfuge on the other!"

"But where is the real Duke of Westbury? And where is your granddaughter, Olivia?"

Lady Edna smiled. "Far away from London in a place that each assumes to be secure. And both most desirous of remaining undetected."

"Then you suspect that your granddaughter and the duke contrived their deceptions independently?"

"I am almost certain of it." Lady Edna chuckled slightly. "My only question is how long each of them shall permit this farce to play out."

Michele began to laugh as she caught the humor in the situation. "David and Samantha will not actually *marry*, will they?"

"I think not, though both of them shall be sorely tempted. I have no doubt that David loves Samantha, and I am certain that she loves him in return. I do believe that their good characters, however, shall stop them short of speaking their vows. Neither one of them shall be able to marry the other under false pretenses."

Michele nodded. "I daresay you are correct, Edna. Shall you expose this ruse then, and demand an explanation from the parties involved?"

"Good heavens, no!" Lady Edna reached out to take her old friend's hand. "I should be depriving us of great pleasure if I were to take that action. We shall sit back to watch and listen as their machinations play out to a conclusion. I believe it shall serve to flush out the duke and Olivia from hiding."

Michele caught Lady Edna's excitement and she laughed. "How thrilling! The duke and Olivia shall both come here to stop the wedding!"

"Precisely." Lady Edna nodded. "This current Season is as dull as dust and it desperately needs a good scandal to spice it up. Just think of the favor I shall be performing for the ladies and gentlemen of the *ton!*"

Sixteen

Samantha bathed her eyes with cold water and glanced in the mirror once again. She had just endured the final fitting of her wedding gown and when the ordeal had come to a conclusion, she had escaped to her chamber to indulge in yet another bout of tears. She had turned into a veritable watering pot and she had no one to blame but herself. Now her eyes were puffy and her flawless complexion had turned an unbecoming shade of blotchy pink, but several more applications of soothing water should serve to return her appearance to a state closely approximating normalcy. Unfortunately, there was no cure for the problem that still plagued her and she vowed not to think of it lest she collapse into tears once again. There had been no word from Olivia in yesterday's post and her wedding was but one day away!

In the wee hours of the morning, Samantha had paced the floor of her chamber, attempting to hit on a plan to extricate herself from her distressing situations if Olivia's aid was not forthcoming. She had thought to flee and leave this dreadful tangle behind her, but she truly had nowhere to go. She had counted what money remained in her purse and realized that it should carry her past the outskirts of London, but she could not leave without breaking her promise to Olivia.

There was also the matter of Lady Edna's sensibilities to consider. In all conscience, Samantha could not take her leave without begging that kind lady's forgiveness. It should be heartless to flee and leave only a letter behind. This had not been a consideration when she had left Hawthorne Cottage. Samantha had known that her Aunt Phoebe should be relieved to be rid of her. But Lady Edna had been kindness itself and Samantha had grown to love her every bit as much as if they truly had been granddaughter and grandmother. She simply could not take leave of Lady Edna in such a cowardly manner. She should have to explain the ruse, beg Lady Edna's forgiveness for her horrid deception, and somehow manage to convince her to release her granddaughter's funds. Only then could she satisfy the commitment she had made to Olivia.

Samantha sighed. The task she had set for herself seemed impossible. Lady Edna should be quite naturally overset to find that she had harbored a pretender in her home. Samantha should not blame her if she called the authorities and placed the full weight of her position behind the punishment of this deception. While Samantha was not certain which particular form this punishment should take, she was aware that she richly deserved whatever penalty was meted out to her. She had earned Lady Edna's trust and affection by trickery, and no amount of public chastisement and lawful correction should mend the injury that she had inflicted on that good lady's sensibilities.

There was also David to consider. Samantha blinked back fresh tears and steeled herself to the inevitable. She should regret it for the rest of her years if she did not make the attempt to explain her actions to him. It should serve no good purpose to admit that she loved him above all others. Even if David had come to share her tender emotions, the Duke of Westbury could never marry someone of her station. The most Samantha could hope was that he should understand and come to forgive her for her duplicity.

Samantha knew full well what was required of her, but the thought of facing both Lady Edna and David, and telling them precisely what she had done, filled her with a dreadful anxiety. When she had written to Olivia, she had agreed to go through with the wedding, but now that she considered it carefully, she was not certain that she could perform this final deception. How could she dance with her beloved at the ball tonight and pretend to be gaiety itself? What sort of beast should she be if she were to smile and accept congratulations for a marriage that had been conceived in deceit?

But there was no choice if she were to keep her promise to Olivia. She must gather all the courage she possessed and continue with this horrid deception. If no word from Olivia came, she must speak her vows, make certain that Lady Edna had signed the papers that Olivia so desperately required, and then steal off into the night like the very thief she had come to be.

David glanced down at the notice that he had prepared for the *London Times*. He would take it round to the publisher early tomorrow morning and shake the dust of London from his feet. The plans had been made and he could not change them, not if he wished to save his friend from the machinations of the Dragoness and Lady Fraidy.

Not for the first time, David wondered what should occur if he were completely truthful with Samantha. He longed to take her in his arms and confess all, explaining the necessity of the ruse he had entered into with Harry. Samantha was most understanding, and David suspected that she should find it in her heart to forgive him. He should also tell her that although the initial meeting between them had been cloaked in deception, the love that he had come to harbor for her was genuine. But even if Samantha shared his sentiments and confessed that she also loved him, she could not marry a man with no title, no land, and no distinguished lineage. Lady Edna should never allow her granddaughter to marry beneath her station, especially since David should be revealed as an utter scoundrel for his part in the ruse.

David's eyes flickered over the neat lines of text that he had written with Harry. Every comma was in place, every sentence carefully calculated. The underlying tone was cold, however, and David took up the sharpened quill to add a final sentiment at the end. He thought he could hear his heart breaking as he penned the words:

> *Please find it in your heart to forgive the ill manner in which I have used you. And know that I shall love you forever, my dearest Samantha.*

The motion of the carriage was soothing and Harry gazed fondly at his companion as she slept. Jane had fallen asleep so early in their journey that there had been no time for conversation. She was clearly exhausted and Harry should have felt like a brute if he had awakened her. Instead, he had used the opportunity that had been presented to him to study the young woman that he had come to love and imagine how fine it should be to have her this close to him for the rest of their lives.

"Jane?" Harry moved to her side of the carriage and placed his arm round her shoulders. The sky was beginning to lighten and soon they should reach the outskirts of the city. "You must wake now, Jane."

She frowned slightly in her sleep and snuggled into the comfort of his embrace. "Not yet, Harry. I need to sleep just a little longer for I am very tired."

"Jane, my dearest. We are entering the outskirts of London." Harry smiled as she cuddled closer and rested her cheek upon his chest. If they could but stay like this forever, he should be the happiest of men.

"We are here?" Olivia sat up blinking, a blush rising to her cheeks as she realized her close proximity to Harry. "Oh, Harry! We have made such marvelous time!"

"Yes, indeed we have." Harry felt a sharp stab of disappointment as she left his embrace.

Olivia pushed herself forward, away from the comfort of the soft velvet squabs and the even greater comfort of her dear Harry's arms, and drew back the curtain to look out. They had traveled at a comfortable pace, stopping only to seek light sustenance and secure fresh horses. Now the lovely carriage was on the very outskirts of London and she must confess her dreadful prank to Harry. Olivia took a moment to gather her courage and then she spoke. "Harry, I simply must . . ."

"My dear Jane, I have a need to . . ." Harry interrupted her, speaking almost simultaneously.

"Let me speak of my problem, Harry." Olivia put a finger to his lips. "If I do not tell you now, I shall never gather the courage to do so again. But you must promise not to utter one word until I am finished."

Harry nodded, motioning for her to go on. Though he desperately wanted to tell her his identity, it could wait until she had divulged her problem.

"Six weeks ago, I found myself quite unavoidably engaged to be married." Olivia sighed deeply and dropped her eyes. "It was my grandmother's doing. She arranged it all, including my introduction to society in London. I was to be married to a gentleman of her choosing."

Harry nodded solemnly. Her story sounded much like his.

"I did not have the luxury of refusing her as she is my guardian. She also controls my inheritance and she refused to release the funds unless I agreed to the wedding she had planned for me. I needed my inheritance, Harry, to finance my painting."

Harry nodded again, but he could not keep from asking one question. "And you could not collect your inheritance unless you married the gentleman of your grandmother's choice?"

"Not precisely." Olivia hastened to explain the complications. When she had finished, she risked a look at Harry and found that he was not frowning as she had expected him to do.

"If it is money you need, my dear Jane, I shall be happy to provide it."

"No, Harry." Olivia shook her head emphatically. "I find that money, or the lack thereof, does not matter nearly so much as I had thought it did. My main concern is for my dear friend. I fear that I have placed her in a dreadful tangle and I cannot think of a way of rescuing her."

Harry's brows raised with his question. "And who is this friend?"

"A lovely girl I had the good fortune to meet at an inn. She had just fled to avoid an unfortunate marriage that her aunt had arranged and she had nowhere to go. When I told her of my situation, she agreed to take my place in London and to pretend to be me."

Harry began to frown. "But what caused you to think that such a ploy could succeed? Did she resemble your appearance that closely?"

"Her appearance did not matter, as my grandmother had not seen me since I was in leading strings. And our ruse enjoyed great success, Harry. It was going swimmingly until only a few days ago."

"What happened to throw it awry?" Harry was curious. Jane's story was remarkably similar to his.

"We had thought that Grandmama should sign the papers to release my inheritance long before this, but it seems that she has decided to wait until *after* the wedding. And the wedding is to be held tomorrow!"

"Tomorrow?" Harry began to frown. David had written that his own wedding should be tomorrow. It was indeed a coincidence that Olivia's wedding should have been scheduled on the very same day.

"She has written to tell me that she shall go through with the wedding, but I cannot let her make this sacrifice. Somehow, I must find a way to save her."

"Of course you must." Harry nodded, reaching out to take her hand. "What is your friend's name?"

"Her name is Samantha. Why did you wish to know, Harry?"

"So that I shall be able to call her by name when I rescue her." Harry began to smile as all the pieces fell into place. It was of little wonder that Jane's story had so closely resembled his. They were one and the same! "What is your true name, Jane?"

"Olivia. I am Miss Olivia Samantha Tarrington."

"Olivia." Harry's smile grew wider. "It is a lovely name. And what is the name of the gentleman that Samantha is to marry?"

"He is Harry Fielding, the Duke of Westbury." Olivia sighed deeply. "From the description that Samantha has written to me, he is an admirable gentleman. Perhaps it is even possible that I could have been content to be his wife, had I met him as my grandmother planned. But I did not. Now everything has changed. It is quite impossible for me to marry him!"

"For what reason, Olivia?"

"Because my heart is engaged by another." Olivia stared down at her slippers, vainly attempting to blink back her tears. "I did not suspect that it should ever happen, but I am most fearfully in love."

"Who is it that you love, Olivia?"

Olivia hesitated and then she bravely uttered the words. "You. I love you, Harry. Please tell me that you love me, too. I could not bear it if you did not!"

"Of course I do. I love you more than life itself, and I want to marry you." Harry gathered her into his arms. He found it difficult to believe that she should want to marry the man that he had represented himself to be, and his curiosity demanded that he put it to the test. "But what of your grandmother, Olivia? Surely she would never give permission for you to marry below the gentry!"

Olivia hugged Harry tightly. "This is true, but I do not care. I shall gladly live in a hovel if you are at my side."

"Are you certain, Olivia?"

Olivia's smile was as bright as the sun that had begun

to stream in the window of the carriage. "Oh, yes! I am most certain! You must remember our vow, Harry, to please only ourselves. Bother my grandmother! And bother my inheritance, too! My only concern at present is for my friend, Samantha."

"You must not worry about Samantha." Harry's smile was broad. "I do believe I've tumbled to a perfect solution to the problem, a way in which you shall please your grandmother and also please yourself."

"What is it, Harry?"

Olivia looked up at him and Harry had all he could do not to burst into laughter. "It is simplicity itself and it shall serve to save Samantha from this unfortunate tangle. The wedding shall go off, precisely as planned, and you shall marry the Duke of Westbury."

"What?" Olivia's mouth dropped open. "But Harry . . . I love *you!*"

"Precisely, my darling. And I am Harry Fielding, the Duke of Westbury."

Seventeen

"You are perfection, itself, Your Grace." Mr. Billings stepped back to admire the faultless cascade of snowy white that he had finished arranging at David's neck. "I do believe the Waterfall is most appropriate for this momentous occasion."

David nodded, smiling his approval of his valet's talents. His neckcloth was perfect, as was his entire manner of dress. An expertly tailored coat of black superfine adorned his broad shoulders and his gold patterned vest shimmered softly in the light from the sconces on either side of mirror. His shoes were so highly polished they appeared to gleam with a light from within, and Billings had gathered all the accessories that he should need for this formal evening. "Is the carriage ready, Billings?"

"Yes, Your Grace." Billings brushed an invisible speck of dust from David's sleeve. "I heard Cromley bring it round several moments ago."

David paced to the window and looked out. The carriage that would carry him to the ball was parked directly in front of the door. Pushing down the disturbing thought that this should be the last evening that he would enjoy with Samantha, David crossed the room and descended the stairs.

Mr. Hastings awaited him at the foot of the staircase. The ancient butler was holding a vellum envelope and he extended it to his employer. "A boy brought this round several minutes ago, Your Grace. He said that it was a matter of some urgency, but did not require a reply."

"Thank you, Hastings." David took the envelope and slipped it into his pocket, but as he was about to move toward the door, his butler cleared his throat. "Yes, Hastings?"

"All of us here at Westbury Mansion wish you happy, Your Grace."

David smiled. "Thank you, Hastings. Thank the others for me as well. Was there anything further?"

"No, Your Grace."

Hastings rushed to pull open the door and David stepped out, into the night. Once he had settled himself inside the carriage, he pulled the envelope from his pocket and his eyes widened as he recognized the writing on the envelope. This was a message from Harry. But Harry was in Bath and Hastings had stated that a boy had brought it round to the door. Why had it not been delivered with the regular post?

Once the carriage had begun to move, David tore open the envelope. As he gazed at the message that was written inside, his face lost its color and he gasped in shock. Harry was here, in London!

Harry's words were brief and David groaned as he read them. Harry planned to make an appearance at the ball this evening. His circumstances had changed somewhat, but he should explain all to David when they met. David should say nothing of Harry's impending arrival, especially to Miss Tarrington. He had come to London specifically to shoulder the blame for the cowardly ruse that he had contrived with David, and he was determined to set things aright.

Harry went on to write that he was well aware that his unexpected appearance at Lady Edna's ball might very well set the *ton* on its ear, but that this could not be avoided. After weeks of careful thought and painful introspection, Harry had decided that the Dragoness and Lady Fraidy had been right. It was time he married and gave his family an heir. Harry firmly intended to perform the duty that was expected of him and marry Miss Olivia Tarrington.

Samantha smiled as she glanced in the mirror. Bettina had arranged her auburn curls in soft ringlets and her gold silk gown was perfection itself. The bodice was fashioned in a classic Greek style, reminiscent of those worn by the lovely goddesses that were so frequently depicted in fine tapestries.

The shimmering gold material was gathered on either shoulder by a cleverly designed clasp. From that gathering, it swept down in an ever-widening cascade to cross only inches above Samantha's small waist. The dainty waistline was emphasized by a wide golden ribbon that gleamed in the light, and under it, yards of gold silk had been fastened to make up the skirt. The skirt floated out so magnificently that Samantha had to take care not to brush too close to her dressing table for fear that she should dislodge the objects that graced the surface.

The tips of Samantha's golden slippers peeped out at the hem of her sweeping skirt and she wore a wide golden bracelet on her arm, sprinkled with a score of small diamonds. Her necklace was of the same design, also sprinkled with diamonds, and Bettina had placed a matching circlet of gold amongst her curls.

Bettina stepped back to assess her talents and then she smiled along with Samantha. "You look like an angel come straight down from heaven, Miss Samantha."

"Thank you, Bettina, but I do not believe that angels are quite this immodest." Samantha struggled to adjust her bodice for she thought it far too revealing. "You must fetch a gold lace fichu."

Bettina shook her head. "Oh no, Miss Samantha! It should ruin the lines of your lovely gown."

"But the neckline is far too low." Samantha began to frown. "I should not like to appear improperly dressed."

"You are not in the least improper."

Samantha turned at the sound of a second voice and smiled as she saw Michele in the doorway. "Are you certain, Michele?"

"Very certain." Michele nodded as she entered the chamber. "Your gown is perfection and any such addition should be a travesty."

"But . . . what shall David think of me?" Samantha turned toward the mirror again, blushing heatedly.

"He shall think that you are the most ravishing of creatures. He shall be compelled to count the minutes that remain until you become his duchess."

Samantha laughed. "Do you truly think so, Michele?"

"I do." Michele smiled fondly and handed Samantha a vellum envelope. "A boy just brought this letter for you. He said that it concerned a matter of some urgency, but that it did not require a reply."

"Thank you, Michele." Samantha glanced down at the envelope and breathed a sigh of relief. She had received a message from Olivia at last!

Both Michele and Bettina were regarding her expectantly, and Samantha forced a smile. "It is nothing, I am sure—merely a message from an old friend. She is extremely excitable and nearly everything is a matter of some urgency to her."

"We shall take our leave so that you may read it." Michele signaled for Bettina to follow her. "Your grandmother awaits you in the Blue Salon. Shall I tell her that you will come to her shortly?"

"Yes. I shall be there in a nonce."

The moment that Michele and Bettina had left her, Samantha tore open the letter to read it. The words that Olivia had written caused her to gasp in dismay and she sank quickly down in a chair. Olivia was here in London, but she had not come to stop the wedding. Indeed, the exact opposite was true. Olivia had experienced a change of heart. After careful thought and due consideration, she had decided that Lady Edna had been right all along.

Olivia had written to inform Samantha that she should arrive during the evening's festivities to assume her rightful position. Samantha should not breathe a word of her coming for she had decided that the proper way to accomplish her duty was to present Lady Edna with a public apology for the deception. Samantha should not be in the least bit anxious, for Olivia intended to take all the blame upon herself and beg for her grandmother's forgiveness. Once Lady Edna had recovered from the shock of being so unexpectedly reunited with her true granddaughter, Olivia should announce that she had decided to honor her grandmother's commitment and marry the Duke of Westbury exactly as planned.

"I have just come from her chambers. She is lovely, Edna." Michele took a seat by her employer in the Blue Salon.

Lady Edna nodded and permitted a small smile to grace her lips. "And you have delivered the message that came for her from Olivia?"

"Yes. She is perusing it as we speak."

"I must admit that I am experiencing a twinge of guilt for opening it." Lady Edna sighed. "Do you think I was in the wrong, Michele?"

"No, I do not." Michele reached out to give a comforting pat to her employer's silk-clad arm. "You had need to learn of your granddaughter's plan so that you should be ready to cope with the situation. Have you also read the message that my cousin sent to me?"

Lady Edna nodded. "I have, and it erased all of my doubts in the matter. I am convinced that David is the duke's boyhood friend and companion, David Brackney."

"No doubt our little Samantha shall be grateful to receive that bit of enlightenment!" Michele's lips curved upward in a smile. "Bettina reports that she has been in a brown study all day and I am assured that she loves him with all her heart. I was sorely tempted to tell her to relieve her anxiety, but I followed your wishes, dear Edna. It should not serve to release the cat from its sack so soon."

Lady Edna smiled. "Indeed, it should not! This farce must play out, Michele, with all its required pomp and fanfare, for it shall save all of their reputations in the end."

"But your granddaughter wrote that she intended to marry the Duke of Westbury! What shall happen, dear Edna, when she learns that David is an impostor?"

"She will marry the real Duke of Westbury, Michele. I am convinced that her decision has already been made."

Michele frowned slightly. "But how can this be? Olivia does not even *know* the Duke of Westbury . . . does she?"

"Of course she does! She has been a guest of her painting master's aunt who has a cottage in Bath. And the duke has also gone to his painting master's aunt in Bath, to pursue his painting of landscapes."

"They have the same painting master?" Michele began to smile in delight.

"Yes, indeed. Fate has conspired to have them meet and I am certain that they have fallen in love. They share a common passion, you see, for art."

"You knew this!" Michele's voice held a slight note of accusation.

"Of course I did. It is the reason that I desired them to meet in the first place. Olivia and the duke are together, Michele, and they shall marry exactly as I had planned."

"But what of Samantha and David? They are in love and I am certain that they also desire to marry, but they have deceived each other."

"This is true." Lady Edna nodded. "But that deception shall come to an end tonight. Samantha shall confess her ruse to David long before my true granddaughter chooses to do so. Her love for him shall prompt her to honesty. I am also certain that David shall tell Samantha of his deception in advance of the planned revelation. Love shall triumph in the end, Michele. It reminds me of nothing so much as pieces on a chessboard, moving into position to capture the aging Queen."

"But shall the Queen elude capture?" Michele caught the analogy instantly and an anxious frown appeared on her brow.

"Yes, most certainly she shall, my dear friend!" Lady Edna smiled. "Though the Queen has lived through many games, her strategies are still intact. I shall control the board, Michele. All you need do is observe my movements to see exactly how the game shall play out."

Eighteen

Samantha stood in the reception line, flanked by David and Lady Edna. Though she had affected a most joyous smile for the occasion, her heart was heavy with despair. Her eyes searched the crush of guests waiting to be received, searching anxiously for sight of Olivia. But when the long line of guests had been duly greeted and graciously escorted to Lady Edna's ballroom by footmen dressed in their finest livery, Olivia had not yet put in an appearance.

The ballroom had been decorated lavishly for this important event. All hands had been pressed into service to hang garlands of greenery above the doorways, and huge wreaths fashioned of lush green ivy and colorful roses graced the tall, mullioned windows that overlooked the garden. Bouquets of fresh flowers were everywhere, standing on marble pedestals that had been placed at strategic points round the large room and overflowing from the wall sconces. They released their perfume to sweeten the air and their colors rivaled those of the ladies' formal ball gowns in the glittering light that spilled from hundreds of candles. Though she had peeked in at the preparations on several occasions during the day, Samantha was awestruck as she entered the ballroom on David's arm and observed the magnificent spectacle that Lady Edna had provided specifically for their enjoyment.

The night was warm and the French doors had been opened to the garden. A gentle breeze provided the perfect ventilation and the garden itself was a fairyland of twinkling lights. Faintly, above the low murmuring of the guests as they waited for the ball to commence, Samantha could hear the musical splashing of Lady Edna's stone fountain and the sweet songs of the night birds that inhabited the perfectly groomed trees. It was a magical night, lovely and enticing, and Lady Edna had arranged it all for her one and only granddaughter. Samantha knew that she should have been the happiest young miss in all of London, if only she had been Miss Olivia Tarrington.

David glanced at his intended bride and observed the tears that she quickly blinked back, out of sight. He took her hand and pressed it gently, bending down to speak softly in her ear. "What is it, Samantha?"

"Nothing. It is nothing." Samantha forced herself to smile. "It is only that it is so lovely."

David nodded solemnly. He, too, felt the wonder of this night and the splendor of the ball that had been arranged for them. As he gazed down into Samantha's troubled eyes, he knew that it was time for him to speak the truth. He could not let Harry's appearance come as a shock to the one he had come to love above all others. Perhaps she should not be able to forgive his unconscionable duplicity, but he owed her his explanation of the events that had transpired. "I should like a moment alone with you, my darling Samantha, once the opening dance is concluded. There is much that I must tell you."

"Yes." Samantha sighed as she nodded her assent. "I also have need to speak privately with you."

"Are you ready, my dears?" Lady Edna descended upon them, a fashionable vision in wine-colored silk.

"We are ready." David took Samantha's hand. "I must ask for your indulgence, Lady Edna. Once this dance is concluded I would wish a private word with my fiancée."

"Of course." Lady Edna nodded, and her smile grew warmer as she read the intention in David's eyes. David Brackney loved dear Samantha. And he was about to tell her of his part in the deception. She could only hope that Samantha should do the same and confess all to him.

Samantha turned to Lady Edna anxiously. "Where might we be alone, Grandmama?"

"The garden should be the perfect spot. You must wait until the dance is nearly finished and then slip out together for your rendezvous. In the midst of this crush, I doubt that you shall be missed." Lady Edna reached out to lay a comforting hand upon Samantha's shoulder. And then she broke the rule that she herself had made as she placed a kiss upon Samantha's cheek and hugged her tightly.

Samantha blinked back tears at Lady Edna's very public display of affection, and hugged her back. "Thank you, Grandmama."

"And now we shall begin." Lady Edna smiled at them both and gave the signal to begin the ball.

As the strains of a waltz floated out over the assemblage, David led Samantha to the center of the floor. He took her in his arms and smiled down at her. "Do not be anxious, love. I shall not step on your toes."

"And I shall do my utmost not to step on yours." Samantha whispered the words as her voice was choked with unshed tears. It was small comfort, but at least they should have this one final dance together before her dreams of a perfect future turned to ashes.

Her steps matched with his perfectly as they swirled round the floor. Her eyes were on his, large and luminous and filled with tears. David fought down the lump in his own throat and sighed at the happiness that could have been his. "I love you, Samantha."

"And I love you, David."

They did not speak again, not until the bittersweet dance was nearly ended and they had slipped from the ballroom to find a place of refuge on a stone bench in a secluded part of the garden. Strains of music still floated out into the still night air; David felt a chill that invaded his very soul as he pulled his love into his arms one last time.

Their lips met fiercely in the darkness, desperately seeking that which they both knew they had no right to claim. When they drew apart at last, both Samantha and David were trembling with the emotion of their last moments together.

"I am not . . ." Samantha's voice broke in a rush of tears and at that exact moment, David spoke.

"I have deceived . . ."

Both were shocked into silence at the half-uttered confession of the other. Then Samantha broke that silence with a sob of remorse.

"I am not Olivia. And I cannot marry you, David. Your true fiancée is coming here tonight, to claim you as her own. I am so sorry for my lies and deceit! I did not set out to love you. It . . . it just happened! I know you do not understand, but I do love you with all my heart! And that is why I must go!"

She would have fled the garden then if David had not reached out to hold her. He pulled her into his arms and held her in an embrace so strong that she could not escape.

"You love me?" David's voice was thick with emotion.

"Yes! But a duke cannot marry someone like me. I do not know the identity of my father, and my mother was . . . was an adulteress! I am nothing more than a common orphan who was taken in out of charity!"

"And I am nothing more than a stable master's son. That was what I was about to tell you when you made your own confession." David threw back his head and laughed at the folly that they had almost committed by hiding their secrets from each other. "And you, my darling Samantha, are my very perfect match!"

"You . . . you are not the duke?" Samantha's mouth dropped open in surprise.

"I am not. My name is David Brackney and I have no title at all. I was the duke's boyhood chum."

"But . . . but you were a perfect duke!" Samantha's head reeled at this startling revelation. "How could you play the part so perfectly?"

"I was educated at Eton and Oxford with Harry. The old duke thought to keep my father in his debt by educating me as a gentleman. When Harry was trapped into marriage by the machinations of his mother and his aunt, I agreed to help him by taking part in this unfortunate ruse."

"Just as I did." Samantha shook her head slightly to clear it. Though she was still confused, she was beginning to understand. "Oh, David! I lived in fear that you might recognize me and expose all to Lady Edna!"

"Recognize you?" David frowned slightly, but he did not lessen his hold on the lovely lady he held in his arms.

"From the Two Feathers Inn." Samantha's lips curved upward in a smile as she began to see the humor in their situation. "But you did not give me your name at the time."

Now it was David's turn to be astonished. "You were the girl that I snatched from the clutches of that brute and carried up the stairs?"

"I was." Samantha gave a small laugh. "You assumed that I was a lightskirt, but after one kiss, you quickly discovered that I was not."

David laughed again, a deep, happy sound that was both joyful and amused. "But if you recognized me, you should have known that I was not the duke. A duke would not stop to enjoy hospitality at a place like the Two Feathers Inn."

"You forget that I know nothing of the habits of the nobility. I thought you were a rake as well as a duke." Laughter bubbled up from Samantha's throat and spilled out into the soft night air. "And now I know that you are merely . . . a rake!"

David laughed long and hard, and it was several moments before he could speak again. "A *former* rake. And you need not fear that I shall return to those particular pursuits. I shall have no inclination if you will but agree to marry me.''

"I will!'' Samantha looked up into his eyes, and David pulled her close to kiss her again. They did not speak for several blissful minutes and when he released her, Samantha sighed in exquisite contentment. She would become David's wife. Could any future be more perfect than that? But then an unwelcome thought crossed her mind and her eyes widened with anxiety. Olivia was coming here tonight to claim the man she thought was the Duke of Westbury as her fiancé!

David saw the expression of alarm that crossed Samantha's countenance and reacted immediately. "What is it, my darling?''

"Olivia!'' Samantha's voice was shaking. "She wrote to say that she is coming here tonight and that she intends to marry you.''

"Not me, my love. She is coming to marry the duke. And Harry is also traveling here, from Bath, to marry Olivia.''

"How odd!'' Samantha frowned. "Harry and Olivia are coming from the very same place. Olivia has been visiting her painting teacher's aunt in Bath.''

David began to chuckle. "Would that be Mr. Dawson?''

"Why, yes! You don't suppose that . . .''

"I do.'' David interrupted her. "Mr. Dawson is also Harry's teacher, and Harry went to stay at his aunt's cottage.''

Samantha began to laugh. "Oh, my! Mr. Shakespeare could make a fine play of this, no doubt.''

"Just so.'' David hugged her tightly. "I daresay it should be one of his comedies. I am almost certain that Harry and Olivia shall come here together and announce that they shall be married exactly as the Dragoness and Lady Edna planned.''

"How ironic!'' Samantha shook her head in wonder. "After all this trouble to escape from a marriage that neither of them desired, they meet quite by accident and discover that they now desire it above all else!"

David's expression grew sober. "Shall we tell Lady Edna what we suspect?"

"Yes, we must tell her straightaway. It should not be kind to let her be caught unawares." Samantha nodded quickly. She had known that she must tell dear Lady Edna of her deception, but now that the moment of truth had arrived, she found that she dreaded it most fearfully.

"Courage, Samantha." David held her hand as they retraced their steps.

As they began to climb the stone steps that led up to the ballroom, Samantha pulled herself up to her full height and squared her shoulders to carry the burden of her lies. "I do hope she will forgive us, David. I have come to love her as I should love my very own Grandmama."

"And I have come to love you, too, Granddaughter."

Samantha gasped as she glanced up the steps and saw Lady Edna standing at the top. "Oh, Grandmama! I am so sorry! I have lied to you most dreadfully!"

"And most convincingly." A touch of humor threatened to turn up the corners of Lady Edna's lips. "You succeeded in deceiving me for nearly a day, my dear Samantha."

"You . . . you knew?"

"Of course I knew." Lady Edna waited for Samantha to reach the top step and then she gathered her into her arms. "And you, David Brackney, managed to fool me for much longer than that. I did not tumble to your ruse until but two short days ago."

David saw the humorous twinkle in Lady Edna's eyes and took hope. "You are not angry with us, Lady Edna?"

"Not in the slightest. It has been a most intriguing puzzle and it has amused me greatly. Indeed, I have not enjoyed anything so much in years! I assume that you and dear Samantha will marry, now that you are released from your other obligations?"

David nodded quickly. "Yes, Lady Edna. But first we

must survive this evening. You see, the true Duke and Olivia are . . .''

"Coming here tonight," Lady Edna interrupted him. "I know, my dears. And I am prepared for them. I have devised a way to save everyone's reputation and delight the *ton* at the very same time. Are the both of you willing to perform one final ruse for the sake of Olivia and Harry's happiness?"

"Of course we are!" Samantha stepped back from Lady Edna's embrace, her eyes overflowing with tears of joy.

"David?" Lady Edna turned to him.

"Gladly, Lady Edna." David nodded, taking his fiancée's hand in his own. "It was our concern for their happiness that prompted us to enter into this unfortunate deception in the first place."

Lady Edna's lips curved in a smile that held nothing but fondness for them both. "When Olivia and the duke arrive, you must follow my lead. Now listen carefully and I shall tell you exactly what we must do to extricate ourselves from this dreadful bumble-broth."

Nineteen

"Oh, Harry! I have never once fainted in my entire life, but I am so anxious, I find myself distressingly light-headed."

"Nonsense. It shall all go off very easily." Harry grasped Olivia's arm firmly and escorted her to her grandmother's door. "Just remember that I love you and all will be well."

"And I love you." Olivia took a deep breath and let Harry lead her into her grandmother's mansion. Harry had been masterful when they had devised their plan and she was most impressed with both his poise and his commanding manner. She thought that he should have made an excellent general or perhaps even a king.

Harry raised his brows as he noted the absence of servants. "This is most peculiar, Olivia. I had expected to encounter your grandmother's butler, or at least a footman."

"Perhaps they are all busy elsewhere." Olivia gazed around curiously. It was her first sight of her grandmother's home and she found it splendidly appointed.

"Come, Olivia." Harry led her up the grand staircase. "The ballroom is this way."

"You have been here before?"

"No, my dear." Harry turned to smile down at her. "I am but following the sound of the music."

"Oh. Of course." Olivia felt a blush rise to her cheeks. None but a peahen should have failed to hear the lovely strains of music that floated out of the ballroom to greet them. She was not normally so bird-witted, but the clamor of her own anxious heartbeat resounding in her ears had drowned out all other sound.

"We have arrived, Olivia." Harry stopped just short of the doorway and turned to appraise her appearance. He had taken her to the finest modiste in London and paid dearly for her gown. Olivia had the look of a princess in the cloud of ice blue satin that had been carefully and hastily fashioned to embrace her slender figure. Her hair had been arranged in the latest style by the dresser the modiste had recommended, and her ensemble was complete, save for the velvet-covered jewelry case that he carried in his pocket.

"Am I suitable, Harry?" Olivia began to tremble slightly, knowing that all eyes should soon be upon her.

"Suitable?" Harry smiled gently. "My darling, you are perfection itself! I have never seen anyone more exquisite. There is but one slight improvement that I should wish to make in your appearance."

"What is it, Harry?" Olivia reached up to pat her hair, hoping that the modish style that the dresser had so carefully arranged was still intact.

"It is this." Harry drew the small cask from his pocket and handed it to her with a flourish. "They do not rival your beauty, but I should consider it a kindness if you should wear them tonight."

Olivia's fingers trembled as she opened the cask, and she gasped in delight as she caught sight of the jewels inside. "Sapphires! But they are far too precious for me to wear. What if I should lose them?"

"Then I shall buy more." Harry laughed at her delight, anticipating her reaction when he should present her with the cask of family jewels. The sapphires were merely a bauble. They had not been of the finest quality and he had only purchased them because he had thought that they should complement the color of her gown. "Hold very still, my darling, and I shall fasten them for you."

Olivia held her breath as Harry arranged the jewels around her neck and clasped them. Then he bent down and placed a light kiss on her lips. She saw the admiration in his eyes as he gazed at her and she was filled with happiness. It was at that exact moment that Olivia knew precisely what she wished to say to her grandmother. She would admit that Lady Edna had been right, that she had been cowardly by running away. Had she and Harry both faced their problems straight on, they should soon have discovered that they made a perfect match.

"It is time, my darling." Harry took Olivia's hand in his and stepped into the open doorway of the ballroom. "Courage, dear Olivia. We have but one more challenge to overcome and then we shall to free to enjoy the rest of our lives together."

Samantha's eyes widened as she caught sight of the couple standing at the open doorway of the ballroom. It was Olivia and she was on the arm of a dashing gentleman. She turned to David and pressed his hand. "It is Olivia!"

"Yes." David held Samantha's arm securely, lending her support by virtue of his solid presence. "And we were correct in our assumption, for Harry is with her."

Samantha turned to survey the spot where Lady Edna had been standing only moments before, but she had disappeared in the crush. "Where is Grandmama?"

"She is behind us on the dais. Come, Samantha. She motions for us to join her."

Samantha's legs were trembling slightly as they wove their way through the throng and approached Lady Edna. But Lady Edna did not appear in the least bit anxious as she moved to a position in front of the orchestra, in full view of the assemblage. Once Samantha and David had climbed the steps and joined her on the dais, Lady Edna gave the orchestra a signal and they began to play.

A loud fanfare sounded, bringing the guests' chatter to a surprised halt. The ballroom was perfectly silent as Lady

Edna smiled at her guests and spoke in a clear, commanding voice.

"I thank all of you for attending this celebration for my granddaughter and her fiancé. Rather than the usual round of good wishes, we thought to arrange a truly unusual entertainment for you this evening. Many of you have met my granddaughter and have grown to love her. You have also become acquainted with the duke and have come to enjoy a similar affection for him. Perhaps you assume that you know them well, but our entertainment tonight shall prove to you that, even in this age of jaded sophistication, it is possible to accomplish a most delightful ruse."

There were murmurs from the crowd and a score of puzzled frowns. Samantha bit back a smile as she saw that Lady Edna was succeeding in her plan to pique the crowd's curiosity.

"I should like to formally introduce my dear granddaughter, Miss Olivia Samantha Tarrington. And her handsome fiancé, the Duke of Westbury."

All eyes swiveled to Samantha and David, and Lady Edna gave a delighted laugh. "You assume that I refer to this lovely young couple, but your assumption may be incorrect. Is it possible that you have harbored pretenders in your midst?"

This comment brought several more murmurs from the guests, and the polite smiles on many faces were now replaced by expressions of curiosity and interest. Lady Edna turned toward the young couple in the doorway and motioned them forward. "Olivia? I desire that you and the duke join me."

The murmuring of the crowd grew to a loud swell of excited comments as Olivia and Harry made their way to the dais. Samantha noticed that the only one who did not seem astonished at this turn of events was the esteemed physician, Matthew Baillie. Perhaps she had let slip too many facts about her former life to deceive him. It was quite probable that a gentleman who possessed such a high intellect should discern her ruse quite easily. Samantha met his eyes, fearing that he now should shun her, but that esteemed gentleman did not regard her with censure. Quite the contrary, he was wearing a genuine smile of enjoyment and as he met her gaze, his right eye closed in a wink of pure mischief.

As Olivia and Harry mounted the raised dais, Samantha and David moved apart so that they could take a place between them. This was Lady Edna's doing. She had coached them carefully in what they should do. Samantha leaned close to Olivia, who was visibly trembling, and hastened to reassure her by a whispered word in her ear.

"Just do as Grandmama says and all will be well. She has hit on a way to save us all from hurtful gossip. David is saying the same to Harry." Olivia turned slightly to meet Samantha's eyes and what she saw there appeared to reassure her for she smiled in relief. Then she glanced over at Harry to make certain that he was smiling as well, and gave a slight nod to indicate that she understood.

"I have sought to teach us all a lesson from this unusual entertainment." Lady Edna's eyes crinkled in laughter. "Appearances can be deceiving. We treat our equals with the respect accorded them by their title and position. All others we tend to ignore as inferiors, never seeking to discover their true worth. Perhaps it is time that we regard our maids, and our grooms, and the common shop girls we encounter, with fresh eyes. There may be one among them who is our equal, or perhaps even our better, in the cloak of disguise."

There was an excited buzz as many of the guests discussed the comment that Lady Edna had made. Samantha was certain they were each of them remembering the sharp reprimands or the unkind comments they had made to those of a lower ranking in the past.

"But Lady Edna . . . have you ever known this to occur?" Lady Paxton asked the question.

"Yes, indeed." Lady Edna smiled. "There is one amongst my staff who conceals a royal lineage. Do not think to ask, for I shall never reveal the secret of this person's identity, but had I not encouraged a commodious rapport between us, I should never have known."

There were startled expressions on many faces and Samantha surmised that countless lowly maids and footmen in numerous households should be treated more fairly in future. Lady Edna had given them all cause for thought. But her speech had not concluded and all listened raptly as Lady Edna continued.

"But I have not invited you into my home for a lecture. In addition to this happy celebration, I present you with a delightful puzzle which you must solve before the nuptials that shall take place on the morrow." Lady Edna gestured toward the two young couples who stood on the dais. "One of these lovely young ladies is my actual granddaughter, Miss Olivia Tarrington. And one of these handsome young gentlemen is the real Duke of Westbury. You have the remainder of the evening to discover the truth of the matter by questioning them carefully and observing their actions."

"It is a game?" Lord Danbury's eyes gleamed with excitement.

"Yes, indeed. But unfortunately, Lord Danbury, there is no wagering involved." Lady Edna smiled as Lord Danbury chuckled delightedly. "You shall not know whether you are correct until tomorrow, when they exchange their wedding vows in your presence. At that time, my willing conspirators shall give their true names in a double ceremony that shall join their futures in wedded bliss. And now, my dear friends, let the game commence!"

Twenty

The wedding had been a dream of perfection with two handsome couples instead of one. Olivia had been delighted beyond belief at the lovely wedding gown that her grandmother had ordered made ready for her, laughing in pure joy as Lady Edna had explained that Michele had taken one of Olivia's old gowns to the modiste to make certain that it should be of the proper size. Both Samantha and Olivia had become convinced that Lady Edna was the wisest woman who had ever lived, and in the few short hours that had remained before the nuptials, Olivia had discovered that she loved her grandmother very much indeed.

Immediately preceding the ceremony, Lady Edna had called Samantha aside, saying that she wished a word with her in private. At that time, Lady Edna had declared that although Olivia was her true granddaughter, related to her by blood, she should always regard Samantha as her second granddaughter. She had also asked Samantha if she should mind continuing to call her "Grandmama," as she had discovered that she quite enjoyed that affectionate name as it passed the lips of one she had grown to love. They had shared a fond embrace and a bit of laughter concerning the ruse that had not deceived Lady Edna in the slightest, and then Lady Edna had called David in for a private audience.

David had told Samantha the gist of Lady Edna's comments. She had assured David that she should always regard him as a duke, as he had conducted himself so admirably in that guise. She had also warned him that her "granddaughter," Samantha, was a priceless gem and that he should bring down Lady Edna's full wrath upon his head if he should fail to love and cherish her with all his heart. She had also declared that David should always be welcome in her home and that she should treat any sons and daughters that their union might produce as her very own dear grandchildren.

The invited guests had looked on with excitement as the vows had been exchanged. Lady Edna had planned this also, and since all four of the principals had been stationed with their backs turned toward the guests, not one of the assemblage had been able to discern for certain which young lady was truly Olivia and which young gentleman was the true Duke of Westbury.

At the lavish reception which had followed the ceremony, Lady Edna had risen to give a speech. In it, the dowager countess had declared that she should never divulge the secret, and the members of the *ton* should simply have to accept both couples at their future entertainments, as they should not know which was true and which was *faux!* This announcement had been greeted with a round of applause, for none amongst them wished to exclude the couple who had so delightfully deceived them, and all wished for the amusement to continue when both couples were returned from their wedding trip.

Olivia's dream of flying had been fulfilled as Lady Edna had announced the balloon ascension that she had arranged. A line of carriages had been at the ready outside Lady Edna's town mansion, and the guests had duly been removed to the very center of a small park where several hot-air balloons awaited their pleasure. Olivia had risen into the sky like a bird on her wedding day, precisely as she had always dreamed of doing. When she had stepped from the basket, on firm ground once again, she had rushed to hug her grandmother tightly and declare that every dream of happiness that she had ever harbored had come true.

After several dozen of the more adventurous guests had enjoyed rides that had taken them aloft to the heavens, they had all returned to Lady Edna's town mansion. This had been the time for Samantha to be surprised as she had found a very special carriage waiting for her as a wedding gift. It had been the very equipage that she had described in her devious effort to secure the release of Olivia's inheritance, and Lady Edna had presented it to Samantha and David with great amusement. Lady Edna had also ordered a second cabriolet for Olivia and Harry, which she had presented to them.

There had been a sumptuous dinner to honor the two bridal couples, followed by dancing in Lady Edna's ballroom. At the stroke of midnight, the two happy couples had taken their leave amidst a hail of well-wishes from their friends. They had been handed up into their new cabriolets with much ceremony and had tooled off in high spirits, promising to return to see their dear Grandmama the moment that their wedding trip was concluded.

A week of pure happiness had passed all too swiftly as both couples had found delight in their wedded state. Even their respective futures had been decided, as Harry had begged David not to leave Westbury Park, declaring that he should not relish the thought of surviving without his friendship and his aid. Harry had also approached Samantha, requesting the favor of her services as well, for the veterinarian who tended his cattle was quite elderly and wished to retire. To further swing the decision in his favor, Harry had offered the dower house for their sole use, divulging that before they had set sail on their wedding trip, he had sent a message to David's father requesting that it be completely renovated and decorated especially for them.

David and Samantha had exchanged a glance and then nodded quickly in agreement. The two couples had formed a real friendship and did not wish to be apart.

They should each enjoy their own privacy, but they should be only a short distance away, as only a half mile separated the dower house from the mansion.

On this lovely summer morning, the four fast friends stood at the rail of the ship, straining for a glimpse of the shoreline as the captain had announced that they should dock within the hour. Both Samantha and Olivia enjoyed the comfort of their new husbands' arms around their shoulders, and their glowing smiles gave testament to the fact that both marriages were indeed off to a blissful beginning.

"My only regret is that we cannot continue our ruse on our wedding trip." Samantha sighed as she laid her cheek against the warmth of David's chest. "Once we had secured dear Grandmama's approval, it was such fun!"

Harry grinned as he pulled Olivia even closer to him. "I would much prefer that we *should* continue! We shall be forced to meet the Dragoness in Vienna, and I should prefer to be someone other than her son."

"But why should that be?" Olivia smiled as she gazed into her new husband's fond eyes. "You have accomplished precisely what she intended."

David nodded. "Your bride is correct, Harry. You have married the lady of her choice. How could she not be pleased with you?"

"I have no doubt that she will be pleased about that." Harry's grin grew a bit wider. "I shall gladly admit that she has made the wisest choice possible for my wife. But she will not be pleased when I inform her of the reason that she must remove herself from Westbury Park immediately upon her return."

"But your mother informed you that she wished to reside at Lady Fraidy's home in Brighton once you were married, did she not?" Samantha asked the question.

"She did." Harry nodded. "I doubt, however, that she will be pleased with the news that Westbury Park is to be remodeled as a retreat for promising artists!"

Olivia's mouth dropped open in shock and then she

began to smile. "Harry, that is a marvelous scheme! But are you certain it is what you truly wish to do?"

"It is." Harry's arms tightened around the slender form of his new bride. "I have suffered censure for my painting and I came drastically near to giving it up. I am certain that there are others who have need of a retreat where their efforts are encouraged and they may take lessons from Mr. Dawson."

Olivia's eyes were shining in excitement as she raised her face to Harry's. "Mr. Dawson has agreed to join us there?"

"Yes, he is delighted at the prospect. I received his answer on the day of our wedding and he plans to bring several talented students with him to aid with the renovation."

"You planned all this before the wedding?" David frowned slightly.

"Yes, indeed." Harry smiled at Olivia. "I arranged it all on the day Olivia and I began our journey to London. I sent a message to Oxford, offering Mr. Dawson a permanent position at Westbury Park and assuring him that my wife and I should be delighted if he should choose to join us in our endeavor."

An expression of confusion clouded Olivia's face. "But that was *before* I told you that I was Olivia!"

"Yes, but that was of no consequence. I had planned to marry you in any event and I had vowed that I should not take no for an answer."

"Oh, Harry!" Olivia embraced him warmly. "You desired to marry me even when I was Jane?"

As Harry nodded and pulled his new bride into a closer embrace, Samantha smiled at David. "What of you, my dear husband? Did you wish to marry me when I was Olivia?"

David saw no need to comment. He merely pulled Samantha into his arms and answered her with a loving kiss.

ABOUT THE AUTHOR

Kathryn Kirkwood lives with her family in Granada Hills, CA. She is the author of two Zebra Regency romances: *A Match for Melissa* and *A Season for Samantha*. She is currently working on her third, *A Husband for Holly,* which will be published in July, 1999. Kathryn loves hearing from readers, and you may write to her c/o Zebra Books. Please include a self-addressed stamped envelope if you wish a response. You may also contact her at her E-mail address: OnDit@aol.com.

BOOK YOUR PLACE ON OUR WEBSITE
AND MAKE THE
READING CONNECTION!

We've created a customized website just for our very special readers, where you can get the inside scoop on everything that's going on with Zebra, Pinnacle and Kensington books.

When you come online, you'll have the exciting opportunity to:

- View covers of upcoming books
- Read sample chapters
- Learn about our future publishing schedule (listed by publication month *and author*)
- Find out when your favorite authors will be visiting a city near you
- Search for and order backlist books from our online catalog
- Check out author bios and background information
- Send e-mail to your favorite authors
- Meet the Kensington staff online
- Join us in weekly chats with authors, readers and other guests
- Get writing guidelines
- AND MUCH MORE!

Visit our website at
http://www.zebrabooks.com